Praise for KILL THE BOY BAND

"As fabulously bonkers as its title."
—*Entertainment Weekly*, The Must List

"Boy bands get the *Heathers* treatment in this madcap macabre." —*Kirkus Reviews*

"Wickedly funny."

"Bitingly satirical."
—*Publishers Weekly*

"[For] anyone who's ever had the fortune—or misfortune—of being a 'fan.'" —*Booklist*

"Hilarious. . . . A must-have."
—*School Library Journal*

"I was impressed by how thoughtfully and seriously Goldy treats the subjects of fandom, passion, and being a girl." —Rookiemag.com

"This book is not game-changing. It *is* the game."
—Drew Grant, Senior Editor, *Observer*

KILL THE BOY BAND

GOLDY MOLDAVSKY

Point

For my mother and father,
the world's best storytellers.
—GM

Copyright © 2016 by Goldy Moldavsky

This book was originally published in hardcover by Point in 2016.

All rights reserved. Published by Point, an imprint of Scholastic Inc., *Publishers since 1920*. SCHOLASTIC, POINT, and associated logos are trademarks and/or registered trademarks of Scholastic Inc.

The publisher does not have any control over and does not assume any responsibility for author or third-party websites or their content.

No part of this publication may be reproduced, stored in a retrieval system, or transmitted in any form or by any means, electronic, mechanical, photocopying, recording, or otherwise, without written permission of the publisher. For information regarding permission, write to Scholastic Inc., Attention: Permissions Department, 557 Broadway, New York, NY 10012.

This book is a work of fiction. Names, characters, places, and incidents are either the product of the author's imagination or are used fictitiously, and any resemblance to actual persons, living or dead, business establishments, events, or locales is entirely coincidental.

ISBN 978-0-545-86750-4

10 9 8 7 6 5 4 3 2 1   17 18 19 20 21

Printed in the U.S.A.   40
First printing 2017

Book design by Yaffa Jaskoll

It is always the policy
to speak the truth,
unless, of course, you are
an exceptionally good liar.

—Jerome Klapka Jerome

The most important thing that you should know is that this is not fanfiction. It isn't one of those lonelygirl Tumblr fantasies about meeting your biggest celebrity crush. This is the story of me and my friends and the time we met The Ruperts. You can believe it or not—that's on you. Just because you heard a different account of the events on the news doesn't mean that this one isn't true.

I have to tell it exactly as it happened.

I have to get the truth out.

And I'm truly sorry for what we have done.

PART ONE

1

People have called me crazy.

It's understandable; fangirls get a bad rap all the time. They say we're weird, hysterical, obsessed, certifiable. But those people don't understand. Just because I love something a lot doesn't mean I'm crazy. And I did love The Ruperts a lot. I loved them more than soft-serve vanilla ice cream in summer, more than seeing a new review of one of my fanfics, more than discovering a good '80s movie I'd never seen before.

Just because I was a Ruperts fangirl does not mean I was crazy.

I think it's important that you know that up front. Because everything I'm about to tell you is going to seem . . . well, crazy.

Rupert Pierpont was in our hotel room.

You're probably curious about how we pulled this off. It's

not every day you get to be alone with a member of the most popular boy band ever.

Wait. Let me rephrase that.

It's not every day you get to be alone with the biggest flop in the most popular boy band ever while he is blindfolded and bound to a hotel armchair.

I know what you're probably thinking: What made him such a flop? But we'll get to that. First, Erin and Isabel and Apple and I just stared at him, waiting for him to regain consciousness.

We hadn't turned on the lights yet, so the room was only lit by the afternoon sunlight peeking through the wood-framed windows. It splashed the gray carpet and parts of the plum-purple walls, turning them violet. Overall, though, the place was dark. You could say it matched the current vibe.

The only sound in the room came from the clicking noises on Isabel's phone. The screen wasn't much more than millions of cracks, and the skin was a homemade paper-and-Scotch-tape collage of Rupert L.'s bare chest, but Isabel clutched her phone like it was the most precious thing in the world to her. It probably was. She held the screen to her face as she typed, which cast her in an eerie, campfire-blue glow. She was the first to break the silence. "What *is* he wearing?"

"Hip-hop," I said.

Literally, the words "HIP-HOP" dangled at the end of the chain around his neck. Rupert P. was nothing if not a walking identity crisis. Just two weeks ago he'd been all about the punk thing, with spiked hair and bleached eyebrows. But today he was buried under a jersey, saggy pants, high-tops, and, of course, the chain that spelled the whole ensemble out for you. It felt all wrong, though. The jersey wasn't even a basketball jersey; it was a child-size hockey jersey for some team called the Red Wings. Leave it to Rupert P. to get an identity crisis wrong. "An aggressive style choice."

"He tried it," Isabel snorted.

"I think he looks cute," Apple said, her already full cheeks going fuller with her smile.

"We're all well aware that you do," Erin said.

It was hours or maybe just minutes, but after what felt like an agonizingly long stretch Rupert P. started to stir. He rolled his neck, tried to move his arms, slow at first but then all jagged and frantic and stuck. I was kind of in awe, watching it all. I had no idea tights could make such sturdy knots.

Finally, the perfectly pruned eyebrows that stuck out over the top of his blindfold (BTW, tights also make really good blindfolds) rose in fear, or realization. And the first thing he said was:

"Griffin?"

We all looked at one another. Isabel's phone lost its magnetic hold on her eyes long enough for her to roll them, but there were the beginnings of a smirk curling her upper lip. She went back to thumb-typing with a renewed relish. Apple's forehead crinkled, and having no food on hand to munch on (her go-to when things get stressy), she did the next best thing: She chewed on a strip of her dyed auburn hair. But the two of them were in my periphery because my eyes were focused on Erin. I told her this was a bad idea. But Erin doesn't listen so much as ignore. She says I still have my baby teeth. I tell her there's nothing wrong with being nice. Erin says, "Fuck nice."

Usually she's straightening my collar or tucking my hair behind my ear when she says it, though, and the word "fuck" coupled with "nice" has never sounded so reassuring.

Right then, though, when it mattered most, Erin said nothing. She only smiled.

Erin was all shine and pale golden hues, but her face really lit up when she smiled. Her mouth—lips always painted red—was the standout feature on her face. When she talked, it moved in subtly unexpected ways, like she'd grown up speaking another language, or had an accent once upon a time and English was this new exotic tongue. It was transfixing. I know because I've seen the way boys look at Erin when she says things—often the most innocuous things. They stare at her

8

mouth. Girls stare too. I think part of the reason Erin took to liking me straightaway was because I always focused on her eyes. Unlike every other part of her, they were dark and did not cast spells.

But her smile was like a cavity, a sweetness you were sometimes hesitant to peer into for fear you'd plummet to its sugary depths. Truly a bummer that Rupert P. was too blindfolded to see it.

"No, not *Griffin*," Erin said. Singsong. Sweet. Sexy. Screwed up if you thought about it, but somehow fitting.

Every part of Rupert P. got very still very suddenly, except for his chest, which rose and fell so fiercely it was like it was hooked up to a defibrillator. I could feel the outburst coming. *CLEAR!*

"Who the hell are you people?!" Rupert P. yelled, his posh London accent catching on "hell."

Here's the truth: None of us liked Rupert P., except for Apple, and if I'd had a choice about which of The Ruperts to kidnap, I certainly would not have picked him. Rupert P. was that one boy band member that every boy band must inevitably have: the Ugly One. Historically, ugly boy band members have often tried to distract from their faces by doing the absolute most with their hair (beards, dye, never-cute braids), but Rupert P. couldn't even be bothered to put that mess under a hat.

Flop sweat prickled at his temples, staining the copper hair there a darker shade of mahogany. Rupert P.'s hair was a mushroom cloud of red, which made his face the catastrophic bomb that caused mass hysteria. Okay, I know that's mean, and Apple would disagree with me, but ginger guys just don't do it for me.

Apple, though—bless her heart—she really loved him. Her devotion was truly an inspiration, not only to me but to fangirls everywhere.

Apple knelt down before Rupert P. "It's okay," she said. "Everything is *juuust fiiine*." Her open palm hovered over his white-knuckled fist until slowly, so slowly, she lowered her hand on top of his. Judging by the sharp intake of breath, the furrowed brow, and the little embarrassing noises coming out of her mouth, I was pretty sure Apple had just reached climax.

Rupert P. didn't seem to have the same enthusiasm for touching Apple, though. *"Gerroff!"* he roared.

As I watched Rupert P. try to break free from his restraints, one of The Ruperts' songs popped into my head.

I'm all tied up in your lovin', girl
I'm all tied up in you
But don't ever let me free, girl
Let's take these chains of love and tie you up too

I was holding someone captive and all that was going through my mind was a Billboard Top 40 love song.

I was going to hell.

I knew all along that this was bad, but now that Rupert P. was awake and talking it made it all the more real.

We couldn't keep him.

I would tell the girls how I felt, convince them that this was a stupid thing to do, even for us. I didn't usually take a stand—that was Erin's role—but we needed to do the right thing here. We were all fifteen, but I was turning sixteen sooner than the rest of them, which meant I was the oldest person there. I had a responsibility to be mature about this. Erin was my best friend—she'd back me up. And Isabel would do whatever Erin said. I mean, what were we even going to do with him? No one in this room except for Apple even liked him. Midterms were coming up. I really did not have time to go to hell.

"What do you want?!" Rupert P. shouted. "Do you want me to sing for you? I'll sing for you!"

"Holy flopping hell, is he for real?" Isabel said. She glanced toward Erin and her eyebrows danced on her forehead. I didn't get it, but Erin smirked. An in-joke. The four of us had lots of in-jokes, but this one seemed exclusive only to the two of them. I wondered if Isabel and Erin had marathon chat sessions without me, chock-full of in-jokes. I wondered what they'd do if I mentioned letting Rupert P. go. Would they look at me funny? Would Isabel cast a glance Erin's way, make her eyebrows dance? Would Erin smirk back?

"Is it money?!" Rupert P. said. "Is this a ransom?! Are you a Mexican drug cartel?!"

He had absolutely no idea who we were. At least we had that going for us. If we let him go now we could get away with this, sweep it under the rug, get off scot-free, et cetera, et cetera.

"Please, I'll give you anything you want! Just don't cut off my finger! Bloody hell, don't cut off my *hair*."

"We would never touch your hair!" Apple said, her voice taking on a mouse's squeal, the way it did whenever she got overly excited. "I mean, maybe just the rattail?"

You'd be forgiven to think he had an actual tail coming out of his lower back, but in this case Apple was only talking about the strip of hair down the back of his neck. I tried to spare you this detail for your own benefit, but now it's come up.

"Would that be okay?" Apple continued. If there were scissors anywhere in this room, that rattail would've been in her hands (and possibly in her mouth) an hour ago.

Rupert P. heaved in some breaths, and then the weirdest thing happened: He started to laugh. "Oh. I get it. You're just fans, aren't you?"

Shit. He had us pegged.

12

I tugged on the elastic bracelet on my left wrist and snapped it against my arm repeatedly, trying to think. I had to do something before we gave ourselves away completely. The more minutes that passed the more I realized that all of this was very wrong. Today wouldn't just be the day I kidnapped a ginger. Today would be the day I set a ginger free. That was what was going through my mind, at least. In reality, though, I still cared too much about what my friends would think if I brought any of this up.

"Fans!" Rupert P. yelled. "Stupid-bloody-snot-nosed-crying girls! You're all psychopaths, the lot of you!"

Isabel's face tore open with a grin, not because she was happy about being called a psychopath—Isabel could be kind of sadistic, but even she wouldn't be happy about that—but because, as I suspected, she was thrilled to see a real live boy bander lose his shit. A famous celebrity calling his fans psychos was a newsworthy thing. A headline. A scandal. And there was nothing Isabel liked more than scandal. "Gee, Rupert P., tell us how you really feel."

"D'ya wanna know how I really feel about fans?" Rupert P. said.

Isabel nodded eagerly and held her phone a few inches from his face, the little lines on her voice recorder app spiking spastically in the same rhythm as my heartbeat. "Please speak clearly," she said.

"There's Catholic schoolteachers," Rupert P. began. "Then below that, there's paparazzi, and below that still there's homeless people, and miles and miles below that there are *fans*. You're the scum of the bloody earth, is what you are, innit? As soon as I get free, d'ya know what I'm keen to do? I'm keen to murder all of you. Yeah, yeah, forget telling the police. I will tie you all up like you did me and set you on fire. And then I'll just watch as you burn. How does that sound?"

Harsh.

Isabel tapped the red button on her screen to stop recording. "Well, that should get me a few hits."

"You can't post that!" Apple said. "This is obviously a very distressing situation for him. Can't you see how scared and vulnerable he is right now? Nobody likes being tied up—least of all celebrities."

"Wait, was I being recorded just now?" Rupert P. said. "You have got to be kidding me. Let me go!"

He was getting increasingly agitated, and all we could do was watch, dumbfounded, like this was another Ruperts performance. "I have places to be!" Rupert P. whined. "I was meant to meet up with Michelle! Ugh, she's going to kill me!"

Michelle Hornsbury, Rupert P.'s girlfriend.

Actually, that should read: Michelle Hornsbury, Rupert P.'s kind of/not really/alleged girlfriend.

I'd almost forgotten about her, but I should've known she'd be around here somewhere. She followed Rupert P. everywhere he went.

My phone buzzed in my jeans, and I dug it out to find a new text message from my mom. She worked long hours, and being a nurse didn't afford her many opportunities to call in, so texts were the next best thing.

You girls having fun? it read.

My mom thought I was having a sleepover with a friend. Which was technically true. I'd just neglected to tell her that this sleepover was taking place in a hotel in downtown Manhattan. Lying to my mother was easy, mostly because she never asked follow-up questions. Something as simple as *Which of your friends' houses are you staying at? Can I have their parents' number? Are you sure they won't mind having you over? It is Thanksgiving, after all* would have been enough to catch me in the lie. But that was the thing about being the kind of girl who never gets into trouble: Parents trusted you.

The truth is my mom probably didn't ask any questions because she likely felt guilty about having to work extra shifts over the Thanksgiving holiday. Also, I was showing an interest in something that involved the very social act of meeting up with actual friends instead of talking to them through phones and computer screens. Mom liked me best when I was social and happy, and the therapist I was seeing twice a week agreed with her. It's something that I've admittedly struggled with after everything that happened with my dad.

I texted back.

So much fun!

I wasn't watching Erin, so when she whizzed past me it snapped my attention back to her. The hot-pink tights she tied around Rupert P.'s mouth didn't exactly go with his freckled skin tone, but I guess that was beside the point when they were being used as a gag.

Tights were really so much more versatile than I ever thought.

Erin yanked on both ends, splitting Rupert P.'s lips into an awful grin. "Group meeting," she said. "Right now."

2

Group meetings weren't a thing we usually did. Actually, we'd only had a group meeting one other time.

Almost exactly a month before, the four of us got together at Chocolateburg in Manhattan to hatch a plan to meet The Ruperts. Erin and I rode in together on the subway from Carroll Gardens, Brooklyn—a short ride across the river, but Apple and Isabel were already there by the time we showed up. The boys were having their Thanksgiving half-hour live spectacular in one month's time, straight from NBC Studios in New York City, and none of us had been able snare tix. You can see why this meeting was an emergency.

Isabel giggled as she dipped her spoon into her drink, an order that consisted of runny chocolate, two scoops of blueberry ice cream, and caramel drizzling off of it. She lifted her spoon a few inches over her bowl and watched as the gloopy mess dripped back into it. "This is some Willy Wonka realness."

It was weird seeing Isabel giggle. Hell, it was weird seeing Isabel in a normal, nonstalkery setting. The four of us were friends, but aside from Erin and I, who went to the same school in Brooklyn, none of us ever got together in the real world without the promise of the boys being close enough to stalk, and that only happened whenever the boys had a single to promote. When we did meet up in person, it was usually outside somewhere, standing in the freezing cold, huddled behind barricades for hours on end, armed with nothing but cell phones and CD cases, wielding Sharpies like weapons, and passing the time by discussing optimal ambush tactics. It was a lot like going to war. At least, that's what I imagine going to war is like. Stalking boy bands was serious business.

Anyway, our friendship lived and breathed primarily in Twitter DMs and text messages. That might sound strange, but talk to any Ruperts fangirl and she'll tell you just how important the Internet was in all of our lives. Without it we probably never would've even heard of The Ruperts.

The band was formed on the reality show *So You Think the British Don't Have Talent?*, a weekly talent competition that aired in the UK, where the boys were from. They had each competed separately for the fifty-thousand-pound grand prize, but the producers decided to group them together into a boy band because the four boys were around the same age and all had the same first name. As the now famous story goes, *SYTTBDHT*'s host looked out into the audience one night, saw all the signs that featured the name "Rupert" on them, and said, "Seems the Ruperts are getting a lot of love tonight!"

The crowd went nuts, a million lightbulbs went on over the heads of music execs, and The Ruperts were born.

The group consisted of Rupert Lemon, the baritone who had auditioned with an opera/jazz fusion thing of his own making; Rupert Kirke, who came onstage with an acoustic guitar and got a standing ovation before his song was even over; Rupert Xavier, who explained in his intro reel that along with singing he was also interested in modeling and would be the first contestant in the history of the show who would showcase both of those talents at once; and Rupert Pierpont, the juggler.

I don't mean juggling figuratively; I mean he came onstage with three bowling pins. Let us be clear on something: There were millions of talents that Rupert P. did not possess. One of those was singing. The only reason he was lumped together with the other three boys was because his unimaginative parents looked at him when he was born and bestowed upon him the most common name in England that year. Being named Rupert was the luckiest thing to have ever happened to him.

Their names may have been the same, but as they liked to reiterate in interviews, the Ruperts had their own distinct personalities.

Rupert P.'s likes and passions began and ended with juggling.

Rupert X. was the pretty boy/rebel.

Rupert L. couldn't tell time.

And Rupert K. was . . . well, he was a life ruiner.

Rupert K. was beautiful. He had ruddy cheeks, but the cute kind that looked like he'd always just come from running a marathon out in the cold. He'd had braces when he was twelve, so his teeth were straight and perfect. He had brown hair that he liked to keep short and that he was always pushing back off his forehead, especially when he didn't want to answer a television interviewer's question. He loved fantasy video games, folk music, and baking thumbprint cookies with his grandma. When he smiled, sometimes he would bite the inside of his right cheek. He had a beauty mark on the nape of his neck, right where his heartbeat pulsed on his carotid artery. It was the shape of California and the size of a pinkie nail. Recently, he'd taken to wearing porkpie hats on the crown of his head, something his fans were now copying. He wore sunglasses a lot because his pale green eyes were super sensitive to the sun. He had a tiny scar beneath his lower lip that he got when he fell off the jungle gym when he was six. And he seemed to take pleasure in ruining my life with how perfect he was.

Like I said. He was a life ruiner. All of the aforementioned things would've been enough to have me melting over him, but what really put Rupert K. into the man-of-my-wildest-dreams category was something he'd said in one of the first interviews he'd done.

"Happiness isn't always easy," he'd said. "But it's a priority."

That resonated with me. It felt like he got me.

"Let's focus, girls," Erin said, commanding even the attention of some of the Chocolateburg diners at the table next to ours. Erin was always commanding attention. "The boys will be here in a month. Is there any possible way to get tickets?"

Tickets to *Coming to America: The Ruperts Learn about Thanksgiving!* were free and distributed online by a third party not affiliated with NBC. All 550 tickets were gone 2.7 seconds after they went up. You couldn't even buy them on StubHub. It was the biggest crisis we'd ever faced as fans.

"The only way to get tickets is if we find four fans willing to give them up," I said. "So, we're never getting tickets." I didn't know why we were even bothering with this group meeting, but I didn't say anything like that.

"We could offer to buy the tickets off them," Apple said. She *would* suggest something like that. There were very few things in life that Apple's parents could not buy her. Unfortunately for all of us, these tickets were one of those things.

This is as good a place as any to give you some stats on Apple and her career as a Ruperts fangirl:

Favorite member of The Ruperts: Rupert Pierpont

Number of times she's seen The Ruperts in person: 18

Number of times she's met (this includes getting anything from a selfie to a hug) all/a member of The Ruperts: 8

Apple came from the outrageous ode to wealth and vanity that was Greenwich, Connecticut. She'd grown up there ever since her parents—an elderly, magnanimous couple—adopted her from an orphanage in Beijing when she was one year old. As the story goes, Apple's parents were browsing the orphanage when they spotted the chubbiest baby they'd ever seen eating a piece of fruit out of the trash. I'll give you one guess which fruit.

Living all the way in Connecticut never stopped Apple from seeing The Ruperts in New York. Actually, she'd been to every performance of The Ruperts in New York, New Jersey, and Pennsylvania. (Once she even trekked as far as Montreal.) Erin and I met Apple at one of The Ruperts' shows. It was an outdoor performance for the *Today* show and Apple had pitched a neon-orange tent as big as a circus in Rockefeller Center four days prior to the concert so that she could be in the front row.

It got her on the news.

A reporter interviewed her in front of her tent, asking, "Why are you so devoted to this band?"

"Because," she'd said, "I'm a Strepur for life!"

"Excuse me?" the clueless newsperson said.

22

"*Strepur.* It's what Ruperts fans call themselves. It's 'Ruperts' spelled backward."

The newsperson stared, blinked, smiled, and concluded the interview by asking a passerby how he felt about the growing population of Strepurs.

"I'm all for strippers," the man said.

The clip was a mini viral sensation.

Anyway, Erin and I had convinced our moms to let us leave for the city at two in the morning the day of the *Today* show concert so we could get a good place in line. (When I say "convinced," I mean that Erin told her mom that she was going and I just waited for my mom to leave for her overnight shift.) By the time we got to Rockefeller Center, there must've been at least a thousand people there already. And there, at the front of the line, was that huge *James and the Giant Peach* of a tent. It was a lighthouse beacon, shining the way to the Promised Land. Erin grabbed my hand. Any time she did that it felt like she was pumping life into me. Because if you think about it, the only reason to grab your friend's hand is when something big is about to happen. At first it was scary, but eventually I just started letting her take me. It was almost always worth it. So we waded through the sea of girls all around us, on a quest to reach the tent in the middle of Rockefeller Center.

Apple was all alone in her tent and only too happy to share it with fellow Strepurs. Inside, the walls were wallpapered with posters of Rupert P.'s face, which would've normally been offensive, but I ignored it because it was warm, we were in the front of the line, and the tent got restaurant delivery service.

We'd been friends with Apple ever since.

"Do you think a thousand bucks would do it?" Apple asked, back at Chocolateburg. "Is a thousand too—"

"No one is going to sell those tickets," Erin cut in. "Not for all the money in your parents' bank account."

"We could smoke some ticket holders out," Isabel said. "Threaten to destroy their lives if they don't give 'em up."

You think this is a joke.

This is not a joke.

Isabel had a certain cred on the Internet that stemmed from her massively followed and oft-suspended Twitter account. Oft-suspended because it delivered no shortage of creative (some might say shocking) threats to Ruperts haters or Ruperts celeb girlfriends. Isabel's current favorite target was Rupert L.'s newest girlfriend, Ashley Woodstone. (Or, Ashley "Prancing in the" Woods, Stoned, as she was also commonly known.) Ashley was an actress with questionable new-age ideals, and even though she'd only just started dating Rupert L., Isabel already hated her more than she hated anyone else in her life. Which was saying a lot.

Isabel's infamous tweets ranged from the cartoonish and impossible:

Im going to pull ur tongue out of ur mouth
wrap it around ur neck n strangle u w it so
hard ur eyes will pop out. i will pee in the
sockets.

To the quaint:

Get ur fcking hands off him bitch i will cut u.
#RupertLIsMine ⫻⫻⫻⫻

To the cryptically disturbing:

I watch u in your sleep. ◉◉🤕👍

I would never condone Isabel's scary tweets, but you had to give the girl credit for managing to stay under 140 characters every time.

At this point you may be asking just how much harm a fifteen-year-old fangirl could really do. That is the wrong question to ask. People can do a lot of harm if pushed to the breaking point, and us fangirls lived at the breaking point. If the boys were involved in a scandal, we were at a breaking point. If they got haircuts, we were at a breaking point. If they smiled, we were at a brea . . . You get the idea. Boy band fangirls are a species that are more focused, determined, and powerful in large numbers than just about any other group of people I can think of.

And anyway, Isabel wasn't just any regular fangirl. She was kind of a legend on the Internet for being one of the most aggressive Ruperts stans out there. Also, her entire family was allegedly made up of criminals. Or maybe that was cops. I don't know, we never really asked her, but either way, if they weren't on one side of the law, they were on the other, and that meant Isabel came from tough stock.

You may be asking why I would be friends with a death-threat-happy girl like Isabel. That one is a little harder to answer.

The day I met Isabel was the day I'd skipped class for the first time ever.

Erin met me in front of school that morning and tugged me away from it. "The boys are in town," she'd said. "And I know where."

Obviously, I had to go.

Cut to us sitting on the ground, leaning against the brick wall of a building on the corner of Avenue B in the city, no boys in sight. I was beginning to question Erin's claim when Isabel came to stand in front of us.

Before I ever saw Isabel's face, I saw her boots.

They had too many useless zippers and buckles and straps—useless because the boots looked like they were falling apart. The faux leather tongue spilled over the laces, and the parts over the sides of her ankles folded over too, so that it looked like she'd stuffed her feet into two badly bruised bananas that were halfway peeled.

My eyes swept up over the rest of her——the holey jeans, the cheap-looking denim jacket (it was too blue; the cheap ones are always too blue)——until they rested on her face, and even then I couldn't see it. She was backlit by the sun, so I had to shield my eyes to look at her. Protecting myself from her, even then.

"You guys looking for The Ruperts?" Her voice was deep, skeptical.

It turned out that Erin and I were in the right place, but we would have never been able to get a good look at the boys if it hadn't been for Isabel. She led us to an alleyway, climbed over a Dumpster and then up a fire escape, and when we followed her, Erin and I got our first ever glimpse of the boys. They were kicking around a soccer ball in a courtyard. Our view was partially obscured by a building in the way and they were far from us, but it was the best moment of my life up until that point. I felt so light, watching Rupert K. come in and out of view, that if a strong gust of wind had blown right then, I would've flown right off that fire escape.

The prize for best fan went to Isabel, easy. She knew how to get to The Ruperts. And the truth was, we were lucky to have her on our team.

Stats on Isabel:

Favorite member of The Ruperts: Rupert Lemon

Number of times she's seen The Ruperts in person: 68

Number of times she's met (this includes getting anything from a selfie to a hug) all/a member of The Ruperts: 34 (often multiple times in one day and with a total disregard for school attendance records)

"We can't just threaten people," I said in a hushed voice, hoping the other Chocolateburgers couldn't hear me. "We're just going to have to face the fact that we're not getting into the concert. We can't go."

"The fight hasn't even started and you're already tapping out?" Isabel said.

"I'm not *tapping out* . . ." Maybe I just didn't want to get my karate gi all wrinkled if I knew it was a losing battle. (In my mind, the metaphorical fight she was talking about was a karate match, not a wrestling one. Karate just seemed so much more dignified.)

"You're always too chickenshit to do anything," Isabel said, rolling her eyes. "Your goody-two-shoes mentality is getting way tired."

"Isabel, kindly shut up," Erin said.

I loved Erin in that moment. Because nobody told Isabel to shut up. If anyone did, they'd probably end up on the floor, Isabel standing triumphantly over them with knuckles freshly bruised and bloody. But Erin wasn't just anybody. Isabel curled her upper lip and went back to her phone.

I squeezed Erin's knee, a nonverbal *thanks*, and she, in turn, squeezed mine: *no probs.*

"The boys will still be in New York, there'll be other ways to meet them," Erin said. She dunked a Twix bar into her milk shake and bit off the end of it, making us wait for her to go on. She fixed us with a smile, sly and satisfied, and asked us a question we already knew the answer to. "Where are they staying?"

"The hotel!" All of us said it at the same time.

We turned to Isabel. "Isabel?"

"My sources won't know where the boys will be staying yet, but I'd put my money on The Rondack."

Aside from threatening people's lives every day on Twitter, Isabel ran the most popular Ruperts update site on the Web. She knew stuff about the boys before the boys even knew it themselves.

"The hotel is our best bet," I said, "but everyone goes there. It's going to be packed."

"We could get a room at the hotel," Apple said. "We'd be free to roam around, find out which rooms the boys are in, corner them in hallways, and force them to comply with our every whim." She smiled to herself, lost in a daydream/the boys' probable nightmare.

"I don't think a hotel is a good idea," I said. "Maybe we could—"

"I think a hotel is a fantastic idea, actually," Erin cut in.

I watched her, trying to interpret this new eagerness in her. Erin was never this gung ho about things. Her MO was cool and aloof.

"Okay," I said slowly. "But we won't be able to check into a hotel. We're minors."

"I can get Consuela to check in for us," Apple said.

Consuela worked as a housekeeper for Apple's family, but while that may have been her official title, her role in Apple's life stretched much farther than that. Consuela was Apple's chaperone when she went to Montreal to see the boys in concert. Consuela was actually the one who stayed in the tent at the *Today* show for the first two days before Apple got there. And Consuela was the one who'd nearly gotten herself arrested at Toys "R" Us when she smacked a fellow holiday shopper with her purse trying to get to the last limited edition Rupert Pierpont doll that Apple needed for her collection. Consuela was basically an honorary Strepur, whether she wanted to be or not.

"How much money is that going to be?" Isabel asked. "Because I can't—"

"I've got it covered!" Apple said.

"We'll all chip in for a room," I said. Erin pinched me under the table and Isabel shot me a dirty look, but I didn't care. It wasn't fair to make Apple always pay for everything. Apple grinned at me, and that settled it.

"We're getting a room!" Erin said.

3

The day of The Ruperts' Thanksgiving spectacular, even the city felt more alive than ever. I thought we'd miss the madness of the big parade, since that was in Midtown and we were all the way downtown, but everyone who'd spent the morning perched on Thirty-Fourth Street must've migrated a couple of miles south, because the streets of SoHo were buzzing with life. That is to say, more so than usual. There were people everywhere, shouts and car horns overloud and pulsing in my ears; for all intents and purposes, New York herself was an excited fangirl that day. And her heart, where I could swear everyone in the city was heading to or coming from, was The Rondack.

It was the swankiest hotel in SoHo—maybe the swankiest hotel in all of NYC. Even before everything went down later that night—when the hotel got bathed by helicopter beams from overhead and swarmed by hapless cops on the ground— the place was already crawling with chaos. It was the epicenter of all the action. And my friends and I were poised to make our entrance.

My friends and I and Consuela.

Check-in was at 3:00 pm and we got there just in time, but getting to the front doors was a trip, and not only because Apple's overnight bag was big enough to fit a person. Literally. (I'll come back to that later.) The hotel entrance was congested with people, paparazzi, and a throng of girls just like us, except clearly much less dedicated in their stanning. Because while waiting outside in the cold for seven hours straight until you see your idol had its merits, nothing beat shelling out for keys to the castle.

There was no point being a fan these days if you weren't willing to go the extra mile for your idols. It wasn't enough anymore to send them fan mail and kiss the posters above our beds. These days you weren't a true fan until you engaged in Twitter death threats and endless stan wars. The fandom land-scape was peppered with land mines, and there was no other way to navigate it but to walk until you hit one. You come out the other side a little crazier, yeah, but you're also stronger. You are a true believer. You will do anything for the object of your affection.

Because the truth is, it isn't worth loving something if you aren't going to love it all the way. Apple told me a story once about a couple of girls she met in the pit at a show The Ruperts had at MetLife Stadium. Apple had gotten pit tickets too (which must've set her parents back a couple grand at least), but she said she was worried for most of the show that she'd have to go to the bathroom and lose her prime spot in front of the stage. These two girls next to her told her that they didn't have that problem; they were wearing Depends.

No, you aren't a true fan until you've wept for your love. Bled for them. Threatened lives for them. Relieved yourself in adult diapers at their concert without ever leaving the bone-crushing discomfort of your two-thousand-dollar-a-piece spot.

Because what else does it mean to be crazy about someone?

Plus, being a fangirl was just *fun*. Aside from all the Internet stuff, with fics and gifs and stan wars, there was fandom outside the Internet too. Like the times when Isabel and Erin and Apple and I went for proper stalk sessions. The times when the boys would whiz past us so quick that seeing them was only as brief as catching a whiff of something. I know that doesn't sound like much, but those few seconds of dizzy excitement were worth it just for how alive they made you feel. Tingly and jittery and crazed—in the best way. A natural high, truly. Even the anticipation that came with waiting for them was part of the fun. It was butterflies—the best kind. We might see the boys and we might not, but the hours in between, spent waiting, or racing down streets, or investigating; it was *fun*. We filled Instagrams and Twitters with it. We formed lasting friendships. We were a part of something.

Once, Isabel and Erin and Apple and I had our picture in *Us Weekly*. We were behind the barricades across the street from *The Late Show* studio as the boys made their way in. We were screaming and we were happy. We were the barricade girls.

Coming to the hotel now was only the tip of the iceberg compared to some of the cray things other people had done. If you really thought about it, we were the rational ones. And for one night we would be sleeping under the same roof as The Ruperts. My feelings on the matter could best be summed up with lyrics from The Ruperts' hit "I'm So Excited."

> *Yeah Yeah Yeah!*
> *I'm so excited!*
> *Yeah Yeah Yeah!*
> *Tonight is the night!*

We elbowed our way past weepy girls holding signs that tried to play cleverly on British double entendres (WE WANT YOUR FRANKS AND BEANS) and signs that didn't even try at all (BONERS!). One sign read WILL KILL FOR A KISS, where the word "kill" was drawn in ominously smeared rusty-colored paint (please let that have been paint). We passed a Senior Strepur (a Strepur approaching middle age) whose cleavage-baring top was open so low that you could see a giant tattoo of Rupert X. on her right boob. She'd either gotten implants recently, gained some rapid weight, or had a tattoo artist who secretly hated her, because Rupert X.'s inky face was so stretched out and badly drawn he looked more like Jay Leno than himself. The only way you could tell it was him was because of the the words below his portrait that read RUPERT X. MARKS THE SPOT.

"Nice tattoo," Erin told the lady.

Tattoo Lady looked at me expectantly, surely awaiting my forthcoming compliment. "It's a real treasure," I said.

Erin snorted and pulled me behind her. We weaved through the bars of the huge scaffolding by the entrance that contained all the fangirls within it like a prison. And even though I was a fangirl myself and shouldn't have thought this about my own people, the scaffolding seemed appropriate. Sometimes fans *needed* to be caged, for the good of everyone.

When we got to the doors, our overnight bags hanging from the crooks of our bent elbows, Consuela was the one to speak to the doorman to make him step aside. He leaned on the door for us and held it open wide.

"Hey!" one of the girls behind a barricade yelled. "Why do they get to go in?"

Erin looked over her shoulder and with her sweetest All-American-cheer-captain smile responded, "Because we got a room, sweetie."

I watched the girl who'd yelled, saw her face turn ugly with shock and jealousy. "That isn't fair," she said.

"Womp womp," Erin said. "You guys should probably stay under the scaffolding. It's supposed to rain later."

The way Erin said stuff, with her catwalk confidence and her eat-shit smile, it made me feel giddy and confident too, because I was on her team and when she said those things it was like I was saying them too.

I met Erin last year, at the start of high school, and even though we were both freshmen, Erin was already popular by then. She was popular the moment she stepped foot on school grounds, maybe because she simply decided to be. Where Erin went, so went everything shiny and new, and all she left in her wake were drooling boys and awed stares. She was the opposite of me.

I'd always been a bit of a loner, and it didn't really help matters that my father died in the summer between junior high and high school (two weeks after he died was when I happened to buy my first Ruperts album). It was hard enough transitioning to a new school and trying to make friends when you had your own personal shit going on. Plus, it wasn't like anybody was knocking down my door, eager to befriend the loner/quiet/sad girl.

So you ask yourself, how the heck did I become Erin's best friend? It's simple. I wore a Rupert K. T-shirt to school one day. I probably should have known better. Wearing a boy band shirt in middle school was one thing, but high school was populated by snickering, cruel beasts who fed on boy-band-T-shirt-wearing freshman like me. Wearing that shirt made a statement, and that statement was: *Ridicule me!* But Erin sat next to me at lunch that day. "Is Rupert Kirke your favorite?" she'd said. "Mine's Rupert Xavier."

And so goes the story of our beautiful friendship. See, The Ruperts were the source of all the good things in my life. After Erin and I became friends, things got better. Nobody gave me grief for wearing Rupert K. shirts, for starters. But even when I wasn't in full-on fangirl mode, Erin still had my back. Going down the halls in school was always easier with her by my side. It was self-assurance by proximity; when she was with me I was untouchable, and if anybody ever said anything to me Erin would be there to feed them a nice, warm dish of beautifully prepared shit. Erin floated, and so therefore I did too.

Now she laced her arm through mine and I swear we positively skipped into the hotel lobby together, leaving all the other Strepurs out in the cold.

At this point you're probably asking yourself how all of New York's Strepurs were able to get away from their families on Thanksgiving to stand guard outside of this hotel. You are still asking the wrong questions. Fangirls don't play. We'd cancel Christmas in a heartbeat if Santa got in the way of us seeing the boys. I didn't know what the girls outside had told their parents about skipping Thanksgiving this year, or if they'd told them anything at all, but the four of us had taken care of this detail already.

Like I said, I told my mom I'd be with Erin. Erin double-booked her parents, telling her mom she'd be spending Thanksgiving with her dad and telling her dad she'd be spending Thanksgiving with her mom. (The fact that Erin's parents lived on different islands—her mom in Brooklyn, her dad in Manhattan on the Upper West Side—and didn't communicate with each other directly really worked out nicely for us.) According to Isabel, her Dominican family didn't celebrate Thanksgiving (or any other strictly American holiday, for that matter). And Apple's parents—the only parents of our group who were actually aware of our plan to stay at a hotel for the night and were totally on board with it—threw Thanksgiving the night before. They disrupted work schedules and endured extended family arguments, but Apple was happy and that was all that mattered to her parents.

Inside the hotel I stopped to marvel at the lobby. The front desk was on the right side, with the entrance to the hotel bar off to the left. Every surface was either glass, hospital white, or gold, with the biggest pops of color coming from unexpected accents. Like the ceiling, which seemed to be made up entirely of suspended skateboard decks in the most psychedelic neon colors, hovering above us. The elevator bank was sleek, pristine, gilded, but was disrupted by the ugly appearance of a dirty phone booth right in the center of it. There were scratches in the Plexiglas and graffiti all over its accordion doors, and I wasn't sure if it was a working phone booth, an art installation, or just a symbol of The Rondack's try-hardness, but I appreciated the quirkiness.

Consuela checked in for us, but before handing the keys over to Apple she took me aside. I had no clue why, and as she led me away I turned toward Erin, hoping for some guidance. She only winked and gave me a double thumbs-up. I knew how to read her brand of sign language by now. That particular signal was shorthand for *I trust you to lie your ass off, girl.*

"I do not know you very well," Consuela said. "But I have seen you with Apple. You are the best girl of all you girls."

I couldn't help but smile. She was only Apple's maid—it wasn't like she knew me or was giving me a good grade in school or anything, but it felt like it. I really did like getting good grades. "Thank you."

"You promise you won't get into trouble tonight."

"Trouble? Why would we get into trouble?"

"I do not know. But Apple sometimes doesn't think things all the way. And so many girls tonight outside? I do not get a good feeling. I do not know," she said again, a crease splitting her forehead. "You promise me."

The thing about me—the reason Erin can shoot me the wink-and-double-thumbs-up combo—is that I'm your typical good girl. I dress nicely, but I wouldn't say I'm at the bleeding edge of fashion. I always have my homework done on time. I say please and thank you and adults like me. Because of all these things, everyone always assumes that I'll do the right thing. No one ever thinks I would lie. But I do lie, sometimes.

Because of all of the aforementioned things—because of the way I'm perceived, because people are too trusting—I'm actually quite good at lying.

"We're going to be very good girls," I said.

It was only the first lie I'd tell that night.

Consuela smiled. She gave me the keys and said goodbye to Apple, and I watched as she left through the front doors, struck dumb by the ease of it all.

"We made it!" Apple said, jumping a little in place. "We're going to meet them here, I can feel it."

"Yeah," I said. "I can feel it too."

Somehow I knew we were going to meet The Ruperts. I didn't know yet if I would cry or scream or faint. And I know that sounds like the reaction you'd have while getting mugged or something, but getting mugged and meeting your idols was basically the same thing: a moment of pure hysteria where you lose your mind and all control. The Ruperts could do that to a person. They could do it to me. And I couldn't wait.

Okay, so when I called The Rondack "swanky" earlier I may have been using the term loosely. It was swanky mostly in price, but otherwise it was trying to pull off a motel-for-rich-hipsters vibe. I guess that was what was in at the moment. We got key cards shaped like old brass keys with diamond-shaped key chains, ice machines could be found at the end of every hallway, and if you paid extra you could get crucifixes hung over your bed for the kitsch of it all. We opted out of the crucifixes.

Our room was on the eighth floor of the sixteen-story hotel, so while we weren't in anything fancy, we weren't slumming it on one of the lower floors either. Part of that was Apple's doing. We could barely afford one of the cheapest rooms, but Apple was the one who booked it, so I wasn't totally surprised when we walked into Room 822 and it turned out to be a junior suite.

41

The accommodations consisted of a room with a couch facing a large flatscreen mounted on the wall, a desk, and an armchair in the corner. Then there was the bathroom and, finally, the bedroom.

"Why is there only one bed?" Erin said when she saw it.

"Because one bed's all I need," Isabel said. She dropped her bag on the floor and launched onto the bed, springing so high I thought for sure she'd dent the ceiling. "I call the bed!"

"You can't just call the bed," I said.

"I call the bed too!" Erin said.

"Guess me and Erin are sharin' the bed," Isabel said. There was this crazy demented smile on her face, made crazier by the fact that she just kept on jumping. I shot Erin my best side-eye and made sure she caught it, 'cause since when did she share a bed with Isabel? Since when did she share a bed with anyone other than me?

I waited for Erin to say something about the sleeping arrangements. If I put up a protest I'd be labeled a needy loser who was attached at the hip to Erin, only said with a more growly voice and Isabel's signature sneer. It had to be Erin who spoke up, who chose me. But she didn't. She just scrolled through her phone, ignoring me. I wasn't used to it.

Apple sidled up next to me. "We can share the couch in the other room," she said.

"Bless," I muttered under my breath. There was no way both of us were going to be able to fit on that couch. It wasn't even a pullout. But I just smiled as she went into the other room.

"So what's the plan of attack?" Isabel said. She straightened herself out on the bed and pulled her messy blue-black hair back behind her ears.

"You tell us where the boys are, obvs," Erin said.

Isabel clicked her phone screen on, her thumbs working overtime. "The boys haven't been spotted leaving the hotel yet. Must mean they're still here."

"We have to find out what floor they're on," I said.

"We will," Erin said. "First, though, I'm parched. Apple?" she called into the other room. "Could you get us some ice?"

" 'Kay!"

"I always knew you were thirsty," Isabel said.

Erin playfully threw a pillow at her head. "All day errday, girl," she said.

Another in-joke that I didn't get. Classic.

I decided to flex an in-joke of my own.

"Hey, Isabel," I said. "What time is it?"

"The time is 3:21!" came the cheery English voice from Isabel's wristwatch. I knew I'd killed two birds with one stone when Erin exploded with laughter and Isabel rolled her eyes to mask her embarrassment.

"Did you know it took him *weeks* to record that?" I said.

"Weeks!" Erin howled.

Isabel's wristwatch was the product of a side project Rupert L. had spent millions of dollars on. His one and only flaw, as he so often reminded us in interviews, was his inability to tell time on analog clocks. He talked about it the way other people talked about actual afflictions, like diabetes or gluten allergies, but really he'd just missed that day in grade school when they taught kids the difference between the big hand and little hand.

There was the now infamous TV interview Rupert L. did where he recounted his childhood, growing up never knowing the time. The interviewer held up his watch and asked, "Can you tell me what time it is right now?" And Rupert L., using all of the muscles in his face to try and squeeze his tears back into their ducts, replied, "No, Matt. No, I cannot."

The "telling time problem," or TTP as it had come to be known, won Rupert L. a lot of sympathy from his fans, so he decided to put all of his money on a line of designer watches that literally *told* time. Anytime anyone within a ten-foot radius of the watch said, "What time is it?" his voice would come through to tell you. And you had to trust that it was correct, because there were no numbers to be found anywhere on the thing. As such, it totally failed as a watch in the strictest sense of the word. But it gave us his commercial, which was a gold mine for gifs. You've probably seen it already, but it's too good not to describe in its entirety.

It starts, weirdly, with a close-up of his bicep, muscles rippling beneath dark, tattooed skin. The camera zooms out to reveal Rupert L., hair freshly cut in a '90s-era Fresh Prince hightop taper fade. He's wearing a tank top, and pumping iron in front of a sky-blue backdrop—the same kind they use in school pictures. Then he launches into a whole diatribe about watches and time and how analog watches are a thing of the past. But the best line in the whole thing is this gem:

"It took me *weeks* to record my voice on the watches."

There was something about the way he said "weeks"— loud and squeaky—that always made me and Erin laugh like maniacs. And that was aside from the fact that it had taken him weeks to essentially record himself saying, "The time is" and then counting to fifty-nine. That was all he had to do, really— count to fifty-nine. It wasn't even like he *sang* the time.

"You know what he could've spent all those weeks doing?" Erin said, her laughter not yet dying down. *"Learning to tell time."*

We all liked Rupert L., but that didn't mean we couldn't also harp on him a little bit. He was the group's lovable idiot. (In this case "lovable" is used loosely and "idiot" is used emphatically.)

Isabel was starting to look mad. Well, madder than usual. "You ain't shit for your Rupert L. shade."

You probably think it's a little strange, the way we were talking about Rupert L. You're asking yourself how we could really call ourselves fans of The Ruperts if we were willing to make fun of one of them. I don't know how it was in the days of yesteryear (maybe all fangirls were like Apple—blindly devoted), but the fangirls of today are a way more sophisticated bunch. Loving someone so fiercely gave us permission to also be critical of them. You'll find the biggest Ruperts critics in Strepurs. Sometimes we won't like a tattoo they'll get, or we'll think a haircut makes them look like a drug addict, or we'll make fun of the way they'll pose in photographs. Just because we teased did not mean we didn't also love. Fandom is a complicated culture.

"We should try looking for the boys in the hotel gym," I said. "Rupert L. is always working out."

I waited for either of them to say something, especially Isabel, who would've probably given up her ability to sneer if it meant getting to see Rupert L. sweating those buns of steel off, but she was too busy with her phone, and by that point so was Erin. So I left them and went into the next room to check out the couch/bed situation. But I didn't have time to dwell on that, because that was the moment when the proverbial shit hit the fan and our lives as fangirls changed forever.

*   *   *

It all started with a knock on the door.

I knew instantly that it was Apple. I knew without question that she'd forgotten to take the room key with her when she left to get the ice. Apple forgot things with the frequency and attitude of someone who knew she could simply hire people to remember things for her. So I knew it was her outside the door. What I didn't know was that she wouldn't be alone.

Before I go on, I just want to state for the record that kidnapping one of The Ruperts was never part of the plan for me. When we booked the hotel room, all I knew was that we'd be one step closer to the boys. The best we could hope for was to see them, be close to them, breathe the same air as them. The most we could pray for was the opportunity to possibly get them to see us in return, to stop and talk to us, to love us the way that we loved them. All while taking a zillion selfies and bawling our eyes out.

But we never actually got to do that.

What actually happened, according to Apple's story, was this:

On her way to the ice machine at the end of the hall Apple saw someone already there, getting his own tub of ice. As fangirl luck would have it, it was none other than Rupert Pierpont.

I'll never know if the series of events that unfolded next would have been completely different if it was any of the other boys. If it was Rupert X. getting ice on the eighth floor at the exact same moment that Apple was, maybe none of this would have ever happened. Maybe I wouldn't be telling you this story. Maybe Apple would've just walked away. (Let's be real—she wouldn't have walked away.) But she didn't. And what happened, happened.

Anyway, you can imagine her reaction.

You can't?

Okay, let me help you out. Imagine a big blubbering mess of tear-streaked flesh and dry heaving. Apple did the only thing Apple could think to do. She ran at full fucking speed. Apple did not stop. Apple's overwhelming desire to hug/touch/hump Rupert P. by any means necessary meant nothing was going to get in the way of her flesh touching his. She did not stop until she football tackled Rupert P. to the ground.

Rupert P. was out cold instantly. This was actually kind of a best-case scenario, under the circumstances, because a tackle from Apple could've very well killed him.

I should probably mention that Apple is a beautiful girl who is 267 pounds. I know her exact weight because she tweets about it every day. We all stanned for our respective boys in our own respective ways, and the way Apple worshipped at Rupert P.'s throne was by tweeting him on the daily in the hopes that he would tweet her back. As of today he had tweeted her back a total of zero times. She hadn't stopped trying, though. Actually, she'd started a campaign to lose weight in order to get his attention. So far she'd lost sixteen pounds and he hadn't blocked her yet. (So . . . success?) At five feet four inches tall and 267 pounds, Apple was the lolly to our pixie sticks. And at top speeds I could only imagine she was deadly.

So when I opened the door, Apple was there, just as I'd expected, but she was out of breath and holding Rupert P.'s ankle in her fist, the rest of him draped on the floor behind her, limp as the sack of coal Santa brings for the naughty kids.

"I found one," she said.

And that was how my three friends and I came to be in possession of our very own boy bander.

4

So back to our second official group meeting, now with Rupert P. tied up in the other room.

"What are we going to do?" Isabel said.

We were in the room *not* occupied by the worst boy bander alive, and Isabel was pacing. This worried me. If Isabel was scared, that meant we should all be scared. Like I mentioned before, thanks to her family, Isabel knew of crime. And I was pretty sure kidnapping someone, no matter how irrelevant he was, was a pretty big crime.

I watched as she carved a path in the carpet around the bed, deep focus on her stony face, like a bull circling a red cape before charging. She seemed fine before, but I guess tying up an unconscious flop was one thing and listening to it make threats was quite another. Isabel was post postal.

"*¡Mierda madre culo puta!*" she said. "We need to think!"

When Isabel was mad she cursed in Spanish. I found this out when we were at the side entrance for *Live with Kelly and*

Michael once and Isabel tried to sneak past one of the security guards when he wasn't looking. He was too quick, though, and she ended up on their ban list. I'd never heard so many Spanish obscenities yelled so loud and all at once. But while Isabel might have grown up speaking (broken) Spanish, I'd aced it last year and knew that her curses never made any sense. Like now, for example, all she'd said was, "Shit mother ass bitch." Isabel was a nonsensical Spanish curser.

She turned to me, nostrils flared more than ever. Truly, her transformation into an angry bull was nearly complete. "*¡Que me miras, pendeja!* Think!"

(Roughly translated: "Why are you just looking at me, asshole? Think!")

"There's nothing to think about," I said. "We have to let him go, obviously."

I didn't think that would be such a revolutionary thought, but the way the rest of the girls stopped and stared, it was like I'd just announced that I hated The Ruperts' last album. I mean, yeah, I helped tie him up when Apple dragged him into the room, but really, what else was I supposed to do? What if he woke up and got scared? He could've lashed out at us. It was so Rupert P.'s style to start swinging before he even opened his eyes. Plus, when everyone grabbed a pair of tights to tie around his arms and legs, I wasn't about to be left out. Tying him up may have been a tad cray, but even I knew that keeping him crossed the line into all-out locodom. I thought of what Rupert K. would say if he were here to see this mess. I shut my eyes, and he was standing right next to me. "Not cool, love," he said in his deep, vanilla-milk-shake voice. "You can't very well keep him."

I seriously don't want to.

"Then you've got to let him go," Imaginary Rupert K. said.

A noise a lot like a grunt penetrated the wall and knocked me out of my reverie. It was as if Rupert P. had heard my thoughts.

"We can't let him go," Erin said. Firm. Steady. She was so calm, she even found time to check her cherry-red manicure real quick. "If we do he'll tell. And we don't want that."

It should've worried me right then that Erin was the only one among us who wasn't totally tripping. But I chalked it up to that just being Erin: calm, cool, and creamily complexioned. Usually Erin's levelheadedness in crazed situations was a relief for me, but more and more she was starting to freak me out. Who stayed calm when the biggest flop in the world's greatest boy band was threatening to end you?

"We should hold someone hostage because otherwise he'll *tell on us*?" I said. "Are we back in grade school? What kind of logic?"

"Let's listen to Erin," Apple said. "Right now we have him. If we let him go, we'll lose him. I'm not sure I like those odds."

"That's not how odds work, and I really didn't say any of that," Erin said.

"We should vote on what to do," Isabel said. She stopped pacing. "Anonymous vote."

"Why anonymous?" I asked.

"So that you don't embarrass yourself."

"Fine. Whatever. Anyone have a pen and paper?"

There was a moment of stillness as the four of us looked around, totally clueless. The only things any of us ever wrote with were our phones. And there was no way this was going to be a vote via group text.

"I see a pen," Isabel said, going to the bedside table. "No paper, though."

"Check the drawer," I told her.

"There's only a book in here." She took it out anyway and flipped through it. "No blank pages."

"Just rip one out," Erin said. "We'll write in the margins."

"Maybe we shouldn't r—"

But my words were cut short by the sound of pages being torn off the spine. Isabel handed a page to each of us and let the rest drift onto the bed like snowflakes. There was very little margin space, but I wrote around the heading (something about a Job). We all shared the pen. When we were done writing we crumpled all the papers and dumped them into Apple's orange ski cap.

"Okay, so this is the vote for what to do with Rupert P." It was put on me to read the votes, and the first piece of paper I pulled out was my own. "We let him go immediately," I read.

The second paper only had one word on it. "Sex."

We all turned to Apple. "Good suggestion," she said.

The third piece of paper said, "We keep him until we figure out what to do with him." I couldn't help my own incredulous reaction creeping through my voice as I read. I didn't like the way "what to do with him" sounded at all, but I kept reading.

The last vote was scrawled so severely I could barely make out Isabel's handwriting, but eventually I got it. "Whatever Erin says." I rolled my eyes. So much for the anonymity portion of the anonymous vote.

"It looks like we have a consensus," Erin said.

"Literally, what the fuck?" I said. "Tying him up was one thing—we're young and impressionable—but don't you guys think we're taking our stanning a little too far? I mean, people say all Strepurs are insane, and if we go through with this we'd be proving them right. We can still get out of this with minimal damage done. This probably happens to the boys all the time. I'm sure Rupert P. will understand that we let things get a little out of hand but that we're really sorry. I mean, do you guys really want to go from crazy fangirls to literally crazy fangirls?"

I didn't normally say so much at once. Usually I let Erin do all the talking. Most of the time I let other people convince me of something instead of me being the one to do the convincing. But this was important, and I could feel the gravitas of my statement as I looked around the room. I was the coach at halftime in every inspirational sports movie. My friends were the hapless team who didn't know what the hell they were doing, but all they needed was one measly pep talk to turn things around and come out on top. People were actually listening to me. I'd never felt so much like a leader before. It was invigorating. No wonder Erin always took charge.

Their shadowed lids dropped low over their eyes as they got lost in thought, thinking this over. It was happening. I was getting through to them. This was *working*.

Isabel cleared her throat. "I've given it a lot of thought," she said, "and I think this could be really great for my website."

"Then it's settled," Erin said. "We keep him. For now."

This was not the way inspirational sports movies went.

"This is some mechanical bullshit," I said. "You guys can keep riding it; I'm out."

I opened the door and walked out into the other room. Despite the blindfold, I knew Rupert P. could sense that I was there. He squirmed and squealed.

I really did want to do the right thing, but you have to understand who I was up against. Apple was never going to let Rupert P. go, Isabel was scary enough even when she wasn't in full bull mode, and Erin was . . . Erin. I couldn't turn on my best friend.

I didn't know what else to do. So I left.

5

I now lived in a world where kidnapping a boy bander was as common as asking for his autograph. I always knew that Isabel and Apple were next-level crazy, but the fact that Erin still wanted in on this was the real shocker. And I just ran away, too scared to really do anything. Chickenshit, like Isabel said. But I wasn't about to stay in that room, not when it required spending this much brainpower agonizing over the well-being of Rupert P. And the day I spent my time agonizing over the well-being of Rupert Pierpont was the day I officially couldn't recognize myself anymore.

I needed to think. I went to the hotel bar.

I probably should have left the hotel (in hindsight, I definitely should have), but I stayed. I guess I was hoping that if I could find a place to cool down, the other girls would cool down too and we could talk about it like rational people. Or at least as rational as a pack of fangirls could get.

The bar didn't have anyone posted at the lobby entrance to

card me, unlike the street entrance, which I could see through the glass door was barricaded by a pair of buff bodyguards blocking the Strepurs outside from stampeding through. I'd never been in a bar before, and though I probably shouldn't have been breaking any more laws that day, I couldn't deny that I felt instantly cool perching myself on a bar stool while fancy people chatted around me. It was still early in the day, so the place was mostly empty, but I liked that. It felt less threatening somehow.

The new setting helped to clear my mind. I hooked a finger into the bracelet on my left wrist and pulled it tight until it snapped against my skin. It was one of those bracelets made of white alphabet beads strung on a skinny elastic string. I don't know why snapping it like that always calmed me down, but it did. It was kind of fitting too, since I'd gotten the bracelet to sort of commemorate my dad. It was nice to think that he had a hand in helping me relax.

"How did you get in here?"

I let go of my bracelet and looked up. The bartender in front of me wore fingerless motorcycle gloves and a diamond stud in his left earlobe. And it took me a minute of awkwardly staring at him to realize that he was talking to me. "Oh, am I . . . not allowed to be here?" My cheeks were red. I did not need the mirrored wall behind him to tell me that, but it confirmed it anyway.

"You're allowed. I just meant, how did you bypass security?" He pointed his chin to the street door and the fans outside. "Girls have been trying to get in here all day. One made it past the door, but she was quickly escorted out. She cried a lot."

"I have a room here."

He scrunched his hairy eyebrows and watched me. He was hairy all over, with the hair on his head slicked and parted at the side and a beard that was neat but full. He was clearly one of those hipster guys who thought passing as a Civil War soldier was the height of cool. I pictured him trading his black button-down shirt and margarita mixer at the end of the week for a Union uniform and musket to keep fighting on the weekends. He would probably be one of those soldiers who played a somber song on his fiddle outside of his tent at night and wrote long letters to his faithful wife back home, her frayed, sepia-toned portrait tucked safely away in his breast pocket.

Or maybe he was just from Williamsburg.

"You're a fan, though, right? Of the boy band that's staying here tonight?"

Maybe he knew something about the boys. Maybe he could help me find Rupert K. I leaned forward. "Yeah," I said. "I am."

"And so you got a room here at the hotel," he said. "Wow. I don't know if that's the most determined thing I've ever heard of, or just the saddest."

I pictured a musket ball piercing his chest during battle.

59

"I don't think it's sad."

"You're spending all this money on a room, for what? So that you could maybe, possibly glimpse these guys—who don't deserve your attention, by the way. They're just regular boys, probably not unlike the ones in your own high school. They've got skid marks in their underpants just like any other person."

"Wretched," I muttered.

"What's your name?"

"My name?"

"Yes," he said. "What is it?"

I paused, but only for a moment. "Samantha Baker."

"Okay, Samantha Baker, tell me, because I'm really interested," he said. "You seem like a smart, nice girl. Why do you love The Ruperts?"

As if smart, nice girls couldn't possibly like a boy band. I didn't know if I should've felt offended or . . . Well, I was just plain offended. "Can't I just love them?"

"Of course you can. But I want to know why."

Why did I love The Ruperts? It was a fair question, and one that I got all the time from schoolmates, randoms on the street, concerned parent, but it was still a difficult thing to answer.

Was it their music? It was fun, and I listened to it almost exclusively, but even me, a die-hard Strepur, could admit that it wasn't anything groundbreaking. I'll be the first to defend

60

The Ruperts when people say that their music is just bubble-gum (who doesn't enjoy the simple deliciousness of gum sometimes?) or that it didn't merit any accolades because none of it was written by them (most of the greatest singers in the world don't sing their own music). But I can also call The Ruperts' music what it is: catchy, mindless pop.

Did I love them because they were hot? Because they *were* hot, minus Rupert P., of course. Rupert K. would always be my favorite, but the others had their charms. Rupert L. was a beefcake. A babe. One hundred percent bona fide. And Rupert X. may have been the most conventionally blond-pretty boy I have ever seen.

Did I love them because they were the only boys in my life who consistently told me I was beautiful? Probably.

I loved The Ruperts for who they were, sure, but I mostly loved them for how they made me feel. Which was happy.

The Ruperts made me happy. The simplest thing to be in the world. And the hardest.

After my dad died, happiness was a myth. The Ruperts changed all that.

"You can't help who you love," I said, shrugging.

Civil War Bartender slapped a dingy white dishcloth over his shoulder and leaned forward, his hairy eyebrows rising and falling dramatically. There was wisdom about to be imparted, I could feel it. Bless.

"What you don't even realize now—what you will only come to understand in time, but lucky for you, I'm here to tell you—is you're not going to give two shits about this band in a few years. In fact, I guarantee that this group that you admire so much and that you are putting all of your love and dedication and devotion into will be nothing more than an obsession you will be immensely embarrassed of having had. One day you'll be in college, maybe you'll be at a party, and someone will say, 'Hey, do you remember The Ruperts? How shitty was their music?' and you will have a moment of crisis: Do you admit your former love for them, or do you concede, because you know in your heart that this person is right? And guess what you'll say? You'll say, 'Yeah, their music was utter. Putrid. Garbage.'"

He leaned back again, looking way too proud of himself. I know what I said before, about the importance of being nice, but I have to say this guy was a total douchefuck.

"So, can I order a drink?"

If I had to sit through this lecture, maybe I could get a white wine to go with it. I'd heard white wine tasted better than red. Plus, it didn't stain.

"I can't serve you alcohol."

Classic. "Do you have Sprite?"

"One Sprite coming up."

He had no idea what he was talking about, but he was a Civil War bartender—I didn't expect him to. He was just another adult who forgot what it was like to love something so completely. In fact, he probably only liked things ironically, which meant he didn't really like things at all. And I may have only been a teenager, but I knew a truth that he had obviously never grasped: The joy you find as a teen, however frivolous and dumb, is pure, and meaningful. It doesn't matter that it might ferment and taste different when you're older. That's the whole point of being a teenager—not worrying about the future.

Other people may have seen fangirls as crazy teenage girls obsessed with a fad, but they couldn't understand the small but important joy you can get from indulging in these fandoms. They didn't understand that a new gif of Rupert K. grinning at you could be the difference between a crap day and a beautiful one. They didn't get the friendships that formed, the community of people who shared in your same joy. Maybe it was obsession, but it was also happiness; an escape from the suckiness of everyday life. And when you find something that makes you happy and giddy and excited *every day*, us fangirls know a truth that everyone else seems to have forgotten: You hold on to that joy tenaciously, for as long as you can. Because it's rare to get excited about anything these days. Ask your parents.

All of my best memories have something to do with The Ruperts. Like the times Erin and I spent at her house.

At school, Erin still had her popular friends: a seemingly unending supply of people she'd sit with in the back of classes, girls she'd go to the bathroom with to touch up mascara and trade lip balms, guys who'd carry her books just because she liked the idea of it. And while the two of us had our moments at school—meeting up at my locker every morning, eating lunch together, passing notes in the classes we shared—it was still vastly different from when we would hang out together after school. At Erin's house, we'd lie on our backs on her carpeted bedroom floor and sing Ruperts songs as loud as we could until we were out of breath and dizzy from laughing. Erin would always pop up and grab her hairbrush to sing into, and I would always marvel at the fact that nobody at school ever got to see this side of her—the geeky, fangirly, passionate-about-a-boy-band side. Because being too passionate or excited about anything was never cool. Erin only let me see that side of her.

"There you are!"

Speak of the devil. I spun at the sound of Erin's voice. She marched through the bar until she was beside me, taking the stool next to mine. Civil War Bartender watched us skeptically. Or maybe that was just the look of someone checking Erin out. "I've been looking all over for you," she said.

Civil War Bartender set my drink down in front of me, and Erin didn't even wait for him to ask what she wanted before saying, "Rum and Coke."

"What are you, like, seventeen?" he asked.

Erin didn't betray anything. Not an impeccably mascaraed eyelash moved on her face, but I could tell she was beaming at the fact that someone thought she was older than her actual age.

"Did no one ever tell you it's bad manners to question a woman's age?" she said.

"Do your parents know you're in a bar in the middle of the day?"

"I don't know," Erin said. "Do yours?"

I wish I could talk to him that way. But watching Erin do it was just as good. "What does a girl have to do to get a drink around here?" she said.

"Be not so much a girl," Civil War Bartender said. He smiled at her. He actually smiled! Did he think she was flirting with him or something? That this was some meet-cute banter? He was in for a rude awakening. I braced myself, wishing this bar served popcorn.

"Oh, you don't think I'm woman enough," Erin said. "Come on. I'll show you my tits for a drink."

"Erin!"

"Wow, did everyone just hear that?" Erin said, ignoring me. "The bartender just asked me to show him my tits for a drink!"

"Hey!" Civil War Bartender said.

"Well, I *never!*" She was making a scene. I was embarrassed and enthralled. Watching Erin was like watching a new movie without knowing any spoilers: can't-look-away-edge-of-my-seat realness.

"What is wrong with you?" Civil War Bartender hissed, but he was working hard behind the bar like he was Tom Cruise in *Cocktail*. "Rum and make the Coke cherry," Erin said.

He stamped the glass down in front of her, and she winked at him. "That's a good boy."

Civil War Bartender left us to go to the other side of the bar. He picked up a heavily dog-eared paperback copy of Jack Kerouac's *On the Road*.

Of course.

"It's too bad the bartender is such a shitstain. He could get it otherwise."

"Ew, Erin, he's prehistoric."

She cocked her head to the side and gave him a once-over. "I'd swallow."

"*So* wretched."

She turned to me. "So why'd you run off?"

"Erin, come on. You know this is wrong." We were away from Isabel and Apple. It was just the two of us. She had to agree with me on this.

"I was raised by nannies who never spoke to me. I know very little about right and wrong."

Okay, I guess she didn't agree. I watched as she clamped her crimson lips over the skinny cocktail straw, drinking through it from the corner of her mouth, as always. It was a preventative measure. Erin knew the rule about smokers' wrinkles around the upper lip. She made a vow never to let her lips turn into something ugly and puckered. She even avoided the dreaded duck face in all of her selfies for that very reason, and I had to give her major props for that. But as I watched her now, the red straw looked like a trail of blood at the corner of her lip, like something she forgot to wipe off after biting into someone. It gave me a chill.

I leaned close to her, making sure that no one was near enough to hear, but kept my voice down just in case. "Holding someone hostage in our room is outrageous."

"Isn't it, though?"

"I didn't mean it as a compliment."

"But think of the story you can get out of this. While other girls are sitting in their darkened rooms updating their Ruperts fap fantasy fics, we'll have the real thing to play with. You could write something brand-new."

She was talking about my fanfiction. In real life I never showed my writing to anyone except Erin, but on the Internet

I was kind of well-known for my fics. Most Strepurs wrote fics where they injected themselves into the story so that they could play out some deep Mary Sue fantasy of the boys falling in love with them. My fics were different. While they were still rpfs (real person fiction), they were about real issues. There was one fic I wrote where each chapter focused on a different Rupert and explained the origin stories behind their tattoos. I worked with the concept that the reason Rupert L. had covered most of his chest and arms in twenty-seven different renditions of a bunny rabbit from his favorite obscure British animated show was because he was really self-conscious about his body and wanted to cover it up in nostalgia for a simpler time when he had no body image issues.

See? Totally plausible.

My favorite chapter in the fic imagined why Rupert K. had gotten the words "I do" on his forearm. It was the only tattoo he had and he'd never spoken publicly about what it meant, but in my fic I wrote a whole romantic scenario about waiting to meet the right girl and his ideals about marriage and commitment.

"This isn't exactly fic-worthy," I said.

"Not fanfic," Erin said. "You could write something original."

"Don't you like my fanfic?"

I always emailed Erin my new ideas before I ever wrote

them down, and she was the first person to see the completed chapters before I posted them.

"You know I do," Erin said, but she started picking at her cuticles—something she did when she was getting tired of talking about a topic. "Whatever, forget fics for a minute. Keeping Rupert P. could lead to us finding the rest of the boys. It could lead to a lot of things."

"Like jail," I said. "It could lead to jail."

"The whole situation is pregnant with possibility."

"And I'm too young to be a mother."

She threw her head back and laughed, and a little thrill went through me at the sound of it. Anytime I could get Erin to laugh was a good moment. Anytime I could cause her to be pumped or happy felt awesome, honestly. It was part of the reason she was always the first to get new chapters of fic from me. Her praise was always more important than the praise of hundreds of readers online.

"Be real," she said. "You know what they say. The night is young and so are we."

"We've gone too far, Erin. You know I'm always with you on things, but . . ."

She looked at me expectantly, but it was harder than I thought it would be to disagree with her. Maybe if I phrased it a certain way, she'd see it the way I saw it. "We're kidnapping an international superstar."

"Rupert P. can't even sing."

"I don't care if he's basic, it's still illegal."

Erin put her drink down and brushed her hair back without actually putting any of it behind her ears. Her blonde hair was far too beachy to belong to a New Yorker in winter, but Erin had discovered the secret to effortlessly wispy-chic hair, and she was keeping it to herself. The hair added to the overall allure. She always said she was saving herself for Rupert X., and while lots of girls said the same thing, Erin had the sort of looks where if she ever did get in a room alone with Rupert X., her dreams would very probably come true. And Erin always did get her way.

When she leaned forward, her hair fell around her face, and her hands fell onto mine.

"Have you given any thought to what would happen if we let Rupert P. go right now?" The pause was meant to be dramatic. I let her have it. "We'd be so dead."

"We'll be dead whether we keep him for an hour or whether we keep him for a day. We're fucked sideways either way."

"Or we can wait until we figure it out so we're not," she said. "The answer will come to us eventually."

With her hands in mine, she smiled at me, and I guess it put me at ease. I'd always trusted Erin before; why shouldn't I trust her now?

"Wait, did you just leave Rupert P. up there?" I said. "With Apple?"

"Don't worry, Isabel's there to make sure she doesn't molest him."

"Did you at least warn them not to get him wet or feed him after midnight?"

I smiled at my *Gremlins* joke, but Erin just stared at me blankly. Honestly, I know all of Tumblr is obsessed with the '90s right now, but if you just go back a little further to the '80s, you'll find a treasure trove of retro awesomeness. The movies are super vintage, and the fashions are a trip: I'd take big hair over chokers any day.

"And you trust Isabel?" I said, getting back on topic. "She's probably too busy stoking the fanwank in her site's comments section to care what Apple does."

"Quite frankly. I trust Isabel. She's chill."

"She's *chill*? I didn't realize you guys had gotten so chummy." I tried to sound casual, bring up the topic in a non-chalant way, but I really was curious: Where was I when Erin and Isabel decided to become BFFs?

Erin cocked her head to the side and smiled, a look on her face like she could read my mind, which made me slightly happy and slightly scared. "Aww." She pinched my cheek. "You're still my best girl."

I averted my gaze, but smiled too, reassured. Maybe I'd been making too much of in-jokes and bed sharing. And then I saw her, sitting alone at a small round table in the corner. "Holy shit. Michelle Hornsbury."

Michelle Hornsbury was gorgeous, even from this distance. Impeccable waves of brown hair cascading down her shoulders and back. Posh Brit. Dewy skin. Permanent rosy blush. Eyes that sparkled. Rupert Pierpont's girlfriend, in the flesh.

Erin whipped out her phone. I thought she was going to citizen pap her, take a discreet pic, but when she showed me the screen, it was only Michelle Hornsbury's Twitter. "Michelle Hornsbury just posted this five minutes ago."

> Rupie is showing me the sites in NYC.
> Love him. #bestboyfriendever #lovinlife
> #NooYawk #fuggedaboutit #xoxo #blessed
> #bae #baegoals #bagels

Michelle Hornsbury was a gorgeous girl. And she was a liar.

"We should go talk to her."

"Are you crazy?"

"I think we've proven today that we're all a little crazy," Erin said. She hopped off her stool. "I'm doing it. And if you don't come after me, I might say something really stupid, like that we accidentally kidnapped her boyfriend."

She left her rum and cherry Coke barely touched on the bar. Of course, I followed her. I always followed her.

"Hi!" Erin said when we got to Michelle Hornsbury's table.

She looked up from her phone, all doe eyes and sparkly pink lip gloss. "Hello," she said. Doe eyes, lip gloss, and wariness.

"You're Michelle Hornsbury, aren't you?"

Michelle Hornsbury smiled and looked as she always did in pictures: somehow frightened and unsure. A bunny rabbit who suddenly realized she wasn't alone. "Why yes, I am."

"I'm Erin. And this is my friend—"

"Diane Court," I said. I knew Erin was giving me a look, even though I wasn't watching her.

"Pleased to meet you," Michelle Hornsbury said. "Are you girls Hornies?"

You'd be forgiven to think Michelle Hornsbury just asked us a very inappropriate question. In fact, she was only asking if we were fans of hers. "Hornies" were what Michelle Hornsbury fans called themselves. Terrible fan name, I know, but what else do you expect from fans who came up with the name "Strepurs"?

While Michelle Hornsbury had no discernible talents, and therefore no reason to be famous whatsoever, some of Rupert P.'s fans spilled over into becoming fans of his girlfriend.

I always thought obsessing over a famous person's significant other or parent or sibling was dumb, but there were still a lot of people who did it. Michelle Hornsbury's fans were dedicated enough to build websites in her honor and send her cookies whenever she said she was feeling sad on Twitter.

So, were we fans?

"Quite frankly!" I lied.

"Can we sit down?" Erin said.

Michelle Hornsbury's smile was still present, as ever, but dimmer now, even more unsure, if that was possible. "Uh, I don't know . . . I really should get back to my . . ." She looked around the totally empty table, the candy-colored cosmo in her hand, her phone. "Emails. I've got loads of emails to read."

Erin sat down anyway. Not wanting to stand around like an idiot, I sat down too.

"Well, alright," Michelle Hornsbury said. She was originally from Derby, England, but she must have cleaned up her Midlands accent in the time she became Rupert P.'s girlfriend, because now Michelle Hornsbury was All Posh All The Time.

"Where's Rupert P.?" Erin asked. She just dove right in. I kicked her under the table. Kicking under the table was the universal sign for *You're so bad!* But Erin didn't even flinch.

"Oh, he's busy working away," Michelle Hornsbury said. "Working hard to get ready for that concert for you girls. Will you be attending?"

"We couldn't score tix," I said, suddenly hopeful. I thought maybe she'd have an extra pair in her purse that she was just waiting to give away to the first person who asked. Surely that was how fame worked?

"Shame," Michelle Hornsbury said.

I guess that was not how fame worked.

"How did you girls get into the hotel, by the way? Security seems pretty tight." She looked around like someone in need of said security.

"We have a room here," I said.

"Here? At this hotel?"

"Yes," I said.

"How did you manage to find a room? I thought the hotel had no vacancies this week."

"Actually, we booked our room a couple of nights ago," Erin said. "And there were a few others available too."

"Oh," Michelle Hornsbury said. Her Bambi eyes looked into the bottom of her glass.

"Michelle," Erin said. "You just tweeted about being with Rupert P. five minutes ago."

"I was," Michelle said, her eyes going big again. "He was

just here. And now he's gone. Like I said. Work. Always working. Such a workaholic, that boy, bless him."

"We actually just saw Griffin Holmes earlier," Erin said.

Griffin Holmes, stylist to The Ruperts. I could not believe Erin had just brought him up. She did it to get a reaction out of Michelle Hornsbury, I was sure of it. And judging by the way Michelle stood up abruptly, she had. "Lovely to meet fans, as always," she said. "Unfortunately, I must be going now. Toodles!"

We watched her go, and then Erin and I looked at each other. *"Toodles!"* we said in unison.

"So you're Diane Court now?" Erin said, eyebrow arched and perfectly skeptical. "I thought Andie Walsh was your go-to."

"It felt like a *Say Anything* moment."

Erin didn't get it, but also didn't care enough to stay on the topic. "Okay, *Diane*, tell me that wasn't *delicious*."

I shrugged, noncommittal. I felt slightly guilty about how we'd just conducted ourselves.

But Erin wouldn't let it go. "Tell me that was not crème-de-la-crème, four-star delicious."

Erin's biggest talent in life was making being bad feel so good. Because there was no way I would've enjoyed that if Erin wasn't there. And yet, I couldn't lie. I got a tiny kick out of it. "Okay," I said. "It was kind of delicious."

"Know what's even more delicious?"

Erin tucked her fingers under the strap slinked over the back of Michelle Hornsbury's vacated chair. She pulled up a purse and dangled it before me.

"She forgot her purse!" I said. "We have to return it to her."

"Would you loosen the pretty white bows in your hair just once? Let's have some fun with it first."

"We can't just take her purse."

"We aren't going to. We're just going to look through it for the proverbial shits and giggles."

"Erin, this is next-level wrong."

She ignored me.

In retrospect, we should've just left, but we didn't. We never should've touched that purse. But Erin had to open it. She had to look through it. She had to take a souvenir.

Michelle Hornsbury's purse was basically a first aid kit if you ever found yourself walking down the street and needing to transform into a Proper Girl ASAP. There was every type of makeup a person could possibly need, the requisite feminine products, snacks, even a mini bottle of tequila.

"Is Michelle Hornsbury secretly a lush?" I asked.

Erin shrugged. "Who knows, but let's start the rumor that she is." She pulled out a fuchsia alligator-skin wallet first and rifled through it. "Only five bucks American, the rest are pounds." She put it back and then took out a tube of lip gloss in Pink Lemonade, the same tint that Michelle Hornsbury had been wearing. "I say we go back to our room, show this to Rupert P., and tell him we ain't fuckin' around." Erin laughed, really gleefully. It was pretty infectious.

"So now you want him to think we kidnapped his girl-friend too?"

She shrugged one shoulder. "Why not?"

In the grand scheme of things, if I really thought about it, this probably wasn't even the craziest thing a Strepur had done to The Ruperts. There was that girl in Australia who dressed as a maid at their hotel, got their room key, and watched them sleep for the whole night. She recorded it with night-vision video. Thanks to her, we now knew that Rupert X. snored and that Rupert L. cried out in his sleep. She was a hero among us, really.

Was doing crazy stuff to show your love just part of the Strepur tradition? Was pretending to threaten the life of Rupert P.'s girlfriend worth it if it was just in good fun?

While Erin's schemes were normally exciting, now she was genuinely starting to scare me. Erin had always been edgy, but this was veering into sadistic. She'd definitely been spending too much time with Isabel.

"You're not serious about the lip gloss, right?" I said. "We can't torment Rupert P. like that."

"We're already off the rails," Erin said. "Might as well make it a true pileup."

"I don't know . . ."

"Remember that time we went to the mall?"

How could I forget? When you lived in New York City, going to one of the malls here wasn't a thing people normally did. But one day Erin and I got it in our heads that we wanted to be like Real American Teenagers, and Real American Teenagers went to the mall.

"You made up this elaborate lie that got us both out of school," Erin said. "It was totally Ferris Bueller of you."

Erin referencing an '80s movie? She really did know the way to my heart.

"We took the subway to the Manhattan Mall," I said.

"What a shithole."

"And you stole that cardboard cutout of Rupert X. from Claire's!"

"Rupert X. had no business displaying tween jewelry anyway."

"Your klepto ways are a thing of legend," I said.

We'd taken the cutout and run like hell until we found a photo booth. I'd always wanted to have those strips of photo booth photos you only ever saw in movies. Erin and I spent all of our pocket money posing with Rupert X.'s cutout, and he actually came out pretty lifelike in the pictures, except for the occasional glare off his forehead and the fact that he never changed expressions.

Erin liked trouble the way some people liked chocolate:

Too much could become a problem, but a little once in a while could be a naughty guilty pleasure. The way she thrived on it was contagious, and now, sitting across from her in the hotel bar, I was itching.

"Do you think we could get Rupert P. to give us concert tickets out of this?" I joked.

"That is so ransom of you. I like the way you think, girl."

I took the lip gloss from her hand. "We're leaving this here, right?"

"Of course," Erin said. "I was only kidding about that."

I was relieved. Maybe Erin wasn't as sadistic as I thought.

"Come on, we can't keep Rupert P. waiting," she said. "It's getting late."

"If only we had one of Rupert L.'s watches to tell us what time it is."

"It's like a cuckoo clock for your wrist," Erin said.

"I'll tell you what's cuckoo . . ."

She cracked up and I joined in the laughter. The thing about me and Erin was that we could always make each other laugh. That trumped everything else.

I got up to go first, with Erin following behind me. When I turned around I saw her put the pink lip gloss tube into her pocket.

6

Back in the room, we found Apple straddling Rupert P.'s lap and dragging her tongue along the side of his face.

"What the fuck everlasting?!" Erin said.

"Oh, hey, guys," Apple said. "I was telling Rupie that everything would be a-okay with just a lick and a promise. The promise part was my full devotion to him."

Rupert P. moaned through the tights.

"Isabel, you were supposed to watch her," Erin said.

But the only thing Isabel was watching was her phone, like I knew she would be. "She's only licking him," she said, lying cross-ankled on the bed. "It could be so much messier and you know it."

Erin pulled Apple off Rupert P.'s lap. He tried to bounce in place, move around some, but the chair was one of those really ornate and heavy armchairs that wasn't really going to budge unless you meant to do some damage, and judging by

Rupert P.'s spaghetti arms, I wasn't sure he was strong enough to move it an inch, let alone tip it over if he wanted to.

He gave up all attempts to escape almost immediately, though he still moaned. The tights around his mouth were soaked, either with his own saliva or with Apple's. Maybe the moisture around his cheeks was from tears. My gut suddenly twisted with a sour feeling of guilt and sympathy that I could not ignore.

"Was he crying?" I whispered to Apple, low enough so that Rupert P. couldn't hear.

She shot me an icy glare. "Are you implying he was crying because I was just sitting on his lap? You think I hurt him? You think I'm fat?"

Her appearance was one of Apple's main hang-ups. Fat was what she saw in the mirror every day and the conclusion she always jumped to when things didn't go right in her life. And, I'm certain, it was also the reason she chose Rupert P.—out of all the Ruperts—to love the most. I have this theory that choosing which boy to love in a boy band says a lot about a person. I think Erin loved Rupert X. because she believed she was hot enough to love such an attractive person. I think Isabel loved Rupert L. because she felt she was tough enough to love someone with muscles so big. I think I loved Rupert K., deep down, because he was the most approachable one in the bunch.

And I think Apple loved Rupert P. because she couldn't even envision herself being loved by one of the cute boys. She loved him because he was the only one who she thought could possibly love her back.

I think that boy bands don't worry about having a snaggletooth of an ugly member in their otherwise perfect row of teeth—boys—because they know that there are girls like Apple out there. Girls who really don't like themselves enough to aim higher.

Honestly, if I thought about it too much, it broke my heart.

But it was just a theory I had.

"No, Apple, I'm not saying you're fat. I'm implying he was crying because he's being kidnapped."

"We're not *kidnapping* him," Apple insisted.

I waited for her to explain just what exactly we *were* doing, but she didn't add anything more.

"Did any of you see any of Rupert L.'s tweets recently?" Isabel said. She didn't wait for us to answer and proceeded to read off her phone: *"To the girls outside of the hotel please be careful. It is not safe to stand beneath the scaffolding by the entrance."*

Isabel read it nicely enough, but I still imagined his tweet with all the spelling errors and grammar mistakes it probably contained.

"This is from half an hour later: *We've just been informed cops are having trouble with crowd control outside of the hotel. Be safe.*"

The four of us stared at one another for a moment, then ran to the windows at the same time. There were two windows in the room, and Erin and I took one while Isabel and Apple took the other. The wind was too loud when we opened the windows, but even so, I could hear all of our gasps. The crowd outside was even bigger than it was when we came in only an hour ago. Girls flooded the cobblestone streets. There were even girls across the street, as if they'd even be able to see the boys from there. It didn't seem right, this many people on what was heretofore a quiet city block. It was like they were stretching the narrow street, forcing small SoHo to conform to their overindulgent size. I could make out a few figures in dark blue, officers making sure there was a walkway and that cars could pass, but there weren't enough to come between a stampede of teen girls and their favorite boys.

"That isn't safe," Isabel said. "It won't end well."

A normal person would've maybe been concerned while saying those things, and they certainly wouldn't have a demented smile on their face, but then this was Isabel we were talking about. "Best," she whispered.

I tried to pretend she didn't just secretly wish for a full-on Strepur revolt.

Erin stepped back from the window. "Isabel, what else is Twitter saying?" she asked.

Isabel turned away from the window too, her phone her main focus once again. "The Strepurs outside say they haven't seen any of the boys yet, but supposedly Rupert K. left really early in the morning and he's not back yet."

Classic. The only reason I was here was to see Rupert K. and he wasn't even in the hotel.

"We have to find out where their room is before they all head out," Erin said. "Hey, Rupert, what room are the rest of the boys staying in?"

He shook his head. Obviously, with the tights in his mouth he couldn't answer, but it was clear that he also *wouldn't* answer.

"I'm not sure if you realize this, but you're the one who's tied up," Erin said. "You're at our mercy."

He stayed silent for a minute but then nodded his head. Erin pulled the tights off his mouth so they were ringed around his neck but left the blindfold on. "I'm not telling you anything until you untie me. Bitch."

"We're not untying you until you tell us something."

"Guess it's a Mexican standoff, then, innit?"

"First the drug cartel and now this. Is he obsessed with Mexico or what?" Isabel said.

"I'm not at your mercy, YOU'RE AT MINE!" Rupert P. yelled, and it was something awful, fierce and violent. It made us all suck in a breath. "As soon as I get out of here—and I WILL get out of here—you're all done for, do you understand? All four of you. Yeah, I can tell how many of you there are by your voices. And it all depends on my testimony just how much trouble you'll get into. So it's up to you. Either let me go now and get off with a lenient punishment, or keep me tied up longer and go to jail for it. Choice is yours, ladies."

We were silent, and I knew what it was that had shut us up. That word.

Jail.

Suddenly I was in the pit at a concert, hundreds of bodies crushing me against the barricades, cutting off my air supply. It felt like that, except for the exhilarating part.

I went to the bathroom door and opened it, motioning for everyone to follow me inside.

"Oi! Where are you going!" Rupert P. yelled, but his voice was drowned out when I shut the door.

"I am not going to jail," I said.

"No one is going to jail," Erin said.

"I watch *Orange Is the New Black*," Isabel said. "If I go down, you're all coming with me."

"Rupert P. would never press charges," Apple said. "I know him better than anyone, and he's got a huge heart. He would never put us through that. And anyway, I'm sure we can work something out with him. If it comes down to it, I'll volunteer to perform sexual favors."

"In exchange for us not going to jail?" Isabel said.

"Yes, also that."

"Get a grip, girl," Erin said.

"Fine, I could try talking to him first. We should get rid of the blindfold. If I could just look him in those stunning amber eyes—"

"The blindfold stays," Erin said.

"Preach," Isabel said. "Once the blindfold is off, he makes us; once he makes us, we're jailbait."

"No one is going to jail!" Erin snapped. She didn't exactly lose her cool, but it was the first time all day that she'd been close to it, and she seemed to realize it too. She ran a hand through her hair and shook it. It seemed to at once calm her down and revitalize the volume in it. Neat trick.

"Do you guys not realize that we have all the power right now?" Erin said. "Because he realizes it, and it's got him going schizo. So long as Ginger's terrified, we've got the upper hand."

"Shit, Erin, I'm not in the business of terrifying gingers," I said, unsure but still determined to talk some much-needed sense. "You think we'll get anything out of him? He won't even give us room numbers. And I'm not going to sit back and watch while Apple gives him a rubdown. We need to let him go."

I watched Erin carefully, trying to gauge what was going on in her mind, trying to find her tell. I hated that she could so easily read my mind sometimes but her mind was still largely a mystery to me. She was our unspoken leader, always had been, and for one reason or another we always listened. I didn't know if I expected her to call me out for being such a pussy about this and not sticking it out, or if she'd agree with me. And then I saw something in her: a twitch in her lips, a furrow in her brow. Still imperceptible to the other girls, but not to me. I'd known her the longest. I knew her most intimately. I knew she was thinking this through. She was coming around. The old Erin was back and was about to get on my side on this.

"Well . . ." she said.

But then someone's ringtone cut her off. On instinct we all checked our phones, but the noise wasn't coming from inside the bathroom. We opened the door and followed the sound. It led us straight to the one place none of us (except Apple) wanted to go. Rupert P.'s lap.

That was the moment something changed in Erin. There was a renewed vigor, and it was like nothing was ever said in the bathroom. That one little moment where I saw her resolve blink, that moment was totally gone now. Her eyes were wide open.

"Get his phone!" she said.

Of course, this was Apple's job, and she took to the task no questions asked. She squeezed her fingers into one of the pockets in his jeans, ignoring his yelps of protest. Then she went to the other pocket. After a moment she went back to the first. "Oops. It was in the first pocket all along."

She handed the phone to Erin, who took it from her and smiled down at the caller ID.

"It's Griffin," she said. "Should we answer it?"

"Don't you dare," Rupert P. said.

"We should let this go to voice mail," Erin said. "I'm sure the message will be very enlightening."

It stopped ringing, and we all listened for the ting of the voice message alert. "You can't listen to that voice mail," Rupert P. said. "And not only because I absolutely do not allow it, but because you haven't got the password." He began to laugh. "Joke's on you, you psychopaths! Go ahead, keep my phone. It's completely useless to you without the password. And you'll never get it out of me."

"Apple?" Erin said. A smile was spreading on her face the way blood spreads when it's spilled.

"Try P-I-M-P," Apple said.

Erin's index finger bounced around the screen four times, and the phone turned as bright as her smile.

"Bloody hell," Rupert P. murmured.

Erin put the newest voice mail message on speaker.

"Babe," came the deep male voice on the phone, *"where are you? I've been waiting in my room all this time. Just went out for a bit of ice, did you? I hate when you . . . You can be such an arsehole some-times! But then you're well aware of that, aren't you? I'm done waiting. You can spend the night in your own room."*

And just like that, I knew that we had him.

And that Erin wasn't about to let him go.

7

Rupert P. was gay.

I guess I should've mentioned that earlier, because—full disclosure—all of us kind of knew it already. All of us except Apple, apparently.

She marched up to me, grabbed my hand, and led me to the farthest corner of the room. "Why would Griffin call Rupert P. 'babe'?"

In case you're not up on the major players in The Ruperts' camp, allow me to educate you. Griffin Holmes was the stylist for The Ruperts. It was his job to outfit each of the boys in the clothes they wore on tour and for events. Also, he was rumored to be Rupert P.'s secret boyfriend.

"And why was Griffin's name the first thing Rupert P. said when he woke up?" Apple said.

Maybe Rupert P. gets tied up a lot, Apple. Maybe Griffin's the one doing the tying. Maybe that's their thing. "I don't know."

I should've told her then, but I couldn't. Rupert P.'s sexual orientation was a point of much speculation among the fans. Except Rupert P. fans. Which should not come as a surprise; if they were willing to overlook the fact that he was a disaster of a human being, they were willing to overlook the fact that he was gay. If I told Apple what the rest of the world and I secretly already knew, it would break her heart.

"Apple, calm your tits," Erin said, her tone as level and patient as a teacher's. "No need to lose your chill because your lover boy likes dick."

Leave it to Erin to do the job for me.

"I do not like dick!" Rupert P. said.

"He does not like dick!" Apple said.

"Well, that settles it," Isabel snorted.

Erin walked up to Rupert P., and the way she was looking at him was the way a cat might look when you tossed it a shiny new ball of yarn. She swept an index finger along his jaw, down to his chin, and there was absolutely nothing sweet or romantic about it. Frankly, it scared me.

"Is Griffin your boyfriend?" she asked, her voice so saccharine it made my teeth ache. "Do you want us to get him for you?"

Why was she acting like this?

Apple stepped in front of Erin. "Rupert P. and Griffin Holmes are just friends," she said.

"Sure they are," Erin said. "Just like your always-a-bachelor uncle Patrick and his roommate Alistair are just friends."

"Uncle Patrick doesn't like to live alone!"

"Can we get back to the tea here?" Isabel said. "We have his phone."

It was then that we all realized, with the same instant force of clarity, that Rupert P.'s cell phone was an unearthed treasure trove. It didn't matter that none of us except for Apple liked him. A person's secrets were worth something. And a phone was nothing if not a keeper of secrets. I got what Erin meant about having all the power. I was starting to feel it.

Rupert P.'s phone was everything we could hope to get our hands on.

It was one hundred times more valuable to us than he would ever be.

It was almost as good as meeting the boys in person.

Almost.

It was friggin' comical how fast I dropped my resolve to release Rupert P. in favor of having all that info on his phone.

But even though Isabel and Apple and I all lunged for it at the same time, Erin took a step back, keeping our new toy out of our overeager hands.

She looked to Rupert P. "On behalf of me and my friends,

I apologize. I think we may have accidentally caused a tiff between you and your boyfriend."

"Alright, alright, I surrender," Rupert P. said. "I give in. You've had your fun now. Do you want to make a deal? Let's make a deal!"

"Do I look like a fucking game show?"

"Please," Rupert P. said. "You give me back my phone, I walk out of here and I don't say anything to anyone."

"Don't you have a girlfriend also?" Erin said. "Girls, doesn't Rupert P. have a girlfriend?"

"Michelle Hornsbury," Apple said. "She's quote-unquote nineteen, a quote-unquote university student, a quote-unquote model—"

"Don't forget beard," Erin interjected. "She is also a very dedicated beard."

"Quote-unquote?" Rupert P. asked meekly, hopefully.

"No," Erin said. "She is very factually performing her duties as a beard."

"Wait, what's a beard?" Apple said, stroking her jaw.

Isabel cleared her throat and spoke in an authoritative voice. "A beard is someone who dates a gay person of the opposite sex in order to make that person appear heterosexual."

"What?" Apple said.

I tried to explain it this time using simpler words. "It's when a girl dates a gay guy, making him look straight."

"I still don't get it."

"Damnit, Apple, do we have to draw you a fucking Venn diagram?" Erin snapped. "Michelle Hornsbury is only Rupie's pretend girlfriend so that he may maintain a straight image in the public eye." She turned to Rupert P. "Am I warm?"

"You know nothing about my relationship with my girlfriend!"

"Quote-unquote."

"We met Michelle Hornsbury downstairs," I said.

"Ah yes, lovely beard, that beard," Erin said.

"You met Michelle Hornsbury downstairs?" Apple whispered fiercely. "Was she stunning in real life? Are the rumors true? Does she smell like cotton candy and the tears of Rupert P. stans?"

"It would break her heart if she found out about Griffin, wouldn't it?" Erin went on. "Or is she in on it? Oh shit, is it like an arrangement between you two? Why, I *never*."

"Walk me out of here with my blindfold on," Rupert P. said, the desperation in his voice so thick you could spread it on toast. "Put me in the lift, I swear I won't look at any of you. I don't know who any of you are—you'll never get in trouble."

"Fuck that," Erin said. Behind me, Isabel giggled. No matter how often they were popping up these days, Isabel's giggles never sounded quite right, and that was especially true now. Like spotting a clown at a cemetery.

"Do you want autographs?" Rupert continued. "Is that it? Do you want me to sign something? A body part, perhaps? Your breasts?"

"Ew, no."

"Wretched."

"Child, please."

"Quite frankly!" Apple squealed. She pulled on her shirt, but I stopped her before she got the whole thing off.

"We should take the deal," I whispered to Erin.

"Don't be such a spaz." She held up the phone, her eyes blazing but leaving me feeling suddenly cold. "We have all the power now, remember? We can make him our bitch."

She turned to him and said, "Time for you to start bargaining, cowboy. Think that's something you can *juggle*?"

"I'll give you whatever you want. Just please don't go through my phone. That's private."

He told her not to go through the phone, so of course she had to. The first stop was his gallery. As much as I knew this was wrong, as much as I felt bad for Rupert P., whose posture was suddenly stick straight, his head high, his ears perked—a puppy who thought it heard a noise at the door—I couldn't not look at his phone. I was weak. Don't judge me.

We all crowded around the phone and Erin started scrolling through the pics, the minutes filling with our excited squeals every time we saw one of our boys in photographs from backstage on tour. There was a series of shots of Rupert L. bench-pressing with his shirt off, and all the orifices of Isabel's face went round: her eyes got extra big, her mouth formed a silent O, even her nostrils flared with pleasure. "Iconic," she whispered.

There were a few hidden camera–style shots of Rupert X. playing with his hair, and then a few more where he was looking directly at the phone with a pressed expression on his pretty face.

And then there were the pics of Rupert K.

In a lot of the pictures he was posing for selfies with Rupert P., smiling, happy. I was looking at never-before-seen pictures of Rupert K., and it was starting to hit me that we truly had unprecedented access to the boys. Somebody send help.

But then Erin stopped scrolling. At first I couldn't make out the image. It wasn't an image at all, actually. There was a PLAY button in the middle of the screen, surrounded by an eye, lips, an elbow? Then I realized what it was.

Isabel's eyes lit up. "What a time to be alive," she said.

"That's not real. That's photoshopped," said Apple.

How to explain that you couldn't photoshop videos?

"Jackpot," said Erin. "The boy planted his own evidence. *Quelle surprise.*"

Erin's red-nailed finger clicked the PLAY button, and we all watched as Rupert P. made out with a guy. Definitely Griffin Holmes.

Erin stopped the video before it could get any further.

There was the sound of a whimper, and for a moment I wasn't sure if it came from Rupert P. or Apple. I patted her shoulder in a show of support anyway.

"You and Griffin make a cute couple," Erin said. She actually sounded sincere for once. "I don't know why you'd try to hide your love."

Rupert P.'s head fell forward and his shoulders slumped. "Why do you all hate me so much?" he said. "What have I ever done to deserve it?"

"Well, there was that time The Ruperts canceled their second American tour because you said you had mono when you were actually seen all over Vegas gambling hundreds of thousands of dollars for four weeks straight," Isabel said.

"He has a debilitating gambling problem!" Apple said. "It's nothing to joke about."

"Or that time you held a private juggling performance for that dictator's son's birthday party," Erin said.

"He had to pay off his gambling debts somehow!" Apple said.

"There was the famous nose-picking incident at the Video Music Awards," I said.

"The fact that you're a Roman Polanski sympathizer," Erin said.

"The time you punched that baby in the finger," Isabel said.

"That baby had it coming!" Apple said.

"The time you drunkenly called in to that radio station and spoiled the ending to *Game of Thrones*."

"Everyone had already read the books!" Apple said.

"The time you threw up on the entire first row at the Berlin concert," Isabel said.

"He had bad shellfish!" Apple said.

"Bad shellfish and a bottle of absinthe."

"Do you realize how much effort it takes to get every *single* person in the front row?" Erin asked. "Green slime everywhere."

"All of those girls agreed it was really easy to wash out of their hair!" Apple said.

"The nudes."

"Come on," Apple said. "Everyone and their grandma has leaked nudes these days!"

"The racism."

"The ageism."

"Not to mention the sexism."

"The well-documented hatred of your own fans."

"The bordering-on-disturbing Troll doll collection."

"Did we miss anything, girls?"

"That about covers it," I said. And that, ladies and gents, is what made Rupert P. of The Ruperts such a spectacular. Fucking. Flop.

"So what did you ever do to deserve this?" Erin said. "You're a cold sore on picture day. You are a fart in a cramped elevator. You are the gum on the bottom of my Louboutins. You, Rupert Pierpont, are a *miracle* of awful. But hey, you do you."

"Alright, alright," Rupert P. said. "Just tell me what I can do so that you don't show anyone those videos of me and Griffin. Please!"

Erin walked over to his chair, stood right before him. He couldn't see her, but something told me this wasn't about him so much as it was about Erin. She stood tall, looking down her nose at him. "Why don't you beg for me, love?"

Something about the way she said it—the way she made the word "love" sound so cruel—brought me to my senses. I pulled her by her elbow and dragged her to the corner of the room. I got in her face, and what I saw, unbelievable as it was, was something that amounted to tears in her eyes. At the very least they looked awfully glassy. I'd never seen Erin cry, or even come close to it. But then she blinked. She fixed me with a pressed gaze, and I said, "What you're doing isn't cool."

"And what is it that I'm doing?"

"I have no clue," I hissed, keeping my voice low enough so that only she could hear me. "But taunting him like this? Using Griffin against him? Your actions are bordering on the homophobic. And I don't know what you might be thinking, but it isn't a total scream."

"Do you honestly think I'd *out* him? Contrary to some of my actions today, I'm not a raging asshole. I'd never do that to someone."

"Yeah, well, Rupert P. doesn't know that."

"The point: You're finally nearing it," she said. "Rupert P. has something to lose. I'm not going to give him special treatment just because he's gay. If I did, that would be the real injustice here, wouldn't it? Think of how far it would set us back as a society."

Behind us, Isabel had taken over Erin's role, and now she was the one standing over Rupert P. "What suite are the boys staying in?" she asked.

"Room 1620," Rupert P. said.

"Where is your room key?"

"Back right pocket."

"I volunteer!" Apple shouted.

"Let's go!" Isabel said.

"Wait, you can't just go into their room," I said.

"She's right," Erin said. "What if they're there now?"

That was not what I'd meant at all. But she did have a point.

"Where is the rest of the band?" Isabel asked Rupert P.

"I don't know."

"We can ask them." Erin took Rupert P.'s phone and typed out a group text to the rest of the boys, whose names were clearly marked in the contacts.

Where are you?

The first text came back from Rupert X.

I told you to never fckin txt me u stupid ginger gint.

"*Drag* him!" Isabel said. "Rupert X. might be my new favorite Rupert."

The next text came from Rupert L.

I'm heer. Wear r u?

Ever helpful. Sometimes, I couldn't figure out why Isabel loved Rupert L. so much. He was super cute, sure, and he may have been built like a bag of rocks, but he was also dumb as a bag of rocks. His tweets were always littered with typos. It figured his text messages would be too.

"Autocorrect can be a bitch," Isabel explained.

Finally, the text from Rupert K. that I was waiting for came in.

Sound check at NBC. Are u close?

Isabel spun to face Rupert P. "Wait a minute. How did everyone leave the hotel without being spotted?"

"Maintenance entrance in the car park below the hotel," Rupert P. said, calmer now. "It's the reason we picked this place. I need to be at sound check, so can you please let me go now?"

Rupert P. could've said a whole bunch of things just then, but Erin and Apple and Isabel were too distracted to pay him any more unnecessary attention. They had the boys' room key and the promise that they weren't around. They had the keys to the castle.

"Let's go!" Isabel said again, getting antsy, bouncing in place.

Erin took a step but I took her hand. It felt suddenly like if I let her go I'd lose her for good. "Erin, he's willing to let us get out of this mess scot-free," I whispered. It felt necessary to keep my voice low, as though what I was saying was too important and fragile to state out loud. "Don't you think this has gone on long enough?"

The way she looked at me just then, the way her eyes crinkled with some of the glassiness of before but none of the sadness—for the first time, that look scared me. "It hasn't even started yet."

Neither of us could know then just how right she would turn out to be.

8

Rupert P.'s head hung low. With the girls out of the room I felt I could be nice again. And something about the way he looked, the way he was literally bent out of shape, made me feel like being extra nice. "You don't have to be ashamed," I said. "It's okay to be gay."

He didn't say anything. For a second he was so still I thought he might have fallen asleep. And then I had the creepy thought that he was dead or something. Amazingly, it was only the first time that night that I'd have that thought. But then his lips twisted ruefully, and in that moment I knew not only that he'd heard me, but that he also hated me.

"It's okay to be gay, is it?" he said, his voice mocking and nasal. "Well, thank heavens you're here to tell me that. I never would've thought so until this very moment. That's all I need, yeah? A Rupert Kirke fangirl to share her infinite wisdom with me."

Yep, he hated me. It made me feel uneasy. But I guess it was too much to ask of the person you were kidnapping not to hate you.

"It's okay to be closeted too," I continued. "You should come out in your own time. And if and when you do come out, your fans are still going to love you. I don't know if you know this or not, but there's hardly anything that fangirls love more than gay boy band members. I mean, I don't particularly subscribe to that faction myself, but you'd be surprised how many slash rpfs there are out there."

"Slash rp——? What the hell is an rpf?"

"Real person fics . . . fanfiction." "Fanfiction" was one of those few words people didn't say in real life. Like "shit" blurted in a kindergarten classroom. It just wasn't done. And it felt weird to say it now. I thought briefly of writing down everything that was happening for a future fic. Sort of a true crime rpf. I was pretty sure it'd never been done before. Then I realized it would probably come off way too unrealistic. It'd have to be an AU fic. "Forget it," I said.

"Bloody hell, how is this my life?" Rupert P. said. "How am I taken prisoner, listening to a teenage girl talk to me about *fanfiction*! How the fuck did I even end up in the bloody band! I can't sing, you know! I can't even bloody sing!"

"I know."

"Shut up! You don't tell me I can't sing! I'm the only one who's allowed to say it. Me!"

"Sorry," I muttered under my breath. "How did you know I was a Rupert Kirke fan?"

"What?"

"When you said I was sharing my 'infinite wisdom' with you, you called me a Rupert K. fangirl. How did you know?"

"You stink of it."

"Excuse me?"

"You're wearing his perfume," he said.

All the Ruperts had their own separate fragrances. They were a big hit, along with the requisite nail polish and hair accessories. You could smell like your favorite boy *and* wear his face on your head at the same time. Rupert K.'s fragrance smelled of jasmine and baby's breath flowers. I was wearing it now. But I'd only dabbed it on my neck and wrists. I was sure Rupert P. was exaggerating about the strength of it.

"And Rupert K. is everyone's favorite," he said.

"Not my friends'."

"Lovely bunch, they are."

"I'm sorry about them," I said. "But I'm not like them. I'm going to let you go."

He looked up, unseeing but disbelieving. He let a moment pass, maybe wondering if I was going to end that sentence with a "Just kidding!" But I wasn't. Without the rest of the girls and their majority rule, I realized I could finally set him free. And I had to do it before I lost my courage. But I had to think of how. There were a few things that could happen after I untied him. At best he'd punch me in the face and leave me unconscious on the floor; at worst he'd set me on fire like he'd promised before. Plus, there was the blindfold to worry about. I wondered if we could work something out, where I promised to let him go only under the condition that he walk out with his blindfold on. And there was the issue of warning my friends to get out of the penthouse before Rupert P. found them.

"What are you waiting for, then?" Rupert P. shouted, suddenly animated, bouncing in the chair and trying in vain to move it. "Let me go!"

His voice knocked me into action, and I instantly forgot about all the possible consequences of setting him free. I had a new fire in me, a determination to do some good. "Yes! Okay!" I crouched down before him and started working on the knot around his right ankle. It was a double knot and extremely tight, made tighter because Rupert P. had struggled against it.

"What's your name?" Rupert P. said as I worked.

"My name?" He wanted to know my name. "It's Baby."

"Baby? What kind of name is that?"

"Well, actually it's Frances. But everyone just calls me Baby. I was named after the first woman in the c—"

"I didn't ask for your bloody history. Your friend . . ."

"Which one?"

"The bitch." Erin.

"There's a reason she didn't want to let me go, isn't there? She's planning something."

I let go of the knot. "What do you mean?"

"Have you asked yourself why she still wants to keep me?"

"She wants to get concert tickets."

"Does that make any sense to you? I give you concert tickets and then neglect to inform the police of your seat numbers. Brilliant."

I had to admit it did sound kind of ridiculous. But maybe there was more to Erin's plan than that. Maybe there was something else she wanted that she'd forgotten to tell me about. Maybe there was a reason she was acting totally OOC, making me forget that she was a good person once— scaring me.

"She's *lying* to you," Rupert P. said, piercing my thoughts. "She's got something up her sleeve. I know it. You know it. You're just turning a blind eye to it."

"Erin is my best friend. I trust her."

"She doesn't trust you if she won't tell you what's going on."

He didn't know what he was talking about. He didn't know anything about me and Erin and our friendship. So why was what he was saying cutting into me?

"What's taking so long?" Rupert P. said. "Isn't there a knife around here you can use?"

Right. A knife. The faster I got him out of here, the faster I didn't have to dwell on all the things he'd just said. I stood up straight and looked around.

"You know what?" Rupert P. said. "Forget I said that. Last thing I need's a demented fan wielding a knife. *Demented fan.* Apologies for being redundant."

I searched the desk, every drawer, looking for something sharp, but there wasn't so much as a letter opener to be found. I went to the bedroom and made a beeline for Isabel's bag. If anyone was likely to pack a knife in her luggage it was Isabel, but all I found were dark-colored clothes, her laptop, and a framed pic of a shirtless Rupert L. I spied polka-dot fabric, and even though I had to move on I was too shocked to find polka-dot *anything* in Isabel's things to do so. I pinched the fabric carefully and then held it up by both ends. It was underwear. Isabel wore polka-dot underwear. I dropped them immediately.

I went to Apple's bag next. It was humongous, and I was already dreading having to go through all her things, but when I pulled back the zipper there was—no joke—nothing but popcorn inside. Loose popcorn, a seemingly endless supply, spilling out of the bag like she'd just raided a concession stand.

I went to Erin's bag next. There were overnight clothes and a red bikini that opened in the front. I guess she thought there'd be time for swimming on this stalking trip. I didn't expect to find much else in Erin's things, except I sort of did. Unbelievably, there was a tiny dagger in Erin's bag, hidden in a side pocket. It was about the size of my pinkie, attached to a silver chain, its edge about as sharp as that of a spoon, but it was a dagger nonetheless. I recognized it immediately. It was an exact replica of the dagger Rupert X. used to wear around his neck. Any Strepur would remember it; he'd famously posed with it between his teeth for a *Rolling Stone* photo shoot. In the black-and-white photograph Rupert X. had been shirtless, the dagger necklace the only thing he'd worn. I didn't know Erin got a necklace that looked just like it. I wondered why she never wore it.

"Oi, where'd you go?" Rupert P. yelled from the other room. "Waiting to be set free here!"

I came back to stand before him. "I'm sorry," I said. "I can't find anything sharp." The dagger was just a charm, too tiny, the edge too dull. Useless.

Rupert P.'s head rolled back, resting on the top of the chair. "You were only teasing me."

"No, I wasn't."

"You were never going to let me go."

"I was. I *am*."

"My nose itches," Rupert P. said suddenly. "Will you scratch it for me?"

I walked forward and scratched his nose with my right index finger. I didn't see it coming when he grabbed my left hand. Even though his forearm was tied to the armrest, he could still reach his fingers out, and they wrapped themselves around my wrist. His grip was strong. I couldn't shake free of him.

"Let me go!"

"I heard that one before," Rupert P. said. "Oh yes, it was me saying it. Not so fun now, is it?"

I pulled my arm, but it was like it was trapped in an iron cuff. "Is your kidnapping of me just a deep-seated manifestation of your daddy issues?"

I froze, my arm going limp in his grip. "What?"

"Your bracelet." He turned up his nose like he'd just smelled something bad. "It says 'Daddy.' "

I looked down at my arm, his fingers digging into my wrist, my bracelet peeking through between them. He must've been able to see in the crack between the blindfold and his nose.

"You don't know anything about me."

"Does he spoil you rotten?"

I tried wrenching my hand free again.

"Is he the shoulder you cry on whenever people surely make fun of you for being a weirdo?"

111

"Don't talk about my father."

"I hope I'm not out of line when I tell you that wearing a 'Daddy' bracelet is absolutely the creepiest kind of jewelry a girl could wear," Rupert P. said. "You must get loads of dates."

"It's something to remember him by."

I shouldn't have said it. I knew I shouldn't have said it when Rupert P. turned his face up, looking directly at me, even with the blindfold on, and smiled. "So he's dead, then."

I didn't answer. I guess that was confirmation enough for him.

"Let me guess," Rupert P. said. "The Ruperts have personally touched your life in a very trying time, yeah? Has Rupert K. taken over the role of the most important man in your life now? That's rather disturbing? Call it armchair psychology if you must, but I am in an armchair and in the presence of a psycho. I think that means I have some authority on the matter. No, you're not spoiled rotten. You're just a rotten girl."

I yanked my hand with enough force that I stumbled back. My arm finally came free of his hold, but his fingers still clutched my bracelet. I landed on the floor with a pathetic thud just as the elastic broke. The white beads that spelled out "Daddy" spurted onto the ground, bouncing all over the carpet and rolling away from me.

"Your daddy would be so proud."

I want to tell you that his words didn't affect me at all, that he was just saying mean things because he was pressed about being tied up, obviously. But that wouldn't be very honest of me. I wiped my cheeks as soon as I felt them become wet.

I got on my hands and knees and crawled, collecting all the beads I could find, and the string, even though it was broken. And then I crawled toward Rupert P. and grabbed the knot again, blinking back my tears so I could better focus on the task of untying him. You're probably wondering how I could be nice to him after the things he'd just said. But this wasn't just about being nice. At that point I just wanted to set Rupert P. free so that I wouldn't have to hear him talk anymore.

The knot was coming loose when I heard the door open behind me. I'd hardly turned around to see who it was before Apple was on top of me.

"What were you just doing?" she said.

"Get off me!" I said.

"Were you about to molest my Rupie?!"

"Crisis, Apple, get a grip!" I said. "Not even if you *paid* me."

"She was about to cut him loose," Isabel said. Her arms were loaded up with things—mostly clothes—like she'd just looted someplace. I guess she had.

"Did you manage to leave anything in the room?" I asked. My voice sounded fine, and I hoped they couldn't tell I'd been crying.

"Don't change the subject," Isabel said. "Erin's gonna wanna hear about this."

Apple stood up, helping me up too. "Sorry," she said. "It's just when I saw you crouching in front of his lap like that . . . Let's just agree that I'm the only one who is ever allowed that close to his lap, okay? And let's also agree never to do something so rash like letting Rupert P. go."

"Fuck my life," Rupert P. said in one long exhale.

"Look what I got," Apple said. She pulled up her flowy knee-length skirt and revealed a pair of bright orange tighty-whities worn over her tights, the name "Rupert Pierpont" written across the waistband. "Shh," she said, mouthing the words. "Don't tell him."

"Where's Erin?" I said.

"She's still up there."

"Better go see what she's *really* up to," Rupert P. said.

I left the room and took the elevator to the sixteenth floor.

9

I stood before Room 1620 expecting someone from The Ruperts' team to swing open the door—a manager, maybe, or a PR person. Someone to catch me snooping and say something terrifying like, "Hey! You there!" But nothing happened when I knocked. Nothing happened the next three times I did it either. "Erin," I called. "It's me."

I almost turned back, thinking Erin must've already left and I'd missed her somehow, but then her muffled voice came through the door. " 'Me' who?"

"Your Bestest Bestie?"

"How do I know it's really you?"

I rolled my eyes, pointless since she couldn't see me. After all the shit with Rupert P. earlier I was really not in the mood. "Who else knows that you like to take your Rupert X. cutout and p—"

The door swung open. "You promised to never mention that again," she said. "And anyway, I got rid of that thing."

"You did?"

She stepped aside to make room for me. "You're not going to believe this place."

She did not lie. I could not believe the place, and everything Rupert P. had said about my dad and about Erin being shady totally flew out of my head and was replaced by the awesomeness of the hotel room. The suite was enormous, with floor-to-ceiling glass walls that opened up to a terrace. The light must've been incredible in the morning, but I could only guess at that because it was dark out by now. There were beanbag chairs, and a taxidermied deer head on the wall with a life jacket around its neck and a pig snout mask on its nose. There was a tiny plaque next to it that explained that it was only a fake deer head and could be removed by calling the front desk if you found it offensive.

There were two framed pictures on the wall, displayed with spotlights above them like they were museum artwork. One was a large, abrasively yellow poster for some movie called *The Stupids*, and another was a much smaller print of René Magritte's *The Treachery of Images*. I guess The Rondack designers all agreed that those two things should be displayed on the same wall.

But the weirdest part of the suite was the dining table. It was large enough to seat eight, but it was hard to imagine anyone eating on it, since the whole thing was covered in what appeared to be a scale model of SoHo. Right there in the center was a miniature version of The Rondack itself, one of the taller buildings in the neighborhood. The Rondack within The Rondack. Trippy.

There were things strewn about, clothes and papers, and I didn't know if it was the boys who were messy or if it was just the debris that lay in Apple's and Isabel's wakes. But I really didn't care about the small stuff at that point. I didn't come with the intention of ransacking the boys' things, but Erin was already walking toward one of the bedrooms, and my feet started following her of their own accord. My heart rate spiked. I realized what was happening.

I was excited.

I *wanted* to ransack Rupert K.'s things and find personal items, things that he'd packed himself and couldn't live without.

I was a horrible, horrible person. But I was also a fangirl in my idol's room. How could I shut my eyes to it all?

It was just like The Ruperts' song "Your World."

Baby, let me watch you sleep
Let me come inside, I want to see your room
I don't care what your mom thinks
Show me your world and let our love bloom.

"Rupert X. and Rupert K. are staying in the same room," Erin said.

"Double wedding!"

Erin laughed. "Double wedding" was a thing we said whenever Rupert X. and Rupert K. did anything that linked them together. We liked to think they were each other's closest friends in the boy band, and if me and Erin, who were best friends, loved two boys who were also best friends, it meant a double wedding was very possibly in our future. It was a dumb joke, but it made it us laugh, so we continued to tell it.

"How do you know they're sharing a room?" I asked. But when we walked into the bedroom the question answered itself. Two beds: one of them had a pair of pillows with the letters *RX* monogrammed in the corners of the silk pillowcases. Obviously, that was Rupert X.'s bed. Whenever an interviewer asked him about his skin care regimen, he would always bring up the importance of sleeping on silk pillows, which, he liked to point out, was not only good for the skin, but for the hair as well. And Rupert X.'s hair definitely added to his overall allure. His golden pompadour could rival a rooster's. The other bed just looked like a standard hotel bed, but on the nightstand was an inhaler. Only one of the boys in the band needed an inhaler. My boy.

Erin walked up to it and tossed it into the air, catching it a second later. "What do you say: perfect souvenir?"

"I can't take that," I said. "Rupert K. needs that."

Really, he had no business being a singer with his asthma. It was common knowledge that he escaped backstage at least once every show to take a hit off his inhaler. It was usually after one of the more upbeat numbers, where he was jumping around a lot and losing more breath than he was taking in. But that was just another reason why I loved him: He lived to perform even though it could kill him. How could you not admire his commitment? There were always at least a few fan signs at concerts that said things like, RUPERT K! LET ME GIVE YOU MOUTH TO MOUTH or RUPERT K. I CAN'T BREATHE WHEN I'M AROUND YOU or I'LL TAKE A HIT OFF YOUR INHALER ANY DAY.

Girls would fight to the death to take a hit off this thing, to be able to hold in their hands an object that Rupert K. regularly put into his mouth. And there it was, on the palm of Erin's hand. Beckoning me.

"At least hold it for a minute," Erin said, handing it to me. "Take a hit if you want, I won't tell anyone."

Don't worry, I didn't take a hit off Rupert K.'s inhaler. I wasn't that sick.

I only pressed the mouthpiece against my lips.

Erin had already wandered off to Rupert X.'s side of the

room, and I was grateful that she allowed me this one moment to have this middleman—a thing that both Rupert K.'s lips and mine had touched. In a way—if you squinted—it was like we'd just kissed.

Obviously, I've thought about what it would be like to kiss Rupert Kirke. Okay, yes, it's a little embarrassing to admit, but every Rupert K. fangirl fantasizes about the same thing, and I'm certainly not above it all. I actually have a whole little scenario of how it would go down. We'd be in this dangerous situation, or maybe just an adventurous one—I haven't decided yet—but then when we were finally alone and we'd had a moment to catch our breaths, he'd look at me as if he was seeing me for the first time. He'd put the palm of his hand on my cheek and gently caress it with his thumb. His own cheeks would turn super red, the way they do when he's shy or out of breath, only this time he'd be shy and out of breath for the best reason. He'd lean in really slowly and I'd know that he wanted to kiss me but he'd make me wait for it a little bit. He'd fish for the kiss (because fishing for the kiss is always the most adorably romantic way to go, natch), and then finally his lips would be on mine. They'd be soft. They'd be perfect.

That's what I imagine a perfect kiss would be. I haven't had a perfect kiss yet. (You need to have at least actually been kissed to have a perfect kiss.)

"Are you done making out with his inhaler?"

I quickly put the inhaler down, but Erin wasn't even looking at me. Her back was to me as she sat on the edge of Rupert X.'s bed, looking through something I couldn't see.

"I wasn't making out with it."

"Right."

I walked around Rupert K.'s bed before sitting on it. When I did, I did it as carefully as possible, not wanting to put too much weight on it and disturb it somehow. But then I thought, screw it, and just full-on lay down and stretched out. It wasn't warm like I'd hoped, but that didn't mean it wasn't still good.

Holy shit, I was lying on Rupert K.'s bed.

Yes, on the one hand we'd kidnapped someone, which was bad, I know, but on the other hand, it had facilitated the fact that I was now lying where Rupert K. *slept*, which was oh so *swoon*. And the swoon, at least at that very moment, totally outweighed the bad.

I was in Rupert K.'s bed.

I was in Rupert K.'s bed.

Carrie Underwood, take the wheel—I was *not* okay.

I shut my eyes and Rupert K. was lying beside me, looking at me through his lashes, lazy and long, his hair bed-heady, sticking up in all the right places. "My love," he said. "You're in my bed."

"I know!" I squealed.

"What?" Erin said.

121

"Huh?" It was probably a good thing Erin snapped me out of my reverie before it got too NSFW. "I can't believe I'm in here. How are you not more excited about this?"

I watched Erin's back, waiting for her to answer, but her shoulders only rose and fell in a shrug. A toned-down response regarding all things Ruperts was not exactly the norm for Strepurs, but was becoming exceedingly common for Erin, and continued to confuse the hell out of me.

I realize I haven't given you the fangirl stats on Erin yet. Might as well do it now.

Stats on Erin:

Favorite member of The Ruperts: Rupert Xavier

Number of times she's seen The Ruperts in person: 5

Number of times she's met (this includes getting anything from a selfie to a hug) all/a member of The Ruperts: 0

Erin and I had the same stats, except we liked different Ruperts and I'd only seen them four times (the *Today* show concert and three other times when Isabel took us stalking and we got glimpses of them as they got on and off their vans outside a couple of TV studios in Manhattan). The one time Erin saw the boys and I wasn't there was on her trip to Dublin six months ago.

Erin's parents had just gotten divorced, and as a special divorce treat, they each proposed taking Erin and her twelve-year-old sister, Richie, on a trip. Individually, that is.

Her dad wanted to take them on a cruise to the Bahamas, but her mom wanted to take them to Dublin to visit her grandparents. It actually made the divorce messier than it already was, because now her parents were fighting over who got to take the girls where, and they each kept throwing special incentives into the trip to try and play favorites. Erin's little sister opted for the cruise solely based on the fact that it had a kids' club on board and she was really desperate to have her first kiss already and was fairly certain that if it was ever going to happen it would be on the high seas while an *NSYNC cover band played under sparkling disco lights.

Erin, to her family's surprise, chose the Dublin trip. Of course, I knew she chose that destination because The Ruperts were going to have a show there. Erin's mom brought her new boyfriend along on the mother-daughter bonding trip and was too busy with him to care that all Erin wanted to do was go to the concert. She dropped her off at the arena and told Erin to have a good time.

She was so lucky her parents got divorced. I would give anything to fly to Europe and see the boys in concert.

Erin never even held it over my head that she'd gone to see The Ruperts without me. Actually, she never spoke about the Dublin concert. I always took it as her trying to spare me the jealousy.

"Find anything good over there?" I said.

Erin twisted her head around and held up a maroon Moleskine notebook. "Only Rupert X.'s diary."

I sat up with a start. "Where did you get that?"

"Bottom of his suitcase."

I sat on the edge of the bed and waited; I knew she'd read it for me.

Erin cleared her throat. "*Dear Diary, Dr. Slalom says I should start this. Says she won't read it but I should do it for my own sanity. Diaries are lame. She says I should call it a journal. Still lame. Dot dot dot. Fuck this. Good night.*"

"Adorable."

"*Dear diary,*" Erin continued, "*Today I had whole wheat toast and jam.*" She looked up. "That's all he wrote for day two."

"Riveting stuff."

"You have no idea. *Dear Diary, I hate my life.*"

"No," I gasped.

"*No one can possibly understand what it's like to be in a band where everyone's name is Rupert. Someone will say, 'Hey, Rupert!' and we'll all turn round. WE'LL ALL FUCKING TURN ROUND.*" Erin stopped. "He put that part in all caps," she explained. Then she continued, "*All we do is sing pussy music. The lads are pussies too. Fucking can't stand them. Yesterday we were stuck in the hotel because of all the girls outside. I had to spend the whole day with L and P. L stuck his entire fist in his mouth and expected me to be impressed. P was*

124

*his usual little gingerqueer self. Fuck my life. Dot dot dot. I had eggs
Benedict for breakfast. Highlight.*"

"I don't believe it."

"You can't make this shit up. It seems like he takes the
journal thing more seriously later," Erin said. "Listen to this:
*Every day I look around me and am deeply plagued by the unfairness of
life. It is everywhere. All around me. Why is life so unfair to so many
undeserving people?*"

"Wow," I said. "Deep."

"*I have everything a person can want in life and yet I find it exceedingly unfair that I can say, with absolute certainty, that I will always be
more attractive than whatever girl I am with at any given time.*"

"Okay, the deep end just got kinda shallow."

"*I have been with a plethora of girls already. And while they were all
very hot, not one of them has surpassed me in beauty. Why was I chosen
to be so good-looking? Every time someone sees me with another girl they
think, 'He can do so much better.' And they are right. I will go through
life thinking I can do so much better. Thus, this is the tragedy of my life.
Plagued by beauty. Who can I turn to, dear diary?* And in parentheses
he writes: *Consider submitting this to our writers to create new song.
'Plagued by Beauty' as title. Secure a writing credit.* Then he just drew
a bunch of dollar signs and wrote, *Boom! Shakespeare, bitch!*"

"Yikes," I said. What else *was* there to say? "Who knew
Rupert X. was so . . . plagued?"

"By beauty, of all things." Erin took her phone out of her jacket pocket and skimmed through the pages again, snapping as many pics of them as she could.

"Why are you doing that?"

"Because when you catch a fish this big you don't just throw it back in."

"Yeah, but what good could possibly come out of information like that? Especially the stuff about him hating the band. That could cause serious backlash for The Ruperts."

"I think it was Mark Twain who once said, 'YOLO.'"

Reading Rupert X.'s diary was fine, but why take pics unless you meant to do some major damage? And why was Erin so hell-bent on keeping Rupert P.? What Rupert P. said rang in my head again. I didn't have the answers, not right then, but something about this wasn't sitting well with me.

"We should probably get going. We aren't supposed to be here."

"Ugh, why are you constantly clutching your pearls?" Erin said. "If I ever teach you anything in life it's that you need to stop being so *safe*. It's just a tiny bit of trouble we're getting ourselves into. The water's nice. Jump in."

"The boys could come back any minute, though."

"So? Wouldn't be the first time they find girls in their room."

"Are we going to be *those girls*, then? Might as well take our clothes off and just lie here waiting for them while we're at it. Whore the place up a bit."

Erin shot me a look. "How very slut-shamey of you."

I was only joking, but she was right. It wasn't cool of me to say that. And by the way the air around us turned suddenly chilly, I knew even before she'd said anything that I'd said the wrong thing.

My phone buzzed.

How's everything going?

Another text from Mom. I started typing.

Gr8. Erin's mom let us make the pumpkin pie but we dropped it on the floor so we had 2 do it again. 2nd pie = perfect. We wanted 2 top it off with confectionary sugar but the corner bodega didn't have any so we bought something called Inca Kola instead. Can't wait 2 try it.

"If you want to go so badly, then leave," Erin said, interrupting my typing. "There's still a few things I want to check out."

I hit SEND.

I was certain by then. Something was definitely up with Erin.

10

When I walked back into our room Rupert P. was looking at me.

He was looking at me because the tights/blindfold lay at his feet.

I stared into the abyss and the abyss stared back. With a smile on its face.

Rupert P.'s face was busted all on its own, but when he smiled he was an assault to my retinas. I'm sorry, I know I should stop being so mean about Rupert P.'s looks, something I know he can't help (though he hasn't really tried either, has he?). Actually, no, you know what? I'm not sorry. Erin says girls apologize too much. We say "I'm sorry" almost as much as we say "Hello." And you have to believe me—Rupert P. really was *so. Ugly.* I can't even describe it. He looked like an ostrich.

"Who took his blindfold off?"

Isabel was in the corner of the room, on her phone, natch, while Apple was in another corner, on her phone too, but looking way more guilty.

"I recognize your voice," Rupert P. said. "Have a nice chat with your bestie, did you?"

I reached for my bracelet but then remembered what he'd done to it. I marched over to where Isabel stood. "He's seen our faces now. How the hell could you let this happen? You were the one who kept reiterating the importance of the blindfold! He couldn't *make* us, remember?"

"Yeah, well, Golden Delicious over there just *had* to look into his eyes to assure him that everything would be hunky-fucking-dory. By the time I realized what she was doing the blindfold was off and Rupert P. was looking me in the face. Fugmonster's got that Medusa stare. I'm still spooked, man."

"Apple!"

"Okay, okay, I know you're mad," Apple said. She was next to us suddenly, a meddlesome apparition. "But I think I'm getting to him. Showing him some kindness may be just what he needs right now if we want him on our side."

"Bull to the shit," Isabel said. "She just wanted selfies."

This could not be happening. This wasn't an actual conversation we were having. I snatched Apple's phone out of her hands, ignoring her cry of protest, and clicked on the gallery icon. I just wanted to be proved wrong. There *could not* be pictures of Apple posing with our kidnappee.

There were a dozen pictures of Apple posing with our kidnappee.

She was sitting in his lap in all the pictures, sometimes throwing her head back so her auburn hair cascaded over her shoulders, other times bowing her head toward him, trying to manipulate an intimate scene. Pic after pic, Rupert P. looked utterly unamused. Actually, in the first few pictures he looked enraged and even panicked, but by the time I got to the final few he was just dejected, rolling his eyes in some. And in all of the pictures, Apple had her shirt off.

"Apple, what is wrong with you?"

"Everything," Isabel chimed in.

Unbelievably, just by the way her face fell, I could tell that Apple was expecting me to congratulate her on how good she looked in the pictures. "I did it . . . for science," she said.

"Why is your shirt off in all of these?"

"Wardrobe malfunction." She took the phone from me.

"Delete them!" I said. "Delete them immediately!"

"No way. I wasn't going to post any of them anyway."

"Sure you weren't. Just like you didn't post that Vine of you gyrating against that Rupert P. life-size pillow, despite all common sense and better judgment."

130

"That pillow and me looked really good together!"

"If you Instagram any of those I will kill you," I said. "I will peel you, I will slice you, and I will bake you in a pie, Apple. That is not hyperbole!"

"How dare you talk to me like that?" Apple said. "You're taking your frustrations out on me because you know you can't talk to your dear Erin like that. And Isabel is too scary to talk to like that. But just because I'm the normal one in this group doesn't mean everyone gets to walk all over me!"

"*You're* the normal one? You've been trying to sexually molest Rupert P. since you dragged him in here by the ankle!"

"Semantics!" Apple said. "I love that boy! Look at how precious he is!"

I looked over at Rupert P. He was drooling.

"How can you deny all the sexual tension between us!" Apple said. "This might be the greatest day of my life and you're ruining it."

"The greatest day of your life involves a guy tied to a chair?"

"You're purposefully choosing to focus on the negative!"

"Isabel, she's acting schizo," I said. "Back me up!"

But Isabel didn't say anything. She was too busy trying not to drop the two phones in her hands. Rupert P.'s phone didn't stop vibrating. "He keeps getting messages wanting to know where he is," Isabel said.

"They want to know where I am because the television special is starting soon," Rupert P. said from his chair. "What time is it?"

"The time is 7:53!" said Isabel's watch.

"Oh, you've got to be kidding me," Rupert P. muttered.

"Hey, Isabel," I said. "Did you know that when Rupert L. looks at a watch face his eyes cross?"

She really did not find that one funny. Perhaps it wasn't the best time for a Rupert L. watch joke.

"Listen to this." Isabel clicked on one of his voice mails and put it on speaker.

"Where are you?!" A man's voice, gruff and agitated. I could tell by their expressions that neither Apple nor Isabel knew who he was either. Maybe he was The Ruperts' manager, Larry Lee. We'd never heard his voice before, but we'd seen his picture tons. He was balding and overweight and looked like someone who always sounded gruff and agitated. *"There are screaming girls waiting, do you hear me?!"*

As soon as that message ended Isabel clicked another.

"Twenty bloody minutes to show!" The same man. I tried to picture him, and he was pink all over with steam comically coming out of his ears. *"You're not at the hotel, you're not here. Michelle doesn't know where you are and neither does Griffin. Yes—we resorted to asking Griffin. He's not much of a secret when the shit hits*

the fan like this. A secret we've been keeping for you, and this is how you repay us, you little shit!"

That message finished, and then a new voice came on. "Hullo, Rupert." I knew that voice. I would recognize it anywhere. "It's me, Rupert . . . Rupert K. . . . obviously. Listen, mate, where are you? The lads are going a bit mad. I'm trying to sort them out but they won't listen. This is a big show, you know that. I'll talk to them, though. We won't do anything until you get here. Just call me back, alright? Right."

End of messages.

Isabel put her phone in her pocket and focused solely on Rupert P.'s. "Let's answer all of them at once."

I wanted to know what she was going to do. No, not what she was going to do—what she had up her sleeve. Because that was how Isabel operated. She didn't merely do things; she schemed. But I was also afraid to ask.

"There," Isabel said. "How did people live without Twitter?"

I didn't have to look at my phone to know that Isabel had just done something very bad. Her devilish smile told me that all on its own. I checked my Twitter feed. A new tweet from our very own Rupert P.

Apple got to it first. "Crisis!" she said. "Crisis!"

I looked down at my phone's screen. "You didn't," I said, incredulous.

133

"I did," Isabel said.

"What are you all going on about?" Rupert P. said.

"Baby, you just quit The Ruperts!" Apple said.

"What? No, I didn't."

"Just as I predicted you would on my website an hour ago," Isabel said. She sighed. "Do you know how much traffic this will drive in? I can't with how good I am."

"I didn't quit the band!"

"But you just said so, right here on Twitter."

Isabel set his phone down on his lap, faceup so that he could read the tweet. Just two words.

I quit.

Cryptic enough to make his phone go silent for an instant, and then for it to light up again incessantly. It buzzed on his thigh until it slid off and then skidded on the carpeted floor. The phone was the only thing moving in the room until Isabel finally did what I never thought she'd ever do to a phone. She turned it off.

"Why would you do that?!" Rupert P. yelled. "I thought you girls were supposed to be fans!"

"Quite frankly!" Apple said. "He can't quit the band! If he's not in the band . . . do I even like him anymore?"

"You should be thanking me," Isabel said to Rupert.

"Thanking you?! Are you mental?! You're destroying my life!"

"Actually, I just got you some really good publicity. The whole world is going to tune in tonight to see if it's true. The band will be in every news story tomorrow morning."

"You should really get into public relations," I told her.

She shrugged, all faux modest. "I see no lies in that statement."

"Do you think anyone will believe this?!" Rupert P. shrieked. His voice got higher the angrier he got, like he was experiencing puberty all over again. "Tomorrow morning I'll tell the whole world you did this!"

"You'll tell the world a band of teenage girls kidnapped you and forced you to post that you quit on Twitter? I think the real concern here is, will anyone believe you?" Isabel said.

The door flew open and Erin blazed in, breathless. "Whose brilliant idea was it for him to quit the band?" she said, her phone in her hand and a grin on her face. Though the grin was short-lived, disappearing as soon as she saw Rupert P. She didn't say anything, and neither did we. We only watched her, waiting to see what her reaction would be. For his part, Rupert P.'s eyes narrowed, and there was something behind his gaze. A kernel of recognition. Erin looked scared, like she was dreading something. I couldn't make out what, though. I didn't have all the information yet.

Erin sped right past him and went into the bedroom. We all followed her like she pulled on invisible leashes and we were helpless to take off the collars. Apple headed for the bathroom, though. "Where are you going?" Erin hissed.

"I'm taking off his underwear," Apple said. And here I was in blissful ignorance, having forgotten that she still had that nasty thing on. "He quit the band. I'm not going to go around wearing the underwear of a *former* member of The Ruperts. *Gross.*"

She went off and Erin turned to Isabel and me. "Why is his blindfold off?" she asked.

"Why bother whispering?!" Rupert P. shouted. "I can still hear you!"

Erin walked out of the bedroom and the leashes tugged us along. She reached for the tights on the floor, but Isabel grabbed her wrist before she could do anything with them. "Wait. He should see this."

Apple came to join us just as Isabel turned on the TV and flipped to Channel 4. It was eight o'clock. Time for The Ruperts' Thanksgiving spectacular.

All there was on-screen was an empty stage. Well, the backup band was there, listlessly playing instruments— the starting chords to "Can I Get a Bite of That Sandwich, Girl?" to be exact—and there were spotlights roaming the stage, as if they too were looking for The Ruperts, to no avail. The only way you knew there was a live studio audience was because there would be an intermittent shout for someone's favorite boy bander every few seconds. After a moment, two hosts skipped onto center stage, and for all the smiling and laughing and sweating under stage lights, it looked like they were bracing through the pain.

All of us in the room—even Rupert P.—watched with bated breath.

"Well," said the female host. "Looks like we're going to start with a video clip first!"

"You never know what'll happen on a live show, folks!" said the male host.

"Not that anything's wrong!" the female host said.

"Nothing is wrong at all!" the male host said. Then both of their hands went to their ears, and they nodded, and the male host said, "They're telling me to cut to the video."

"That's what they're telling me too, Stu."

"Let's see what the boys got up to when they paid a visit to Isla Pardon's house to learn about preparing a turkey!"

"Sounds scrumptious *and* adorable!" the female host said.

They cut to a video of The Ruperts inside a beautifully sunlit kitchen with famed chef Isla Pardon looking lost in between them. This was obviously a prerecorded bit because there was Rupert P. with his arm around Isla, clueless to the fact that she looked none too pleased about it.

"That was our song 'Can I Get a Bite of That Sandwich, Girl?'" Rupert L. said to the camera. "And speaking of food, let's see if we might learn how to slaughter a proper American turkey for Thanksgiving!"

Isla giggled, or maybe coughed, and said, "We won't be slaughtering a turkey—just cooking one, boys."

"That's what I meant." Rupert L. rolled his eyes and laughed.

The boys proceeded to mess around while Isla took the recipe seriously. Rupert X. pinched some salt and threw it over his shoulder while Rupert L. dipped his finger into a bowl of powdered red stuff and then tasted it, grimacing. "I'll have the breast, please!" Rupert P. said.

"*Turkey* breast," Rupert K. said quickly. "He meant turkey breast."

"OMG, I don't think the boys have ever talked about *breasts* this much," Apple said.

"Twitter is probably exploding right now," I said.

Rupert L. thought it was the most original thing in the world to make the turkey look like it was dancing around; Rupert X. drank directly from the bottle of cooking wine; and Rupert K. tried to get Rupert P.'s hands out of the mixing bowl. They ended the segment with a turkey stuffing food fight.

"There's no way they're going on with the show after this, not without me," Rupert P. said.

"No one is checking for you," Isabel said.

"They're all backstage right now, trying to find where I am. They're going to cancel it. They are going to come out and apologize. You heard what Rupert said. He talked to the lads. They're not doing anything without me."

They cut back to the studio again, the camera focused on the stage. The backup band was still out, the girls were still screaming.

"Are The Ruperts really going to perform without Rupert P.?" I asked.

"Prayer circle," Erin said.

The guitarists played the opening riffs of "Love U-FO," and suddenly Rupert K.'s voice broke through the silence. *"I think our love might be extraterrestrial,"* he sang. The three boys came out and started jumping around, hyping the crowd and messing up their synchronized dance moves, as usual. And all we could do was watch, shocked, confused . . . amazed.

Isabel walked up to the TV, slack-jawed. "I can't believe it," she said.

I couldn't believe it either.

Apple chewed her hair.

And Erin smirked. "Would you look at that," she said. "It's amazing how much better this song sounds without a *fucking juggling break* in the middle of it."

I kept watching the screen. The Ruperts were performing flawlessly, maybe better than ever. It was almost as if they'd always been a three-man band. The point is that what was happening on TV was because of us. In a twisted way, we'd made history. The need to let Rupert P. go seemed almost beside the point now. I mean, yeah, it was still criminal, but something way bigger was happening. We'd changed the band.

We'd bettered it.

"What a time to be alive," Erin said.

"I told you no one was checking for you!" Isabel said, bouncing on the balls of her feet.

I looked at Rupert P. His face was glued to the TV too, and he looked more shocked than any of us. Even he had seemed to forget about my plan to set him free.

"This is giving me life right now," Isabel said. "This is giving me so much life I might be immortal."

She was thinking of what must've been happening online. Her phone was already in front of her face, her chipped navy fingernails already dancing over the screen.

Sometimes I wondered if Isabel was all bandwidth and hot spots. The Internet, and the shenanigans that transpired within it, made her spark to life like nothing else. Her heart was her site, pulsing with life every time the comments section exploded after a good scoop. She came alive with the chaos. I think she loved it more than she loved the band itself.

This was a next-level scandal, and to Isabel, scandal was the only thing that pulled back the curtain and showed us who our idols truly were. Without the scandal we only saw something manufactured, created by music execs and publicists. For the first time, I kind of got it, and suddenly, I couldn't wait to see the fallout. How would The Ruperts deal with this shake-up in the coming days? It felt like Pop Rocks. Like I'd just emptied a whole bag of them into my mouth and they were just starting to burst. Delicious.

The song ended and the hosts came back onto the stage and asked the boys some questions.

We waited for them to ask about Rupert P., to address the redheaded elephant in the room. Would they say that Rupert P. was sick and couldn't perform? That his tweet was fake; that he'd been hacked?

"We're noticing that one of the members of The Ruperts is missing," the male interviewer said. "Rupert Pierpont is no longer with us?" There was a slight uptick in his voice at the end of the sentence that turned it into a super-bleak-sounding question.

"Rupert Pierpont quit," Rupert X. announced.

Gasps, from the studio audience and from us.

"We're absolutely gutted," Rupert L. said.

"But we wish him all the best," Rupert X. said.

I waited for my Rupert to say something, but he stayed silent.

And that was it. The hosts smiled, a new song started up, and the new Ruperts were born.

Rupert P. had been wiped out. It was as if he'd never even been in the band to begin with.

And no one understood that better than Rupert P. himself.

"You're all going to pay for this!" he yelled. He'd gone batty with rage, and I guess the anger gave him some adrenaline or super strength or something, because suddenly his right arm slipped out of its restraint. And once that one was free he could get his left arm out too.

None of us moved. We probably should've tried to stop him, but I think we were all scared of what he'd do in his demented state. His hands were free now. Anything was possible.

He seemed shocked that we didn't move to tie him again, but he only froze for a moment, and then he started on the tights around his ankles.

"You're all mental!" he said, his fingernails picking at the knots. "I never understood fans, you know? The worship—that I understood, but the way you all imagine yourselves with us. You call us your *boyfriends*. It's so dumb. You think any one of us would get with you?" He stopped and looked up at Isabel.

"I'm not being funny, love, but you look and act like a bloody barbarian. There is not a single graceful or feminine thing about you. You think any of The Ruperts would look twice at you if they saw you in this hotel? You look like you work for housekeeping. The only time we'd ever look your way would be to throw our dirty sheets at you."

Isabel looked angry. Well, she always looked angry, but now her fists were clenched balls at her sides, stiff as frostbite, and her lips were a tight line. But underneath all of that I saw something on her face that I'd never seen before.

Hurt.

"And you!" Rupert P. said. "Your name can't actually be Apple. You don't mean to tell me that your parents named you after the fruit whose shape you most resemble. You're a beached whale! You realize that the only way you were able to get anywhere close to me is because you're twice my size and I didn't stand a chance, right? When you charged at me it was like you eclipsed the world. Pretty sure I saw my life flash before my eyes." He laughed. "That's exactly what it was. Even if I were straight I'd never love you! No one could. Look at yourself! You really are rotten, Apple. Though I'm sure that's not the first time you've heard that one."

Tears sprung to Apple's eyes with shocking force. Well, not that shocking, I guess. I knew Rupert P. was an asshole, but seeing it up close was a visceral experience. It was the kind of 3-D that makes you dizzy and induces vomiting. That was Rupert Pierpont to a T. Apple couldn't look at him, or any of us for that matter. She took out her phone and gave it all of her attention instead.

"And you!" He turned to Erin, and I really wanted to hear this because, yes, Erin could be a bitch depending on if you misinterpreted her confidence, but on the outside, Erin was beautiful. He could say all he wanted about her personality, but he couldn't touch her looks. And as Rupert P. took her in, it was like he was doing so for the first time. He seemed stumped for an insult, quiet and contemplative. And then he said, "I know you."

Erin's eyes went slightly bigger than usual, and Rupert P.'s lips curled from a grimace into a smile. "Bloody hell, now this all makes sense. You're the Dublin girl."

Dublin girl? "What does he mean?"

"He doesn't know what he's talking about." Erin raced to him and picked up the pink tights on the ground, so quick that Rupert P. didn't even have time to try and snatch her. But I was quicker. I pulled her hand away before she could gag him. This time I didn't turn to her for answers, though. I turned to Rupert P.

"How do you know who she is?"

"He's delusional and butthurt," Erin said. "Don't listen to him."

"You *were* at the Dublin show," I said.

"She was more than just *at* the Dublin show," Rupert P. said. "She *was* the Dublin show."

"You went backstage?" Isabel asked.

"You met the boys?" Apple said, looking up from her phone.

"No wonder you did this," Rupert P. said. "Don't tell me this is your way of getting back at us." For some reason he looked at me then. And he laughed. "What did I tell you? Can't trust your own best friend."

"What is he talking about, Erin?"

"I'm done talking," Rupert P. said. "You girls will destroy yourselves from the inside. Don't need me to muck it up for you."

"Apple, hold him down," Erin said.

"Oi!" Rupert P. said. But Apple was already on him, and just as he'd said, she was clearly stronger than him. She held his arms behind the chair. Erin used the same pair of hot-pink tights she'd used the first time. She wrapped them twice around his mouth and then used the ends to tie his hands behind his back. Every time he tried to move his arms the tights got tighter around his mouth. Who knew Erin was such a mastermind at tying people up?

Who knew anything about Erin anymore?

I looked at her, but she averted her eyes.

"Well, I'm going to the concert," Apple said. Her tears had already fallen, and apparently were long since forgotten.

"But you don't have tickets," Isabel said.

"Actually, I do." She held up her phone. "Consuela has been standing outside of NBC this whole time. She just texted that a Rupert P. fan was so upset by his absence that she walked out. Consuela snagged her ticket." Apple left the room.

"Well, this was anticlimactic," Isabel said. "The Internet's blowing up right now, and I need to be on top of it." She left the room too.

Erin looked at me but neither of us said anything, a silence so icy I shivered. Even Rupert P. looked interested in it, his eyes darting back and forth between us, riveted like a fan at Wimbledon. But we weren't about to indulge him. Or at least Erin wasn't. She walked out of the room.

11

My plan to set Rupert P. free would have to wait. Right now I needed to follow Erin.

Story of my life.

But this time I followed Erin with the intention of getting some answers. She jammed her finger into the elevator button, still not saying anything, not even looking at me. After a few seconds of waiting she huffed and pushed through the stairwell door. I followed her. I followed her down eight flights. For a moment I was stupid enough to think she was trying to get me to come with her someplace private, but by the time we got to the lobby she was taking so many sharp turns around corners that it hit me that she was actually trying to lose me.

"Wait up!" I said as I followed her into the Valmont room.

I didn't know what the Valmont room was for, but it was a huge space with rows of chairs divided in the middle to form an aisle. Maybe they held weddings there, or seminars. Right now it was empty except for me and Erin.

She finally stopped, a lone rose standing tall among a field of ugly brown chairs. She spun on her heel to face me. "Yes?"

As if I was a pesky gnat she couldn't get rid of. As if I wasn't the one friend she told all her secrets to. "What the hell was all that about?"

"I don't know what you mean."

"You *were* the Dublin show?" I said, echoing Rupert P.'s words. "What was he talking about? How does he know you?"

"He must've seen me at the concert." Picking at her cuticles, wanting to change the subject. But I wouldn't.

"Stop lying to me, Erin. At first I thought it was only a little weird that we were taking a boy bander hostage, but now I feel like you're writing a story and I'm just playing a part in it, because all I got from everything that went down in there is that (a) Rupert P. is an unmitigated asshole and (b) his being in our room right now is maybe not the fluke that I thought it was. What the hell is going on?"

She took a deep breath, and I could see from the look on her face—cheeks filled with color, lips twisted, resigned— that she would tell me something she'd never told me before. That she would be honest with me. Maybe for the first time.

"Rupert P. being in our room *is* a fluke," Erin said. "How could I have known what Apple would get up to when caught alone in a hallway with the love of her life and an ounce of determination?"

I took this in, but it sounded like truth by omission. It sounded like there was more. "What *did* you know?"

She took a deep breath and it all came out. "I knew that Griffin had a room on the eighth floor, and that Rupert P. would probably be spending most of his time there."

"And why did you know that? Or want to?" I asked. "It wasn't because you thought that would get us closer to the boys."

"No," she said. "I wanted to know where Griffin and Rupert P. would be so that I could catch them together off guard. I was hoping to maybe get a picture. Citizen pap the hell out of them. The plan was always to blackmail Rupert P. Everything that happened with Apple—Rupert P. ending up in our room—that was all serendipity. It expedited things. I never dreamed the blackmail would go this far. Or that it would work so well."

"But why would you want to blackmail him?"

"To make a dent in the group. Which would be the start of my plan."

I was afraid to ask, because I was afraid of what the answer would be. But I needed to. "What is your plan?"

"To kill the boy band."

12

Oh.

Like it was the weather.

Sunny out and 30 percent chance of *kill the boy band*???

"Figuratively speaking," Erin added.

Because that made it so much better. "Do you mean The Ruperts specifically, or boy bands as a concept?"

"Both, actually."

"Oh," I said. "What the fuck?"

"Calm down," Erin said. "I just want to destroy them till they're an unrecognizable shell of their former selves."

"Erin, *what the fuck?*" I said it again. And again. I think I may have repeated it a dozen times, because Erin came to sit next to me (I must've also taken a seat at some point) and put a hand on my shoulder.

"Are you okay?" she whispered. "Do you need some time?"

"*Do I need time?* I need more than time, Erin! I need an explanation. Do you realize how crazy you sound right now?

Oh no, you've had a psychotic break, haven't you? This is your *Black Swan* moment. It's okay, it can happen to anyone. I need to get you help."

I pulled out my phone. In my mind, at that moment, that was all I could think to do. Erin wasn't herself and she needed help. Luckily, I had my therapist on speed dial. "Dr. Schwarcz-Levinsohn is great," I said. "She'll whip you right back into shape."

Erin yanked the phone out of my hands. "Get a grip," she said. "I'm of sound mind. Actually, my mind's never been sounder. You may not understand my actions right now, but one day you'll come to realize that what I'm doing is really great. No, not just great—*right*. Boy bands need to go. And we're going to be the ones to eradicate them."

I stood up. I had too many feelings racing through me— spilling out of me—to just sit there and listen to this. "Where is this all coming from? We love boy bands, Erin. *You* love boy bands. You love The Ruperts."

"I hate The Ruperts."

"What?"

"I hate The Ruperts." It was like she liked saying it, liked the idea of it, liked the way the words bounced around on her tongue.

Liked the way my face fell upon hearing it.

Erin always could make anything sound seductive, the way she spoke. But not this.

"How many hours have we spent watching their videos together?" I said, incredulous. Maybe all she needed was to be reminded of how much she loved The Ruperts. "How many times have we gone to your house and laid on the floor in your room and sung their album at the top of our lungs? We've told each other stuff. We've told each other our deepest fantasies about Rupert X. and Rupert K. All we do is talk about them!"

"All *you* do is talk about them," Erin said calmly. "And you've obviously not noticed, but lately all I do is listen. I'm sorry, but I'm done listening. The boy band is everything that is wrong with society."

"Jeez, Erin, it's just a boy band. It's not that serious."

"Tell that to a world of girls who worship them. Do you see how many girls there are outside of this hotel? Thousands of girls, screaming their throats raw. And for what? A quartet of trendy haircuts who don't even know they exist. Those girls outside are lobotomies. They're zombies. Only instead of brains they want stupid boys with mediocre singing voices. I've seen the light, and I'm not going to be part of the trend anymore. I won't just stand around and watch as a whole generation of us devolve into a sniveling puddle over some . . . *boys*."

"A whole generation of girls? You're the one who always said boy bands have a shelf life of two to four years."

"That's my entire teenage life!"

Now she was angry. She stood from her seat and finally raised her voice, the loudness of it matching the panic in mine. And it made me realize that I'd only seen the tip of the iceberg of some new blackness in her heart. The Erin I knew didn't just suddenly start hating the boy band that she'd once obsessed over. There was so much more to this that I didn't know.

"What happened at the Dublin show?"

She looked down, combed her fingers through her hair, and it kind of made me sick that I was still focused on how beautiful she was despite the fact that she was also obviously upset about something. "My mom dropped me off and told me to call her when the concert was over so she could come pick me up. I told you that part."

I nodded.

"What I didn't tell you is that after the show I managed to sneak backstage. It's really not that hard when you know how to talk to certain people. I found Rupert X.'s private dressing room. And then I took all of my clothes off, sat on his couch, and waited for him to find me."

"You didn't."

"Yeah, I did. I still can't believe I did that. I was such an idiot."

She'd never told me any of this, and hearing it was shocking. This was big. This was huge. This was story-worthy. It was especially something you'd tell your best friend. If not as soon as it happened, then at least some time within the six months since it'd happened. "Wait a minute. You're doing all of this because Rupert X. rejected you?"

"Who said he rejected me?"

I sat down again, my knees suddenly giving out. "Are you saying . . . ?"

"I told you I was saving myself for Rupert X. And I did."

"What the fuck?" There I went again. I said it a bunch more times, differently now than how we'd started this conversation, but still with just as much meaning behind it. Erin's admission was shocking on so many levels. Not just because she was talking about sex with her actual favorite boy bander, which was a mindfuck and the most improbable thing ever, but because Erin had had sex at all.

And didn't tell me about it.

This was huge. Sex was huge. Here was Erin, having actual sex (with arguably the hottest boy on the planet, no less) and here I was, thinking we were best friends. But best friends told each other this sort of thing as soon as it happened. How could she keep it to herself all this time?

"When Rupert X. came into the room he was looking down at something on his phone, so he didn't notice me at first," Erin said. "But then when he finally did he had the strangest look on his face. His eyebrows sort of scrunched together, but he smiled. He looked at me like I was a puppy who'd managed to find some hidden treat or something, and Rupert X. couldn't be disappointed because it was so damn adorable. He didn't even look particularly surprised. He didn't turn me down. But obviously I didn't want him to.

"After we were done he took pictures of me on the couch. I thought, 'Wow, he must like me so much he wants to remember me.' But then he said, 'I'm going to send these to the lads.' Don't you just hate it when they call each other 'lads'?"

"Erin . . ."

"I told him not to send the pictures to anyone. I told him that I wanted him to delete them. But he just kept talking like he hadn't even heard me. He said, 'I think I'll title the message Party in My Room.' I said, 'Please, don't.' I started to cry. I pleaded with him not to send those pictures to anyone. I asked him, 'What do I have to do to keep you from sending them out?' And he said, 'I want you to beg for me, love.'"

The words echoed in my mind. I'd heard them before. And then I realized I heard them when Erin herself had said them to Rupert P.

"So I begged. He stroked my face, and gave me this 'poor you' smile. And then he sent them anyway. A second later Rupert L. and Rupert P. came bounding through the room. Now that I think of it, Rupert P. looked like he was just coming along 'cause it was something to do, not because he actually wanted to see a naked girl. Rupert L. looked way more excited.

"I took one of the couch cushions and tried to cover myself up, but it wasn't really enough. And then Rupert X. held my clothes up and said, 'Looking for these?' I tried to grab them and he said, 'It was just a Snapchat, love. Are you really going to go?' He laughed, and then he gave me my clothes. And I ran out of there."

I couldn't imagine Erin like that. Naked. Vulnerable. At the mercy of someone who wasn't partial to her charms. "And you took his dagger necklace," I said. It wasn't a replica I'd found in her bag. It was Rupert X.'s actual necklace, the one he hadn't been seen wearing for the last six months.

Erin's eyes were dark and shimmery and distant, like she was back in that room. "Do you have any idea how much it hurt?"

I didn't know if she meant emotionally or physically. Probably both. I couldn't believe that anyone was capable of hurting Erin. I couldn't believe that someone had succeeded. And I couldn't believe that the boys—our boys, who we loved so much—could be so horrible. "I'm sorry, Erin. Why didn't you ever tell me?"

She shrugged, and when she blinked part of the shimmer in her eyes went away, and it was like she was back in the present. "I was embarrassed," she said. "I was stupid. But I refuse to be stupid any longer. That's why I need to do this."

"We already got Rupert P. out of the band. How much more damage do you want to do?"

"As much as I can."

I swallowed hard, confused and more than a little scared. "Do you realize what you're saying, though? You want to destroy people's lives."

"Four boys for the price of millions of girls. I think it's a fair trade."

"Those girls outside the hotel—all the Strepurs of the world—love those boys. Who are you really hurting here?"

"Strepurs don't know what they want. Those girls outside the hotel could overthrow governments with their passion! They have the potential to do so much more. To make music, or art, or to write something that isn't rpf fanfic!"

A slap in the face. A thunderclap that shook me to my gut. "I thought you liked my fic."

"You're so talented. You could be using your skills to do so much more than just that."

"And you could be using your skills to do more than destroy a boy band! Erin, you can't just go destroying people's lives because Rupert X. screwed you over."

Poor choice of words, I know, but it was too late to take them back.

"This isn't about Rupert X. anymore. He's just a stupid fuckboy. But he did make me realize something. I'm not just going to be a victim. I'm doing something about it."

"How could you involve me in this?" I said.

"You could've walked away from this at any moment. But you didn't."

It was the truth, and it particularly stung because it meant I couldn't just blame Erin for this. It was no one's fault but my own that I never walked away, that I never freed Rupert P., that I never even had the balls to stand up to my friends. I was always following Erin blindly. I was a coward.

I wasn't going to give her the satisfaction of admitting that, though. "You're being psycho."

"I'm the psycho? At least Rupert K. isn't a recurring guest star in my daydreams."

Another slap in the face. They were starting to sting.

I'd told her about that in confidence.

"Think of all the things you've sacrificed for this band," Erin went on. "Friends—"

"I have friends."

"Friends who you don't communicate with on the Internet. Discovering other interests. You've got this tunnel-vision obsession that's keeping you from seeing real life."

I couldn't believe she was saying this to me. I knew other people didn't understand me, didn't understand why I cared so much about these boys, but the one person I thought got it was the one person who was throwing it all back in my face. I always thought we were in this together.

I was so wrong.

And I think that hurt more than anything.

"Why am I even here, then?" I said. "Why did you invite me along if you knew I would be opposed to this?"

"I hoped you'd see my side of things. You're my best friend. I want to save you too."

I'd chased her all the way in here, but suddenly I wanted to be as far away from her as possible. "I'm so grateful," I spat. I tried saying it with as much venom as I could, but Erin was always the one who had a way with words.

13

There was this girl at school who used to taunt me sometimes. Leslie Hamilton. She was a sophomore and I was a freshman, and this was early on in the school year, the worst the bullying ever was. She didn't do anything major, just spewed shit consistently. Stuff about my clothes, my hair, about how I didn't have a dad—really childish stuff. One day in the locker room, while everyone else headed into the gym for PE, Erin took my hand and pulled me back. The two of us were the only ones left.

"I have something for you," she'd said. Her hair was up in a high ponytail, her lips still super red, even for gym. She held out a pink water bottle for me to take.

"Thanks," I said. "But I'm not thirsty."

"It's not for you, silly. That's Leslie's water bottle. She keeps it locked in her locker because she occasionally enjoys a bit of vodka in her post-gym refresher. But combination locks are a breeze, and no match for me." She held it out again, shaking it a bit. "So here, take it. I think you should pee in it.".

I read her face, trying to make out if this was some sort of joke, but she was serious. "What?"

"Pee in the bottle. She deserves it."

"Erin," I said. It was more of a shocked laugh than a name, the way it came out. "I can't just . . . I can't just pee in someone's water bottle."

"Why not?"

"Because it's really mean."

Erin sighed and dropped her hand, the water bottle colliding limply with her thigh. "How can you stand the way she treats you? I can't."

"Yeah, but what you're proposing isn't any better. It isn't nice."

I thought she'd drop it then, that she'd see the error of her ways, but Erin only came closer, smoothed out the shoulder of my gym T-shirt, and said, "Fuck nice." She held out the bottle again, giving it a little shake. She smiled.

I was enthralled by everything about her. By the fact that she was so appalled by Leslie Hamilton's treatment of me that she'd steal the girl's water bottle. By the fact that she wanted to get revenge on Leslie Hamilton simply because she cared about me.

I loved that memory of Erin sticking up for me in her own way. And I especially loved the look on Leslie Hamilton's face when she spit out her water in disgust. Now, after everything, that memory seems tainted somehow, and I just see the situation for what it was: shady as fuck.

Because the truth was, my best friends were psychopaths. Officially.

I mean, there really was no denying it now. When they weren't kidnapping boy band members, they were plotting to destroy them.

I thought of going back to the bar again, but then I also felt like I needed a change. So instead of going down I went up. I took the elevator as high as it would go, and then when it wouldn't go any higher I found the nearest stairwell and kept going up til there was nothing but a door. I pushed it open, and a gust of wind assaulted me. It whipped my hair in all different directions and shouted in my ears. The fresh air was violent, but I felt better already.

I took out my phone and clicked on Twitter. My feed was blowing up, just as I knew it would be. It was a volley between Rupert P. fangirls tweeting threats to kill themselves or anyone else if the news of Rupert P.'s departure was true, and other Strepurs being surprisingly excited by the news of Rupert P.'s exit. My Tumblr dash was a mess too, with people reblogging tear-stricken selfies and hundreds of posts of girls freaking out. Buzzfeed already had a slew of lists up, from "Twelve Signs That Rupert P. Was Bound to Leave The Ruperts" to "Sixty Reasons Why The Ruperts Will Be a Better Band Now That Rupert P. Is Gone." Isabel's website was my last stop. She'd already posted about the whole debacle, speaking about it as if she had some sort of insight on the matter. Well, I guess she kind of did. She was promising more updates soon. I tried scrolling through her comments section, but it seemed impossible to get to the bottom of the page. Her site was extremely popular, but I'd never seen her get this many comments. She must be somewhere right now high-fiving herself or threatening people's well-being, or whatever it was Isabel considered celebratory.

My battery was down to 30 percent. I put my phone in my pocket and walked over to the edge of the roof. The wall at the edge came up to my waist. Normally I would've been scared. I was really high up, and if I leaned too far out—splat—it'd all be over. But fear hadn't done me any good today. Fear had stopped me from confronting Erin about all this. From making up my own mind. I looked over the edge. Down below were the screaming girls, a whole ocean of them. I may not have been down there with them, but I was one of them.

I loved being a Strepur. Maybe I was obsessed, but so were millions of other girls. I wasn't out of my depth. And I was happy in my obsession. But was Erin right? Was I just a drone, wasting my time and potential on boys who would never know I existed?

I stuffed my hand into my jeans pocket and fished out the elastic string of my bracelet and the few beads I'd managed to find after Rupert P. broke it. I pinched one end of the elastic and strung the remaining beads onto it. Some of the letters were missing, and I only managed to spell out "Ddy."

You know that feeling you get when you're about to cry? When your chin quivers and the back of your throat twists and hurts? I hated that feeling. I blinked, trying to stave it off. I sighed deep and shut my eyes, tried to think of something better, and then . . .

"Please don't jump."

The new voice frightened me, and I spun to see where it came from. And then I froze. Because standing behind me was . . . my boy.

My life ruiner.

My Rupert K.

My face at that moment was that Heart Eyes emoji.

"Please, think about what you're doing," he said. He was coming toward me with careful steps, his arms outstretched before him as if ready to catch me if I fell. Was it bad that a part of me wanted to just so he could? "It gets better. Life is precious. Uh, life is beautiful?" He cursed under his breath and squeezed his eyes shut for an instant, embarrassed by his trite-ness. "I don't know what people usually say in these sorts of situations. Just, please don't jump."

He was standing right next to me. He wore a gray peacoat over a white shirt, buttoned all the way up to the collar, and he gripped his black hat onto his head with one hand.

This wasn't real.

This was not happening.

I was losing my mind. I was absolutely losing my mind. But I didn't care. Rupert K. was trying to talk me out of killing myself.

This was the best day of my life.

"Please, step back," he said. He said it as if I could move— as if I had any sort of control over my limbs in his presence. "If you move I will be forced to take matters into my own hands."

Did "matters" mean me?

I lunged for the edge.

Just as he'd promised, Rupert K. grabbed me by the waist and pulled. I didn't have to stumble back and make myself fall on top of him.

But reader, that's exactly what I did.

The two of us were a jumble of limbs on the cold concrete roof. As we were clearly meant to be.

"Are you alright?"

No. No, I was definitely not alright. I was hugging Rupert K. of The Ruperts. Rupert K. of The Ruperts had just saved my life. Not that it was in any real danger to begin with. But I nodded anyway.

"You won't off yourself, then?"

I shook my head. Words. They would've been handy right then. Somehow I mustered one up. "No."

"You sure? You're a sad-looking girl alone on a roof . . ." His voice was London butter. Is that a thing? Let's say it was Marmite, but delicious. He helped me up and I let him.

What was he even doing here? Wasn't he supposed to be at the Thanksgiving spectacular? I guess it had probably ended by now. It was only supposed to be an hour after all. And enough time had passed for him to have come back to the hotel. Plus, I knew Rupert K. well enough to know that he always skipped an after-party.

But why was I trying to figure out why he was here? He just was, and I wasn't going to ask any questions.

"I just needed to think," I said.

Unbelievably, he kept looking at me. He hadn't taken his eyes off me, actually. There was something quizzical behind his eyes, like he thought I might still jump. I didn't dare move an inch. I didn't want to do anything that would make him look away.

"What's troubling you?" he asked. At this point I had lost all manner of speech. I could've been drooling for all I knew. "I'm sorry, it's none of my business. I don't usually get to talk to people my age . . . new people my age. So when I do I can pry a bit. Did you want to be alone?"

"I HAVE NEVER WANTED TO BE LESS ALONE."

I may have said that a little too loudly. To defuse the awkwardness I cleared my throat. Totally saved it.

"We haven't been properly introduced," he said. "I'm Rupert Kirke."

Lulz. Duh.

"I'm Sloane," I said. "Sloane Peterson."

"So, Sloane. Why are you on the roof of The Rondack all by yourself tonight?"

"I just needed to clear my head because . . . well, my best friend sort of betrayed me, I guess? She did something behind my back and now I don't know if I can trust her again."

"Wow. That's exactly the same reason I came up here."

Soul mates. That was what we were. "Really?"

"Yeah," Rupert K. said. "My mate turned his back on me tonight, and it could mess up a lot of things for us. For me."

Okay, so he obviously couldn't know that I'd wallpapered my bedroom with his face and I was currently wearing a total of three pieces of clothing that featured his likeness (socks, tank top under my sweater, underwear), but was he not aware that I knew who he was? I was a breathing fifteen-year-old girl—he must've known that I knew. Why was he being so open with me? Did he see something in me that made him feel like he could talk to me? Thinking about that made me feel instantly guilty. Rupert K. looked so sad, and I was indirectly (or was that just plain directly?) responsible for it.

"Maybe you just need to hear your friend out," I said. "I'm sure if you talk it out you can come to an understanding." Rupert P. could explain the whole thing once we let him free.

"What about you? Do you think you can talk it out with your friend?"

"I don't know," I said. "But you shouldn't be sad. Down there? Those girls are screaming for you."

He smiled. "So you know who I am."

I nodded, my heart beating fast.

"You're not screaming for me."

Oh, I was. Internally I was shrieking. "Screaming wouldn't do you any good right now."

He laughed and leaned over the edge of the wall, looking down at the girls, but they didn't seem as impressive to him as they had to me. His gaze floated up, admiring the skyline as the buildings got higher uptown. "There are so many bright lights."

"*Bright Lights, Big City.*"

"Bright lights, big city?" His eyes went wide, a new idea forming behind them. "That's good. That's really quite good, actually. Do you think I could use that in a song?"

"It's the title of a book," I said. "And a movie."

"Oh. Right, I knew that."

"It's okay, it came out in the eighties—way before we were born, and it's not very popular, you wouldn't have heard of it."

"No, no, I know it," he said. "Yeah, now that I think of it. Course."

He was lying. He always squinted when he lied. It was strange that we were meeting for the first time and I already knew all his mannerisms cold, yet he knew nothing about me.

I leaned over the wall too. A sea of Strepurs growing larger, no end in sight. The crowd had gotten so large it spilled over onto the block across the street. I wondered if you removed the building behind them, would there be more of them still, the way you find bugs under rocks?

"Did you know that if you throw a penny off the Empire State Building you could kill someone?" Rupert K. said.

It was a myth, but I wasn't about to correct him.

"Do you think if I let go of my hat it'll kill one of the girls down there?"

"Uh, probably not," I said.

"Let's test it out."

He let go of his hat, and a second later the wind whipped it off his head and carried it away. I had to fight every urge in my body not to go after that hat.

"Those girls are screaming for the idea of me," Rupert K. said. "They're screaming for the guy whose face is on their tube of toothpaste at home. You know, we even have an endorsement deal with cat food now? *Do you want your cat to eat like a normal cat, or do you want him to eat like a Rupert?*"

I couldn't help but snort at his funny, infomercial-guy voice while simultaneously thinking very seriously of getting a cat.

"I don't mean to sound ungrateful or anything," he said. "I'm very glad for my success. Sometimes it just gets to be too much. Especially when you're in it together with three other guys. It's not as easy as other people think."

"Really?"

"Do you want to know a secret?" He leaned in close. So close that the air next to my cheek felt suddenly warmer. "Sometimes I think about leaving it all."

"Oh?"

"Yeah."

"Wow."

"Yeah," he said. "You've got big eyes."

Non sequiturs were sort of his thing. Some people thought he maybe had undiagnosed ADHD. I was experiencing one of his patented adorable ADHD moments! "I've been called bug-eyed."

"No, they're lovely."

Was I falling? Had I gone over the edge of the roof after all? I had the distinct sensation that I was falling. But Rupert K. was not leaning out to catch me. Guess I was just imagining it.

"Uh. You. Also. Have eyes . . ." I said.

I was an idiot.

His phone rang, a mercy killing of my hopeless gibbering. He pinched it out of his back pocket and glanced at the screen. "I've got to take this," he said. "I hope it works out with your friend."

"You too."

He walked away and disappeared through the door. I was left to reconstruct my brain.

14

Eventually I made my way back to the room. I felt like every character in every teen movie who'd ever been with someone for the first time. You know, that morning after scene where they're walking down a hallway with a knowing smirk, a spring in their step, and badass music playing in the background. Except Rupert K. and I hadn't actually *been together* in the strictest sense. And I also couldn't fully enjoy the moment knowing that I was holding one of his best friends hostage.

It was time to let Rupert P. go. I was kind of hoping the rest of the girls wouldn't be there so I wouldn't have to deal with them and their rationalizations. I just wanted to be done with Rupert P., set him free, back into the wilds from whence he came. But even if my friends were there, I wouldn't let them change my mind anymore. Finally, all bets were off. I was making my own decisions from now on.

I walked down to the eighth floor and opened the stairwell

door. It opened right across from our hotel room. Apple was standing in front of the door, facing it.

"Hey," I said.

She spun around, looking like I'd frightened her. "Hi."

"So how was the concert?"

"Short." She was going to say something more, but both of our attentions were stolen when Erin appeared at the end of the hall, walking toward us. Almost at that exact same moment, the elevator doors opened on our other side and Isabel stepped through them. The four of us met in front of our door, facing one another at an intersection. A weird vibe fell over us. Maybe it was the silence. In all the times we'd been together, we'd never actually been silent. We were always talking about the boys, and when we weren't talking about them we were screaming for them.

Now that we were all together, my first instinct was to tell them about meeting Rupert K., but I stopped myself. It wasn't the right time. Plus, things were definitely still weird between all of us. I knew what we really had to talk about was what was on the other side of that door.

"What are we going to do with him?" I asked. No one said anything. "Apple, do you still want to keep him? After the things he called you?"

She shook her head.

"And Isabel?"

She shrugged. "Fun's over now. I'll do whatever you guys

want." But I knew what she meant was she'd do whatever Erin wanted.

I looked at Erin. I didn't feel like talking to her, but it was her turn to make her opinions known. She looked drained, and I thought maybe it was because of our argument earlier. She raised a shoulder. "Whatever," she said.

So we opened the door to our room.

There was something wrong.

I could feel it even before I knew what it was; something about the darkness in the room, the stillness. Rupert P. was still there, but it was too quiet. His head was bent forward, unmoving. I knew the other girls could feel something was wrong too, all except Apple. We all stayed still while she moved forward. She walked up to his chair. "Rupert?" she said.

Silence.

"Rupie?"

The tights weren't around his mouth anymore. They were wrapped around his neck.

Erin, Isabel, and I may have been the farthest from him, but I think we all got it before Apple did. But when she did get it— when she lifted his head and saw his eyes and mouth bulged open in a silent scream—she was the only one to say it out loud.

"OMG," Apple said. "He's dead!"

PART TWO

15

I know what you're asking yourself. You're asking how a group of teenage girls managed to kill the biggest flop in the world's most popular boy band.

The truth is, I had no idea.

Not right then.

All I knew was what the screams of four hysterical girls reverberating in a very expensive hotel room sounded like. All I could hear was the cacophony of our screeching, and all I could see were arms flailing, tears streaming, hair pulling: the vision of horror. And right in the middle of it—the thing we were avoiding and the source of our hysterics—sat Rupert Pierpont of The Ruperts.

Dead.

I don't mean it like hashtag-dead. I mean, Rupert P. was literally dead.

I never thought my knees would buckle at the sight of him, but here I was, falling. I sat on the ground as the rest of the girls continued flailing. If you muted them and didn't stare directly at their faces, it would've looked like they were prancing. Seriously, I'd never seen Apple more agile in my life. She was leaping from corner to corner on the balls of her feet, twirling her fingers around strands of her hair. The only way you could tell she was at all distressed was by looking at her features, which kept morphing into twisted, wet shapes. Even Rupert P. looked upset by what was happening.

Shit.

My pocket buzzed, knocking me back into reality. I fished my phone out and there was Mom's latest text.

How was the dinner, honey?

I looked up and met Rupert P.'s eyes. He was shocked, outraged, forever.

My fingers shook, but I still managed to type out a message.

So yummy.

Mom responded immediately.

Did you remember to thank your friend's parents?

I scoffed.

Ofc. I'm not a Neanderthal.

Apple bumped into/collapsed against a wall, and the sound snapped me back into reality. Or the nightmare that was my reality. Rupert P. kept looking at me. Where was AdBlock when you needed it?

I put my head between my knees, suddenly feeling light-headed. I took deep breaths. I tried to think. FYI, it is very hard to think in a room full of screaming girls, especially if you're one of them.

"Stop screaming."

None of them heard me. It wasn't their fault—I might have whispered it. I made eye contact with Apple, the loudest of all of us. "Apple, stop screaming." She crouched down beside me, got in my face, and yelled, "I CAN'T!"

"If we don't stop screaming people will hear us and send someone!"

That did it. Our screaming turned into silent heaving as we tried to compose ourselves.

"How did this happen?" Erin said.

"Who was in here last?" Isabel said.

"We're going to need a polyethylene plastic bin and a few gallons of acid," Apple said. We stared at her. "I watched *Breaking Bad*, I know how to get rid of a body!"

For the first time we had just acknowledged that Rupert P. was no longer a person. He was a body. And all of us realized it at the same moment. Though it was just a small moaning at first, the screaming was gearing up again, deep from all of us.

"Everybody calm down!"

They all watched me, but not because of my sudden out-burst; because I was taking control of the situation and that's exactly what they needed. I didn't know where I had gotten this sudden strength. I'm not sure if I could even classify it as strength. A momentary clarity. Maybe my father's death had prepared me for a situation like this. Maybe I wasn't freaking out as much as them because I'd already been touched by death. I knew of it.

The point is, I couldn't just back away slowly and hope my footsteps would lead me all the way back home to Brooklyn. I couldn't just scroll through this. Maybe I was one of those people who handled a crisis with a level head and I didn't even know it. Whatever it was, I embraced it. "We need to assess the situation," I said. "Rupert P. is dead."

"Well, thank shit you're here, Nancy Prew," Isabel said.

"It's Nancy *Drew* and a person is dead, Isabel!" I said. "Because of us."

"Are you saying one of us killed him?" Apple asked.

"Wait, hold up, who said anything about *killed*?" Isabel said, stepping up to me like a panther ready to pounce. "Nobody killed anybody!"

"Then how did he die?"

We all turned to look at the body, a new curiosity. But none of us moved closer to him. "Apple, you check," I said, breaking the eerie silence.

"No way, I'm not touching him."

"You loved him!"

"His death kind of ruined him for me."

"But how did Rupert P. not ruin Rupert P. for you?" Isabel said.

"I'll do it," I said. I could hear the other girls holding their breath, sucking it in and taking all sound with them. The room was a vacuum; just white noise that buzzed in my ears, louder the closer I got to the body.

But then I saw it.

"Oh." Less of a word, more of a gasp.

"He's not dead?" Apple said. "This is all a bad dream?"

"Yeah, Apple, we're all having the same bad dream at the exact same time," Isabel said. "Honestly, the delusion is so strong with you sometimes."

"Would both of you shut up?" I said. "I think I know how he died."

"What is it?" Isabel said. "The suspense is killing Rupert P."

"The tights." The tights that made a great blindfold and even better knots were also an exceptional murder weapon. They were too tight around his neck. Tights that were tight. Whodathunk?

"He was strangled."

The four of us towered over him, our heads almost touching as we looked down at him—really looked—for the first time. He seemed stiff already, even though he couldn't have been dead more than an hour. And his hair was drained of what little orange brilliance it once had, now that it was set against his sallow pallor.

I didn't see my father when he died, so I knew it was the first time any of us had seen a dead body before (I assumed— you never really knew with Isabel). It reminded me of that scene in *Stand by Me* where the four friends find the body by the train tracks and their lives change forever in a profound yet charmingly coming-of-age way. Did this constitute our own shitty rite of passage? Had we just lost our innocence? Were we women now? Because I didn't feel anything except for a vague nausea.

Finding a body and contemplating what it all meant was overrated. It was nothing like the movies.

"Okay, which one of you dicktips killed him?" Isabel said.

"A second ago you said nobody killed anybody."

"A second ago I didn't know he was strangled. So who did it? Not me."

"Not me!" Apple said.

"Not me." Even though it was stupid, I didn't want to be the last one to say it, stuck with the short straw. I turned to Erin, who hadn't chimed in with her "Not me" yet. She was still looking down at Rupert P., but so much more differently than the way she'd looked down at him just an hour earlier. Her eyes seemed stunted open, and she was biting down hard. I could see it in the way her jaw muscles were flexed. I imagined her standing over Rupert P. as he sat, helpless. I imagined her pulling the tights taut against his throat until his veins bulged and the saliva in his mouth gurgled. It wasn't difficult—I'd seen her tie the tights around him twice already. I imagined her pulling hard and not letting go until the capillaries in his eyes burst, the words "kill the boy band" ringing in my ears.

I imagined my best friend as a murderer.

I was the worst best friend in the world.

"Erin?"

"None of us are guilty," Erin said. "Whatever happens, we stick to the same story, alright? We were all together and none of us did it."

"You know what that means, right?" Isabel whispered in my direction. "She totally did it."

"Shut up," I said.

"Um, I know this is an upsetting time, but collect your feels in an orderly fashion. Who do you think you're talking to?" Isabel said.

"Way to stick together, you guys!" Apple said. "Can't we go two minutes without fighting anymore? And let's stop accusing each other. We just need to be honest about where we all were when Rupert P. passed away. I was at the concert."

"I was in the hotel gym," Isabel said. "They have the best Wi-Fi there."

"I was in the bar," I said. Usually I would've blabbed about it to anyone I met—that I had a total "moment" with Rupert Kirke on the roof of The Rondack, where he put his arms around me, saved my life, and said I had lovely eyes—but for some reason I was reluctant to tell my own friends. Maybe it was because they didn't feel like friends anymore. Anyway, none of them would've believed me. Saying I was in the bar was a lot more plausible than meeting the love of your life on a hotel rooftop.

We all turned toward Erin, waiting for her to tell us where she was when Rupert P. died, but she stayed silent. I didn't have time to worry about her silence, because what was creeping me out more was the way she stared at me: steady, unwavering. Like she was seeing right through my lie.

"What if none of us did it?" I said quickly.

"What?" Erin said.

"Look." I pointed to Rupert P.'s arms. "The way he was tied up, his gag was linked to his hands. When we left the room he would've been trying to get his hands loose. What if, the more he tried to free his hands, the more it tightened the gag? What if it slipped off his mouth, down to his neck, and he—"

"Accidentally strangled himself to death?" Erin said.

"Quite frankly."

"You really think that's what happened?" Isabel asked me.

"It's the only explanation we've got. The alternative is one of us is a murderer."

Isabel nodded and started pacing. "Okay. Now that that's out of the way, we gotta figure out how to get rid of the body."

"What?" the three of us responded.

"What, you all thought we could just leave him here? Should we tie the tights around his neck into a nice little bow for the police to find? We need to get him back to his room and let someone else deal with him."

"We can't move him to the boys' room. They're already back from the show," I said.

"And how do you know?" Isabel asked.

Because I met Rupert K. on the roof. "I mean, if Apple's back from the concert, then they must be too."

"She's right," Erin said. "They probably are."

"We need to get rid of Rupert P. before he starts to rot," Isabel said.

"We aren't touching his body," I said. "We need to call the police."

You'd think I'd just announced that the remaining Ruperts had just broken up.

"Have several seats, will you?" Isabel said. "Your arms must be tired of carrying around that huge fucking moral compass of yours. We call the police now and your homecoming court will be a parade of the juvie circuit. I swear, sometimes I think you get off on being a self-righteous buzzkill."

"If Rupert P. did die accidentally, then the police will see that and we won't get into trouble. Not much, at least. The only reason you wouldn't want to call the police is if he didn't die accidentally."

"I could swear you just accused me of murder."

I didn't respond to that, because maybe I kind of had. "You're awfully insistent on getting rid of all the evidence."

I looked over at Erin, wishing she'd back me up. But I already knew she wouldn't. She just stood in the corner, her gaze on nothing and no one in particular. She was almost as devoid of color as Rupert P. was.

"We should have a vote," Isabel said, starting to pace again.

"Another vote?" I was good in a crisis, but I didn't know how far that would take me when it came to standing up to Isabel. It felt like she'd taken the reins somehow, and while Erin had the motive to kill Rupert P.—and might have done it—I still would have preferred her leadership over Isabel's any day.

Isabel was already across the room, grabbing the book from the drawer in the nightstand again.

We all wrote down our votes again. Put the crumpled pieces of paper into Apple's ski cap again. I read them out loud again.

The first vote. "Move the body."

The second. "Call the police."

The third. "Move him."

The fourth vote. "Move the body."

It was like déjà vu, only worse. This was actually real.

I opened the door and walked out into the other room. Rupert P. was in his chair, dead, but still watching me. A shiver ran through my whole body. I couldn't be there any longer. I left.

16

I now lived in a world where murdering a boy band member was as acceptable as asking for his autograph.

Okay, I know we didn't technically murder him. Maybe. But he died under mysterious circumstances that we were directly responsible for. Rupert P., however ugly and shitty a person he was—mayherestinpeace—did not deserve to die.

It was too much to think about.

Obviously, I went back to the hotel bar.

I couldn't just flee the hotel. I wanted to, but I couldn't leave things the way they were: a boy dead in our room and my friends in the lurch. But I also couldn't just sit there and watch them play around with someone's death.

Perhaps the bar wasn't the best place to clear my head, though. It was fuller this time of night. Beyond the windows I couldn't see anything but Strepurs, just piled on top of each other, pressed against the glass. They were the rolling fog in horror movies, the ever-expanding dark blob in *The Blob* (the

1988 remake). I thought back to what Erin said, about those girls being zombies, and now it was all I saw. It was in the glazed-over look behind their overtired eyes; their open mouths, silent from where I was sitting, but eerily cavernous; the drool that fell limply from the corners of them. Were those girls my peers? Was I kidding myself into thinking there was more than just glass doors that separated us?

You could put up a few stanchions, post a pair of guards at the front, but nothing you did could really stop them. It felt like I was the only one who knew the unique and undeniable truth that the only reason this hotel was still standing was because the Strepurs outside of it were feeling merciful. For now. The moment they all decided that nothing would stand in the way of them and The Ruperts, people were going to fall and walls were coming down.

There was a stool open at the bar. I sat in it a second before realizing I'd have to see the Civil War Bartender again. He showed up immediately. Even his beard wasn't enough to obscure the smugness behind it. "I heard about what happened."

I sat up straighter, alarmed. Did he know Rupert P. was dead? Did the girls call the police after all? "I'm—I'm sorry."

"I bet you are. A Rupert quits the band. Smartest guy in the group."

Oh. "You know about that?"

"It's all over the news." He took his phone out and flicked through some things on the screen until a blue glow reflected off his face. He showed me the screen. It was the signature royal-blue background of Isabel's site. If someone as civilian as Civil War Bartender was on it, it had to mean she was getting crazy traffic, which meant she was probably raking it in too. Rupert P.'s death might end up being the best thing to happen to Isabel.

"Come to drown your sorrows?" Civil War Bartender said.

"Will you serve me alcohol if I said yes?" I didn't know how drinks worked exactly. I'd never had any alcohol before, but if movies and books were to be believed, there was a chance I could black out, maybe forget whole parts of the day. Suddenly alcoholism didn't seem like an altogether bad way to lead a life. A drink sounded like just exactly what I needed.

"Still no."

"I'll have a cherry Coke."

He poured me a glass and watched as I gulped it down. I didn't realize my hands were shaking until some of the Coke spilled down the front of my sweater, the ivory cable knit soaking it up like a towel. "Damnit."

"You're really upset about this," Civil War Bartender said.

Why was he still here? He handed me a stack of napkins, and I dabbed them on myself in a futile attempt to get clean.

190

"Chaos for a boy band is always a good thing," he said. "Shakes things up a bit. It'll either make them stronger musicians or they'll disband altogether. Any way you spin it, it can't be bad."

He was starting to sound like Erin. How could two people so different have the same opinion on this?

"Rupert Pierpont was the weakest link anyway," he said. "Wasn't he, like, the one who juggled all the time?"

"For someone who despises boy bands so much, you seem to know an awful lot about them."

"I can't shut my eyes to the world around me. As John Lennon once said, 'Living is easy—'"

"'With eyes closed.' I know. What I don't know is what the fuckall that quote has to do with what we're talking about." I kept dabbing the stain, which seemed to only be growing, in proportion with my annoyance. "Don't you have a Kickstarter to fund or something? I don't have to sit here and listen to you. You don't know anything. You think you're so cool with your beard and your dollar-store philosophies about boy bands and life? You think you have anything to say about the experience of the modern American teenage girl? You have no fucking clue what it's like to be me or my friends. You don't know what we're capable of. So why don't you kindly fuck off!"

I didn't know where any of that had come from, but it felt good getting it out. Is this what it felt like to be Erin all the time? To always make an impact? The few people sitting next to me at the bar gave me long looks before vacating their stools. Even Civil War Bartender took a step back.

"Wow," he said. "Fans, man. You're all crazy."

"Yeah? Write me an open letter."

His gaze left mine to look at someone behind me. He rolled his eyes. "I'll be way over there if you need me."

Erin took one of the newly empty stools beside me. "We need to talk."

"Sometimes, Erin, I think you're the coolest person I've ever met. And sometimes, I can't believe I even allow myself to talk to you." I guess talking to the bartender ripped something open in me. A new confidence, maybe. Whatever it was, I was riding it as far as it would take me. "You betrayed me. You lied to me all this time since you've been back from Dublin. You could've talked to me. I would've *listened*."

"But you wouldn't have changed your mind about the boys," Erin said. "You probably would've judged me for sleeping with Rupert X."

I didn't say anything right away. I wanted to deny it, but I got this twinge in my gut that maybe she was right. Maybe I would've done the unmentionable thing—maybe I wouldn't have believed her, or worse: Maybe I would've slut-shamed my best friend over my love for a boy band.

"I would have believed you," I said, hoping that saying it would make it true.

"Whatever," Erin said. "That's not what I wanted to talk to you about."

"I know what you want to talk about," I said. "He's sitting unblinking in our hotel room."

"We need to——"

"*Come play*, you said. *The water's nice*, you said. And now a person is dead!" My voice had risen a bit, and we both looked around to see if anyone had heard me. But no one was paying any attention to the two teenage girls sitting at the bar. "*Kill the boy band*——those were your exact words."

"I didn't mean *literally*," she hissed. "You . . . you don't actually think I had something to do with his death, do you?"

She looked even worse than she had up in the room. Her hair seemed impossibly limp, and no matter how many times she put her hands through it, it wouldn't cooperate, like even her golden strands were sick of her bullshit. She pushed it back, a nuisance. It didn't look very fashionable. Even the red in her lipstick had faded. I'd never seen the perfect Erin so . . . imperfect.

"No," I said. "No, it was an accident, remember? He did it to himself."

"That's the thing I wanted to talk to you about," she said. "I don't think that he did."

"What do you mean?"

"I called my dad."

"You *what?*" My first reaction was to be scared. But then the more I let it sink in, the more relieved I felt. It made me long for grown-ups in a way I thought I'd grown out of. I wanted an adult to swoop in and help us, take care of everything, clean up our mess and tell us it would be okay. I knew it wouldn't be that easy, but I allowed myself to live in that one second when I hoped it would be. It was warm and safe.

"I didn't tell him anything. I just asked him—hypothetically—if someone could kill themselves through strangulation." Erin's father was a cardiologist. He and Erin didn't speak very much unless Erin needed some urgent medical advice about periods or STDs "for her friends." He was always happy to impart his knowledge to her if it got the two of them to talk, it seemed. "He said probably not."

"Probably not is not no."

"He said the victim would pass out first before they'd ever get close enough to actually kill themselves."

"But the tights."

"Rupert P. would've passed out long before he could pull them tight enough to actually die."

"But . . . there's still a chance he did this to himself, right? I mean . . . It can't . . . We didn't . . ."

"I don't know," Erin said. She wiped her hands over her face. Another thing I'd never seen her do. Erin could go a whole day without touching her face just so that her makeup stayed meticulously in place. "I don't know anything anymore. I just think we have to entertain the possibility that someone did kill him."

"You mean one of us."

She nodded.

"Girls!"

Erin and I turned because, well, we were the only girls in the bar. Michelle Hornsbury rushed to us, all out of breath and unfairly beautiful. She wrapped her arms around Erin first and then me, air-kissing our cheeks once on each side.

To say it was weird was an understatement.

I couldn't remember if we'd returned her purse. I think we just left it on the table. Had someone else brought it up to the bar and relayed the message that it was actually me and Erin who'd found and returned it? It was the only explanation for her sudden turnaround regarding fangirls.

"You don't know how happy I am to see some familiar faces!" she said in her lilting English accent.

"Um, is everything okay?" I asked her.

The happiness vanished from her face, and she looked at me like I was an idiot. "Of course it's not okay. Haven't you heard the news?"

That Rupert P. was dead?

"That Rupert P. quit the band?" Erin said. I had to stop jumping to the dead thing so quickly. "How is he doing?"

I couldn't believe she'd asked that, but I knew what Erin was trying to do. Just like the last time we'd spoken to Michelle Hornsbury, Erin was gauging the situation, seeing where Michelle Hornsbury fell into the grand scheme of things. Trying to catch her in a lie.

"Girls, I have something to confess."

That she was Rupert P.'s knowing beard? That the rumors were true—she really did use cotton candy and the tears of Rupert P. fans as perfume? Both of us leaned forward.

"The truth is, I don't know how Rupie is doing," Michelle Hornsbury said. "He hasn't called me, and I haven't been able to reach him on his mobile. I can't find him anywhere."

Honesty. It was refreshing.

"It's so unlike him," Michelle Hornsbury said, laughing, obviously trying to pass the whole my-boyfriend-is-ignoring-me thing off as a funny anecdote. *He's not ignoring you, Michelle Hornsbury. Rupie's dead. Sorry.*

"I'm beginning to get a little bit worried, actually," she said. "But I'm sure he's just clearing his head at the moment and needs some space."

"Right," Erin said.

"Totally," I said.

"The thing is—and this is why I'm so glad I ran into you both—I'm going to need a place to stay. I was wondering if you two wouldn't mind helping a fellow Strepur girl out?"

I was confused. Michelle Hornsbury had just referred to herself as a Strepur. "Don't you have a room already?"

"I did," Michelle said. She nodded vehemently, like the more she did it the more we'd believe her or something. "I had a room with Rupie, of course." A lie. Rupert P. was staying at the boys' suite when he wasn't staying in Griffin's room. "But you see, he's run off and taken the room key."

"Can't you just get another one from the front desk?" Erin asked.

She and I knew that she couldn't. They didn't give you keys for imaginary rooms. But for some reason we still wanted to catch her in the lie. Clearly, Rupert P. hadn't planned on spending any time with Michelle Hornsbury on this trip. It now made sense why she'd been hanging out in the bar earlier. Was that her shtick? Make an appearance for the cameras walking in and out of various hotels all over the world, holding Rupert P.'s hand for all to see, but then what? Did she just sneak away in the middle of the night when no one was outside? Damn, Rupert P. couldn't even get his fake girlfriend her own hotel room? That was low, even for Rupert P. Mayherestinpeace.

Michelle smiled brightly and blinked. "You know, I tried that, but since the reservation was made under Rupert's name, they can't give a key to anyone but him. You know how it is, with crazy fangirls running amok. No offense, of course."

It seemed like she was waiting for a "none taken," but none came.

"So, what do you say?" Michelle Hornsbury went on. "Will you help a girl out? We can make a slumber party out of it! Oooh, I could tell you *loads* of stories about the boys. Things you've all surely been absolutely dying to know." She leaned forward, raised her eyebrows, and whispered, "Penis sizes?" She said it conspiratorially, like she was selling fake Louis Vuitton purses on a Chinatown street corner and was hoping we'd be in the market for them. *Penis sizes, anyone?*

"Michelle," I began, "we've got a pretty small room and two other friends staying there with us—"

"No problem at all!" Michelle Hornsbury said. She pressed her palms flat against her tummy and said, "I'm so small I could easily squeeze between two people on a bed. Blessing and a curse, really."

"Uh, can't you stay with the boys?"

She cleared her throat. "The boys and I don't really . . . We've all mutually agreed we prefer to spend time apart from each other whenever we can, you know, because we spend so much of it together as it is."

"Huh?"

"How can I put this in terms you might understand?" she said. "I love those boys like brothers whom I hate."

"Uh, look, Michelle—"

"Please," she said. The smile was still there, but her eyes were dimming. "This will probably sound absolutely absurd, and it's truly rather embarrassing, but you must believe me when I tell you that I've got no money, no friends here, and nowhere to go."

Erin and I looked at each other. I wish I knew what she was thinking, that we could communicate telepathically like twins or preternaturally close best friends, but I had no idea what she thought. All I knew was we had to get rid of Michelle Hornsbury.

"Okay," Erin said.

Are you fucking kidding me?

"Splendid!" Michelle Hornsbury said.

"Erin, we should talk about this," I said through gritted teeth. *"Make the decision as a group."*

"Why don't you just go up and tell the girls we've got someone coming." Erin took my hand and pulled me off my stool and away from Michelle Hornsbury. "I'll get rid of her," Erin whispered. "Go up and warn the guys just in case."

I left the bar and made a beeline through the lobby. There was no way Michelle Hornsbury could see Rupert P.'s body in our room, or any of the crap that Isabel and Apple looted from the boys' room. I pressed the button for the elevator as quickly as I could. As I waited for it to come I stared at the phone booth a few feet from me. I wondered if I could step through it and go back in time somehow. I stared at it so long I didn't even realize that I could see through the glass and into the other side of the lobby, toward the entrance. And when my eyes focused I saw him. There, in a corner of the lobby, was Griffin Holmes: stylist extraordinaire and actual significant other of Rupert P.

And he was talking to Isabel.

17

If you were there and saw Griffin Holmes like that, you'd probably be asking yourself the same thing that I did: How the hell did someone so good-looking end up with Rupert P.?

Griffin Holmes's style was on point. He always looked like he'd just stepped out of a Brooks Brothers ad, and I can confirm this is even more true in real life. His Rumpelstiltskin-spun hair was parted impeccably at the side, not a strand out of place. Beneath his tan trench coat (sleeves pushed up to the elbow) his rust-colored tie was pinned to his shirt and his tweed gray suit seemed pinned to his muscular form, which could rival any mannequin's. Honestly, even the way he stood was mannequin-like, with all of his weight resting on one leg, a hand in his pocket, his head cocked just so. His face was made of laser-cut edges. You'd think a stylist would steer clear of a fashion disaster like Rupert P. Mayherestinpeace. You had to wonder: What did the two of them even talk about?

Also, what the hell was Isabel doing talking to Griffin?

I abandoned my post at the elevator. This was way more important than getting back to the room. Well, probably it wasn't. Like, at all. But the curiosity was clichéing me.

I marched right up to Isabel and Griffin, and whatever they were talking about abruptly came to a halt. This told me two things: (a) this wasn't just a regular fan encounter where Isabel spotted him and wanted a selfie or something, and (b) this was the two of them speaking about something secret, and if they had a secret that meant they knew each other.

"Hi," I said.

"Hello," Griffin said, his eyebrows lowering, his mouth falling into a slight pout. Imagine a Marc Jacobs ad where the male model sits on a rock in the middle of a field, looking like he'd just dropped his ice-cream cone on his alligator-skin shoes.

Isabel avoided my gaze, but I squirmed into her line of sight and forced her to look at me. "What's going on?"

"Sorry, who are you?" Griffin said.

"Lydia Deetz," I said, sticking my hand out. "Pleased to make your acquaintance."

Isabel pushed my hand away, which was just as well, since Griffin stared at it like the concept of shaking hands upon meeting new people didn't exist in the beautiful world of magazine ads from whence he came.

"It's okay," Isabel said. "She's a friend of mine. But maybe we should go somewhere else to talk."

"I don't have time for that," Griffin said. He seemed exasperated, not like his usual calm, magazine-photo self. Strepurs knew Griffin from all sorts of behind-the-scenes videos the band put out of them getting ready for awards shows, or going through wardrobe fittings for their tours. Griffin even sometimes uploaded his own videos, talking about fashion and the boys. He was known for ranking their outfits, which seemed kind of ridiculous since he was the one picking all of them. Also, he usually put Rupert P. on top of his best-dressed lists, even when Rupert P. was dressing himself in his everyday streetwear and you honestly couldn't tell if it was Halloween or not. Some fans called Griffin out on it once, explicitly stating that he was ranking Rupert P. higher because the two were in a clandestine homosexual relationship. Griffin started ranking Rupert P. dead last after that.

Of course, the girls and I now knew him from the NSFW video we'd seen on Rupert P.'s phone.

"Look, Isabel, you have to help me," Griffin said. "Rupert wouldn't just leave the band. That's the *last* thing he would do."

I still didn't understand how or why Griffin and Isabel knew each other, but they were letting me be privy to this conversation and I wasn't about to screw it up by saying anything. I just watched them talk, my eyes darting back and forth between them.

"Well . . . what do you think is going on, then?" Isabel

said. You'd think Isabel would be good at lying, but she was actually clearly very bad at it. If I didn't already know that she was hiding something, I'd still think she was acting shady. Her eyes were looking all shifty and unsure. Like, put some effort into it, at least.

"I don't know," Griffin said. "But all of this is highly suspicious to me. He wouldn't just turn off his phone, he wouldn't not answer my calls unless he was with Michelle, and he's *never* with Michelle. And most of all, he would *not* quit the band. You know how hard he's been working on being good. Being kicked out of the band was his biggest nightmare—he told me all the time. Why would he just quit?"

"Maybe he's just playing a prank on everyone."

This was the most plausible lie anyone had said all day. If Rupert P. was known for one thing, it was his penchant for ruining other people's days. Mayherestinpeace.

"Maybe," Griffin said. "But something's still fishy about all of this." He dug his fingers into his hair, though it was so perfectly moussed that every strand fell back into place when he took his hand out again. He narrowed his eyes and his lips fell into a pout. Imagine a male model lying on a bed of women while staring blankly ahead, contemplating the meaning of life. "I'm going to call the police."

"No!" Isabel said. She coughed, trying to cover up her outburst. Not only was she a bad liar, she was also apparently a terrible actress. "You can't do that." She leaned closer to him, and farther from me. "That'll out the both of you. Think about Rupert. Would he want you to do that?"

Griffin glanced in my direction, like he wasn't sure if it was still safe to talk around me now that the word "out" had been spoken aloud.

"I don't care about that anymore," he said. "If Rupert's in trouble then the police need to be involved. Will you do me a favor? Would you just ask around for me? Your resources combined with mine—we could get to the bottom of this."

"For sure," Isabel said.

"Great." He placed his hand on Isabel's arm, and his face melted into something heartfelt. Imagine a male model riding a horse naked. "Thank you, Is."

The sound of screeching metal caught all of our attention. It came from outside, and I'm pretty sure I saw the frame of the scaffolding move.

"That has to be a fire hazard," Griffin said. "There are too many girls out there. That scaffolding is going to come down."

Griffin Holmes: style icon/gorgeous gay prophet.

"I better go," he said.

I watched him walk through the lobby and out the front entrance, and for a second I could feel the heat of the roaring fire of Strepurs outside, their yells licking the doors.

"Do you want to explain what just happened, *Is*?"

"You were there, *Lydia*. You heard the whole thing."

She headed for the elevators and I followed, close on her heels. "What I meant was how the hell do you know Griffin Holmes?"

"He's one of my sources."

The gilded elevator doors opened. Luckily, it was empty, so we could speak openly. "For your site? How come you never told us?"

"I gotta tell you everything?"

"We're friends," I said, and even I could hear how false that sounded now. But I pressed on. "Friends tell each other things like this. Especially if it involves The Ruperts."

She turned to look at me, straight in the eye. Whenever she did that it was intimidating. It was one of the reasons I liked the fact that Isabel was mainly an online friend. Isabel was taller than me. And meaner. And her nostrils were permanently flared, like she smelled something she didn't like and that something was me. She was so much easier to talk to when she was just an icon on a screen.

"Let's not pretend that you're friends with me for any reason other than the fact that I get you the best Ruperts leaks," she said. "I'm a source for you. And Griffin Holmes is a source for me. It's the circle of life, et cetera, et cetera."

Before today I probably would've been offended by her

substituting the word "source" for "friend," but I knew she was right.

"How'd you get him to be your source?"

"I worked on him for a minute. Tweeted him incessantly til he followed me back, and then I shot over a DM right quick letting him know I had proof that he and Rupert P. were coupling it up."

"Did you?"

"No, obvs. He took the bait anyway."

"You blackmailed him."

"And I've been getting insider deets on the boys' every move ever since. You're welcome."

"That's kind of messed up."

"It's not that serious. He spills all the tea and in return I give him scoops from my other sources too. Symbiotic relationship and all that. Anytime Rupert P. and him ever got into a lovers' tiff you best believe I became Griffin's own personal news outlet. How do you think I got those pics of Rupert P. passed out drunk in his house last year? Griff leaks stuff all the time through me. We're actually kind of friendly now."

Griff? "Clearly." And then something hit me. "You knew Rupert P. would be on the eighth floor because Griffin told you his room was on the eighth floor, didn't he? Wait, were you . . . Was there a plan?" My mind was spinning faster than

I could form words to explain it all. Had Erin told Isabel about her plan to ruin the boys? Was Isabel in on this whole thing? And maybe more importantly, was I the only one who wasn't?

Isabel stopped looking at me. Just when I actually wanted her to be straight with me. The elevator doors opened on our floor.

"Talk to Erin." Isabel stepped out of the elevator first. I watched her walk down the hall and I got the strangest feeling, like it was the first time I was seeing her. Maybe it was the first time I was seeing the real her.

And all I saw was hate. Because after a while, obsession without any payoff can breed it—hatred. The boys will inevitably disappoint you somehow. You think a girl that they date isn't worthy of them. You think their songs could be better, that their relevance is weak. You begin to wonder why you still care so much, why you still fight their battles for them over Twitter while they themselves are sipping piña coladas on some Mexican beach, and you realize that at some point your obsession is mostly perfunctory. You've sold your soul to it and now you open up Tumblr and scroll because it's hardwired in you to do it. If you can just get one more piece of info, one more pic, one more scoop, it'll fill that empty feeling in you that you dug unbeknownst in the first place.

This is what I thought of Isabel's obsession. The way fans are necessary to keep a boy band going, the boys became necessary for Isabel to keep her site going, and therefore her life going.

Killing Rupert P. would cause the most chaos. It was the biggest story to ever hit her site. She was on cloud nine—I could see it in the way she walked. She was practically skipping. And Isabel didn't skip.

I pictured her standing over Rupert P. in his chair, wrapping the pink tights around her fists and pulling as hard as she could. I imagined those flared nostrils of hers, and her smile, which was always more of a snarl. It was the kind of smile that was meant to be formed when performing murder anyway.

"Did you kill Rupert P.?"

She turned around slowly, just as she was about to put the key card into our room's lock. "What did you say to me?"

"You heard me." I was scared to confront her like this, but I needed to know. "Did you?"

She marched over to where I stood. "Oh, you *tried* it, *escuincla babosa*." That was not the sort of Spanish they taught in class, but even if I couldn't translate it the message was clear. Isabel was mad. She seemed much taller than me in that moment. Or maybe I was shrinking. I was Alice in Wonderland and I'd just downed the magic shrinking potion. Isabel was the Queen of Hearts. Seriously, I was worried for my head.

She jammed her fingers against my shoulder. The hallway wall behind me broke my fall.

We were alone on the eighth floor of The Rondack, and Isabel very well could've killed me and gotten away with it. "If I'd known I'd have to deal with your whiny ass the entire night, I would've told Erin to keep you home until you were properly housebroken. Just so we're clear, I give zero fucks what you think. But keep reaching, Icarus. Now if you'll excuse me, I have a site to update and a body to dispose of."

Not exactly a denial.

She went to open the hotel room, and I was left to rub the newly blossoming bruise on my shoulder.

When I got to the room Isabel was nowhere in sight, having obviously retreated to the bedroom to update her site or bite the heads off bats or something. Apple sat on the couch. I realized this was the first time we'd dared to leave her alone with Rupert P., but this time was obviously different. There was no fear that she'd try to hump his leg or something. Or at least I hoped not. She just sat there on the couch, looking anywhere but at Rupert P., eating a Reese's Peanut Butter Cup.

I sat next to her.

There was something I needed to find out, before we spoke about anything else. "Apple, were you in on Erin and Isabel's plan?"

She didn't stop chewing her chocolate altogether, but she chewed more slowly, her eyebrows scrunching as she looked at me. "What plan?" she asked through a mouthful.

"You know . . . to mess with The Ruperts?"

Apple swallowed. "There was a plan?"

I let out a breath I hadn't known I was holding. So Apple wasn't in on it. I wasn't the only one who was out of the loop. It made me feel closer to her suddenly. If I had someone on my side, that meant that this whole night wasn't totally fucked. Maybe we could do something to make things right again.

"I'm sorry I blew up at you earlier," she said.

"Me too."

"I guess it doesn't really matter now, huh? The boy we were fighting about is dead."

I had avoided looking at Rupert P., but now that Apple had mentioned him it seemed almost rude not to acknowledge him. He was still in his chair—where else would he be?—and he was privy to our conversation. This was the most pleasant he'd been all day.

"Are you okay?" I asked Apple. "I know he meant a lot to you."

Apple was looking at him too, but I couldn't read the expression on her face. She only shrugged. "He did. But he was also really mean, wasn't he?"

Don't speak ill of the dead don't speak ill of the dead don't speak ill of the dead. "He was an entitled little shitstain," I said. "Mayherestinpeace." I know that sounded bad, but it was the nicest thing I could've said about him.

"He called me a beached whale."

"I'm sorry."

"Do you know how much time I spent loving him?" She looked down at her chocolate, meticulously peeling back the wrapper. "I used everything I had in me. I loved him with my head and my heart. I loved him with every single nerve ending. But he wasn't good."

"No."

"He got what he deserved."

My eyes sprung to her, but she was still staring at the chocolate, her face betraying nothing. She'd said it like it was nothing, but words had meaning. "Beached whale" meant something, and so did "He got what he deserved." But she continued to eat her Reese's like what she'd just said didn't mean anything at all.

I pictured her standing over his chair, a steely resolve beneath the dried tear streaks on her face. I pictured her pulling on those tights around his neck with the same force she'd used to knock him unconscious with love when she saw him in the hallway. Had I overlooked the most obvious suspect? The one who loved him most. The one who would be most crushed by his words.

Isabel stormed into the room and interrupted my thoughts with her pacing. "Where's Erin?" she said. "She's not answering my texts and we need her."

"Still can't make a decision without Erin," I muttered.

Isabel rolled her eyes. "Rush me to the burn unit." She whipped out her phone. "We need to act. Now. We make decisions as a group."

"Well, I'm sure you'll be horrified to know that Erin is with Michelle Hornsbury right now, asking her how she likes her room service because she's offered her room and board *here with us*."

The extra emphasis at the end there had the desired effect. Isabel froze and looked at me. "Are you joking?"

"I think we're way past joking right now."

"Michelle Hornsbury is coming here?" Apple said, mouth full of Reese's. "To stay with *us*?"

"If Erin doesn't find a way to lose her, yeah."

Michelle Hornsbury divided Rupert P. fans into two categories: girls who liked her and thought she was beautiful and perfect enough to be with their favorite boy, or girls who abhorred her, deeming her too ugly and lowly to be with their man. Apple had always belonged to the latter group. In Apple's mind, Rupert P. did not belong with anyone but *her*.

I could see from the look in Apple's eye that she still hated Michelle Hornsbury, despite the fact that she no longer liked Rupert P. anymore. And also the fact that he was dead, obvs.

"I am not spending the night in the same room as her," Apple said.

"Michelle Hornsbury isn't coming here," Isabel said.

"Well, she just might, so we have to hide him. Now," I said.

The three of us looked at Rupert P. He was still so wretched. Mayherestinpeace.

"Hide him where?" Apple said.

"I don't know, a closet or something."

"A closet?" Isabel said. "So that Michelle Hornsbury could just sit in the middle of the room telling us stories about life as a beard while Rupert P.'s body finally flops out of the closet? Cuz you know that's what's going to happen."

A knock on the door. None of us moved.

"Open up!"

It was Erin. "I'm alone, it's safe."

We opened the door. "I got rid of her."

"How?"

"I took her outside and a glob of Strepurs swallowed her up."

Those girls outside were good for something after all.

"We still need to move him," Erin said.

"No way," I said. "This has gone on long enough. We need to call the police."

"No!" Isabel said. "Griffin is already calling the police. They'll come down here, get a real investigation going, put two and two together, and then we're done for, for real. We need to move him out of this room. Make him someone else's problem."

"How can you do that?"

"Watch me."

"Isabel's right," Erin said. "It's our only option. We need to move the body."

"And where are we going to move him?" I said. "The hallways only lead to rooms, stairwells, or elevators. We can't just dump him somewhere."

Isabel picked up the room key on the table next to the door. "The boys' room. We can dump him there."

"What?" This had suddenly become more than just getting rid of the problem—it was now making it someone else's problem.

The Ruperts' problem.

Our Ruperts.

"You want to make them take the fall for Rupert P.'s death?"

"It's us versus them, and I always gotta look out for my girls," Isabel said. "I'm like a feminist. I'm like Beyoncé."

I would have laughed if she wasn't being completely serious. "It's only us versus them because you're making it that way."

Isabel shrugged. "Maybe they wouldn't get in trouble. Maybe they'll call the police right away and the police will see that Rupert P. died accidentally and the matter will be put to death—rest."

"Or maybe not," I said. "Guys, think about this. This could seriously fuck up The Ruperts' whole careers. We *love* those boys."

I looked around the room. The truth was, we all had a reason to want Rupert P. dead. Motivation that, if TV and movies had taught me anything, would hold up in court. Erin had a mission. She wanted to "kill the boy band." Isabel had her site—her need for chaos—a story that would break the Internet, with her holding the sledgehammer. Apple had been put down in the cruelest way by the one person she loved most.

And me? What did I have?

"Everyone's word against yours," Isabel said.

I gaped at her. Yeah, exactly like Beyoncé. "If I don't agree to this you'll all pin his death on me?"

I looked at Erin's face, but she turned away. These were the girls I had thought were my best friends. And they were going to turn on me.

I didn't have a choice.

I really believed that.

And you have to believe me.

"Fine," I said.

Isabel smiled. "You finally decided to level up," she said. "Let's move him."

18

Moving a body is a lot harder than it sounds. Especially when that body belonged to someone as wretched as Rupert P. Mayherestinpeace.

Apple tried Googling our best options, but results varied, and we didn't have most of the materials mentioned (barrels, coffins) on hand.

We went through all of the possible scenarios. The obvious way to go would've been the *Weekend at Bernie's* route. It's this movie where these two guys pretend that this dead guy, Bernie, is still alive by putting him in sunglasses and walking him around with them and stuff. Pretty fucked up if you think about it, but it was nice to know that some movies were still relatable. All we would have to do was find some sunglasses. It'd look like he was just stumbling around drunk, which wouldn't cause any alarm because that was what Rupert P. looked like most of the time anyway.

But then we realized we didn't have sunglasses, and it would look pretty unconvincing if someone stared at him for too long, like if we were stuck in an elevator with other people or something. He had this permanently shocked look on his face that really wasn't helping things either.

Then we thought about Apple giving him a piggyback ride. She could probably do it, and it wouldn't look too suspicious (instead of a stumbling, shocked drunk, Rupert P. could look like a peacefully sleeping child), but that idea was forgotten when Erin thought up an even better plan.

The four of us looked down at Rupert P., halfway inside of Apple's gigantic neon-orange rolling duffel bag and halfway out. (We would've preferred to hide him in something that wasn't quite so ostentatious, but Apple was the only one among us who'd brought a big enough bag.) After emptying it of every last kernel of corn, Rupert P. still didn't fit.

"He doesn't fit," I said.

"We'll make him fit," Isabel said.

That did not sound good to me. Actually, it sounded really bad, and I started to imagine her pulling out a machete from behind her back, but luckily all Isabel did was kneel on the ground and start bending his knees and contorting the rest of him to see how we could better squeeze him into the case. "Are any of you going to help me?"

We all got down on our knees and did what we could. But if I'm being honest, I only touched him when I was sure someone was looking at me. I didn't want to touch him at all. I think Erin felt the same way. Her face remained pinched the whole time as she blindly pressed her fingers against whatever part of him was closest to her. I think her strategy was more to push him *away* from her rather that to push him inside the luggage. It was a good strategy. I copied her. Apple was the least helpful. Who knew all it would take for her to stop touching Rupert P. was him being dead? Thankfully, we had Isabel. She was all business, like this wasn't her first rodeo.

A few minutes later we all stood up and surveyed our handiwork. Rupert Pierpont was stuffed in the bag like a ventriloquist's dummy in a very small trunk, though probably a lot less lovingly. Thankfully, his face was obscured, so I could imagine he was just a pile of clothes. Apple did the honors of zipping the bag closed.

"Should we say something?" I said.

"What do you mean?" Apple asked.

"I don't know. It just feels like we should say something. To honor him. Like what people do at funerals and stuff?"

"This isn't no funeral," Isabel said.

"It would still be nice," I said.

"That's the one thing this death and cover-up is missing," Isabel said. *"Niceness."*

"Forget it."

"Just say something," Erin snapped.

Since Erin had agreed to it, Isabel no longer seemed to have any objections, but now that they were all looking at me expectantly I didn't know what to say.

"Fine, I'll go," Isabel said. She cleared her throat. "Rupert Pierpont was a living wonder. He lived and we all wondered how he did it. Ashes to ashes, dust to dust, may he juggle with Jesus."

We stared at her.

"The end," she said.

It was something. After a moment of silence we got back to the task at hand.

"What if the boys are all in their room right now?" Erin asked.

"Should we text them again?" Apple asked.

"We can't. If we use Rupert P.'s phone now it will definitely look like foul play."

"We're just going to have to risk it," Isabel said. "It's now or never, girls. We wanted to meet the boys anyway."

This was not how I wanted to meet the boys.

But we left the room.

Even though the bag had wheels Apple couldn't drag it

herself, so Isabel grabbed one corner of the handle and pulled him down the hallway with her.

The four (five?) of us waited in front of the elevator doors silently, not speaking to one another, not even looking at one another. When the doors opened we should've looked, or at least said something, because the elevators were going down and I don't think any of us realized it until the doors closed behind us. We were now stuck riding in the same elevator with four girls, all tweens, and a lone mother acting as chaperone, all wearing The Ruperts T-shirts. The mother too.

"Hi!" one of the girls said. "Are you guys Strepurs too?"

I don't know why, but our first instinct—without even consulting one another—was to shake our heads firmly and deny we were fans. Usually it was fun meeting other Strepurs and gushing together about our shared love, but I guess we all just wanted to distance ourselves from The Ruperts as much as possible, given the circumstances. Ironic, I know, since we were heading to their room. And we were carrying one of them in our luggage.

"Oh!" the same girl said. She had dirty-blonde hair. She might have been twelve. I know they were only a few years younger than us, but they still seemed way too young to be cavorting around a hotel.

"Well, we're fans!" Dirty Blonde said.

I don't want to overuse exclamation points here, but you have to believe me when I tell you that every sentence of hers ended with one. I could virtually see them popping out of her mouth with excited aplomb.

"How are you guys in here?" Erin asked.

"We got a room!" the girl said.

Shit, they were us. This elevator was maybe a portal to a different dimension, because we were staring at ourselves in the mirror and the picture wasn't pretty.

Was this what we looked like to the outside world? Imbeciles bouncing on the balls of our feet with stupid grins on our faces and tear ducts ready to flood at the drop of a hat, or more likely, at the bat of a boy bander eyelash? Because I'll tell you right now, it was a scary sight.

"Actually, we just went up to the penthouse floor looking for the boys!"

"You did?" Isabel said. "Any luck?"

"No!" Her face was an emoji. Specifically, the pouty cat with the lone tear on its cheek. "We knocked on every door but no one opened! They're probably hiding out because Rupert P. just quit! Those poor boys are having a really hard time right now!"

"I heard Rupert X. couldn't stop crying," another girl with frizzy hair said.

"I heard Rupert L. is roaming the streets of Manhattan looking all over for Rupert P. so that he can have a real heart-to-heart with him and convince him to rejoin the band."

Another girl piped up. "I heard Rupert K. bought him a really rare collectible Troll doll that he was waiting to give him for his birthday but he's going to give it to him tonight because he feels bad and wants him to come back."

"They're such good guys!" Frizzy Hair said.

"They really love each other!" Dirty Blonde said.

"Nothing can ever tear them apart!" another one said.

"We're from Tarrytown!" the last one said.

The four of us didn't say anything.

I don't think we knew how to respond. They were really hard to understand. Were they even speaking English? Was this how we sounded to people? I tried to convince myself that we were different from them. Cooler. Better . . . Saner. But of the two groups, only one was lugging around a dead body in a suitcase.

Mercifully, the doors opened to the lobby. "BYE!" the four girls yelled.

"Bye," the four of us muttered.

They stepped outside but turned around when we didn't. "Aren't you guys coming out?"

Erin stabbed the DOOR CLOSE button with her finger a bunch of times and didn't stop until the doors were completely shut. Then she pressed the button marked 16.

The four of us looked at one another briefly, dumbfounded, a little scared. Then we resumed not speaking to one another.

The elevator doors opened. We walked down the hallway. Eerily quiet. We stopped in front of Room 1620—the boys' suite. Isabel was ready to put in the key right away, but I knocked first, just in case. We all waited for a minute, and then when nothing happened Isabel put the key in, turned the handle, and we were in.

You don't want the details, right? You don't want to know that untangling Rupert P. should've probably been easier than stuffing him in the bag but was actually just as hard, maybe even harder because now we had to lift him onto a chair. Worst of all, The Rondack was so hip beyond belief that our choice of chair was limited to either high bar stool chairs or beanbags. You're probably thinking the beanbags are the way to go: low to the ground, dump the body on top and go. You have obviously never tried to casually position a dead body on a giant bag full of beans.

Rupert P. sank into the bag easy enough, but no matter how hard we tried to sit him up, he kept flopping over the sides or bending forward so that his forehead lay on his knees. Finally we decided to have him just sort of lie back, feet on the ground, knees bent, eyes on the ceiling.

You don't have to tell me that this was wrong. I knew this was wrong. This was *so* wrong. The mounted deer head on the opposite wall stared at me with his black marble eyes like even it knew it was wrong too. The deer head was judging me.

"So are we going with autoerotic asphyxiation, or what?" Isabel asked.

"If you're implying that we manipulate him to look like he was . . ." Erin made a squick face. "No fucking way."

I had to agree with her. I wasn't going anywhere near Rupert P. or his pants, no matter how dire the consequences.

"You guys hear that?" Isabel said. We all froze, listening. Rustling, muffled—a sound from the hallway.

"Someone's coming," Erin said.

"The Ruperts?" Apple asked. "The Ruperts are coming?" I swear she looked equal parts scared of getting caught and excited to get a close-up look at the boys.

Isabel swore under her breath, but I didn't have time to swear. I looked for an exit strategy. Or at least a hiding strategy. "The closet!"

I didn't know it was a closet until we opened the doors. Two of them, made of rows of slats. I didn't know if that was good because it meant we could peek through them and see outside, or bad because it meant someone could peek through them and see us, but the closet was just big enough for all of us to fit inside of it if we stood side by side. We were also helped by the fact that the boys hadn't unpacked any of their things, so it was completely empty except for a few hangers that hung over our heads.

And as I squinted through the slats, waiting for more noise

and the boys, my eyes caught sight of it: the thing we'd left, bright as a neon sign. "Apple's suitcase!"

Key cards jiggled in the door and a male voice muttered a swear word. The girls gasped, but I must've been crazier than I thought because I jumped out and grabbed the bag. I slammed back into the closet, hoping the newly closed slatted closet doors were enough to cover up the madness behind them. I hugged the suitcase to my chest.

None of us breathed, not even when the boys walked in.

They walked in quietly, but with purpose, and I don't think I'd ever seen them like that before. Usually, in all the behind-the-scenes videos and specials, they were always joking around with one another, climbing on top of one another or poking one another or at least chatting. Now they seemed to be totally in their own heads. They could've each been walking inside separately, the way they ignored one another.

Each of them held armfuls of plush dolls, handmade books, and signs plastered with their faces and essay-long notes scrawled in careful cursive. They must've finally made an appearance at the front entrance of the hotel and met with fans.

Apple, standing to my right, squeezed my hand. Her favorite may have already been dead, but she was still a fan of The Ruperts as a whole, and seeing the band this close was doing a number on her. I knew this because despite everything that had happened, it was doing a number on me too. My guts seized up at the sight of them, and I squeezed her hand back.

I waited for the boys to notice the big dead mess left gift-wrapped for them in the middle of the room, but Rupert X. and Rupert L. seemed more interested in finding the closest trash bin. They didn't lose stride as they marched up to it and dumped all of the fan gifts they'd been holding into it. A teddy bear bounced off the top of the pile, and Rupert X. bent down and picked it up.

"I love you!" the toy squealed. Rupert X. stuffed it face-first deep into the wastebasket. It was only when he was done that he looked up and saw him.

Then Rupert L. saw him.

Rupert K. was reading one of the notes from his stack of fan gifts, still clutched in the crook of his arm. Even in all this craziness he was all shine. There was a slight smile on his face, interrupted when Rupert X. threw the plush bear from the trash at his head.

"I love you!" the bear said again as it bounced off Rupert K.'s head and fell to the floor.

Rupert K. finally looked up, and for some strange reason I was grateful that he was the last one to see Rupert P. He got a few extra seconds to be a normal person instead of someone whose friend was dead in his room. But in the end, the few extra seconds were useless, because I could tell he understood first. He knew, before the other Ruperts did, that Rupert P. wasn't just sitting in a chair. Rupert K.'s hands flew up to cover his mouth, all his fan gifts falling to his feet. I could only see his eyes, bulging and green. I couldn't say "I'm sorry" out loud, but I thought it, and I hoped he felt it.

"What's the matter with you?" Rupert L. said to him.

"Oh shit," Rupert X. said. He got it too. "Oh shit oh shit oh fuck!"

We could always rely on Rupert L. to be the slowest of the bunch. He looked at his friends and then followed their gazes to Rupert P. He walked up to him and tapped him on the shoulder. The two other boys watched, horrified, as Rupert P. did not respond. "Pierpont," Rupert L. said. "P. Hey, P. P. P. P."

"Rupert, stop," Rupert K. said. "Can't you see he's dead!"

Rupert L. took his hand back like he'd just scorched himself, yet he still shot Rupert K. a disbelieving look. "No, he's not." He took a thumb and lifted Rupert P.'s eyelid and still didn't seem to get it, but Rupert K. came and yanked his hand back, forcing him to stop touching Rupert P.

"You can't be serious," Rupert L. said. "Is he really dead?"

Rupert K. placed two fingers under Rupert P.'s jaw and waited. After a moment he said, "No pulse." He touched the pink tights, obviously confused. That was the thing about Rupert K.——you could always see what he was thinking and feeling right there on his face.

Rupert L. started pacing circles around Rupert P.'s bean-bag. He walked over to the wall and threw himself against it, rubbing his palms and cheeks all over it. And then he fell to his knees and broke down. He screwed his face up until tears squeezed out, and I've got to say it shocked me. I never realized he was so sensitive. It was probably all the muscles that made me think he was a tough brute, but obviously, underneath all that, there was a warmhearted softie.

"I always wondered when the band would break up," he said.

A selfish softie.

"I'm not ready for it," Rupert L. went on, dragging his palms along his temples until they met behind his head. "We all know what's going to happen. K. is going to go solo and make it big. X. is going to attempt it and fail."

"Hey!" Rupert X. said. But Rupert L. was totally right. Out of all of them, Rupert K. was the only one with the talent to have a great solo career. Rupert X. would try it, just to stay relevant. He'd probably end up with a gig hosting a celebrity dance show or something, but that wouldn't happen until he was thirty, and by then he'd be ancient anyway.

"And me? Nobody's going to want to see me go at it alone," Rupert L. said. "I'll be a has-been. I'm too young to be a has-been." He was crying so hard. As hard as a child cries when he drops his ice-cream cone on the floor. "Sales for the watches haven't been great, you know. I'm apparently in the red—which my accountants tell me is a very bad color to be in. And Ashley'll surely leave me. She was going to show me how to tell time using the sun."

"Don't mean to interrupt your existential crisis, mate, but *our friend is dead*," Rupert K. said. "What the bloody hell happened?"

"I've got a hunch," Rupert X. said.

"You do?" said Rupert K.

"Yeah, and you know what it is—we're all thinkin' it."

"Yeah, I'm thinkin' it too," Rupert L. said.

I squeezed Apple's hand harder and sneaked a look in her and the other girls' direction. Did the boys' minds automatically go to "crazed fans" whenever something went awry? Were we about to be found out?

"Okay, on three we all say what we're thinking," Rupert K. said. "One, two, three—"

"Autoerotic asphyxiation," the three boys said in unison.

All four of us girls let out a breath.

"I mean, clearly that's what's happened," Rupert X. said.

"Clearly," Rupert L. agreed.

"We need to call someone," Rupert K. said. He took his phone out of his pocket and seemed like he was about to punch in a number when he froze. "Oh no. Griffin just uploaded a video to YouTube."

"So what?" Rupert X. said. "This is no time to check out his latest fashion rankings. Though I am due for a top spot this week."

"I have a feeling we might want to watch this."

The two Ruperts crowded around Rupert K., and although we obviously couldn't see the screen from all the way in our closet hiding space, the volume on the phone was loud enough that when Griffin's voice came on it was clear.

"*This is a message for all Ruperts fans,*" Griffin said. "*I know in my heart that Rupert Pierpont did NOT quit the band. He would never do something so rash. In fact, he spoke to me often about how much he loved the band, how important it was to him, and how he wanted to improve himself to be worthy of being in it. I know all of this because I am Rupert Pierpont's greatest confidante. Actually, I'm his boyfriend.*"

If the boys were surprised by this information, they didn't show it. The three of them were facing the closet, and all I could see in their features was intense concentration, not surprise. Actually, Rupert X. rolled his eyes, which may have been more of a confirmation that the boys already knew about Rupert P. and Griffin's relationship.

"*I'm stating this here, publicly, because Rupert Pierpont is missing. I've called the police and they don't believe me. They think I'm just another Ruperts fan. So here's my message to the police.*"

His voice cut out and a muffled sound came from the phone. It could've been anything, but I definitely heard another voice. It sounded like Rupert P. and Griffin, talking. And then there came a noise that sounded unmistakably like lip smacking. Rupert P. and Griffin, kissing. Rupert L.'s eyes bulged wide, Rupert K. closed his, and Rupert X. looked vaguely disgusted. Griffin must've just shown a video clip of him and Rupert P. together. Probably a similar video to the one we'd seen on Rupert's P.'s phone earlier.

"That should be proof enough that I am without a doubt Rupert Pierpont's boyfriend. I would never betray his trust like this, but I'm worried about him. He isn't answering his phone and no one has seen him anywhere. I called the police to try and get some help, but they said I can't file a missing persons report if it hasn't been forty-eight hours. So that's why I'm posting this video here. If the police won't help, I'm enlisting the next best thing—the fans. I'm calling on all of you, as fans of The Ruperts, to please help. Especially the girls outside The Rondack Hotel right now in New York. Rupert is around here somewhere, and I've never underestimated the power of Strepurs in large groups. Infiltrate the hotel if you have to! Search high and low! I have reason to believe there may have been foul play involved in his disappearance, but I won't go further into that just yet. I have my own theories about what's happened that I'd be happy to share with the police if they'd just bother to cooperate with me. Rupert, if you're watching this, I hope you understand why I had to do this."

There was a moment of stillness as the boys looked at one another, and then in an instant Rupert L. ran for the balcony door. I gasped, but the sound was drowned out by a much bigger one. It came from outside——something awful, like billions of bees dying, or ghosts howling in the woods.

But I knew what it really was.

It was the sound of thousands of Strepurs, unleashed.

"GET AWAY FROM THERE, YOU TOSSER!" Rupert X. roared.

Rupert L. had popped outside for only a second, but it was enough. The sound got impossibly louder. It felt suddenly like we were in medieval times, when armies stormed castle walls, climbing on top of each other, blind with passion and a clear goal. Perhaps this goal was to take Rupert L. Not to hug or to kiss him or to sneak a selfie with him. But simply to *have* him.

He pulled himself back with the effort of someone trying to get out of quicksand, like the power of the Strepurs' yells had a physical hold on him and it was a fight between him and them for his soul.

He shut the balcony door behind him and leaned against it, suddenly weak. "They're climbing the scaffolding," he said. "They're *infiltrating*."

"And you've just shown them where our room is, you marvelous shit," Rupert X said. "Brilliant."

"I can stop them," Rupert L. said, gulping in air and focusing on Rupert P.'s body with an eerily determined gaze. "I know what we have to do."

And then he lifted Rupert P. off his bag of beans.

"What are you doing?!" Rupert K. and Rupert X. shouted at the same time.

Rupert P.'s legs dangled a foot off the ground as he hung limply in Rupert L.'s arms. "We have to show the fans that everything is alright!"

"No."

"No."

"Put him down."

"This is a terrible idea."

"This will not end well."

"Just stop."

But Rupert L. ignored his bandmates' protests and went back to the balcony before anyone could stop him. I couldn't see what he was doing, so I had to rely on Rupert X.'s and Rupert K.'s horrified expressions as they watched. Rupert K. brought his hands to his head, digging his fingers into his hair and twisting. He only did that when things were really bad. I could only imagine that Rupert L. was standing Rupert P. upright with one hand and waving Rupert P.'s arm with the other. (And seeing the pictures later, I was totally right.) Rupert P. had been *Weekend at Bernie's*-ed after all. And I'll bet you anything that movie title has never been used as a verb before now.

Rupert L. (and Rupert P.) came back into the room. "I think that may have been a terrible idea," Rupert L. said.

"You think?!" Rupert X. yelled.

"Why didn't either of you say anything?"

"It's alright, we just need to change the conversation, give the fans something new to talk about," said Rupert X. "We'll get new haircuts."

"That's it, I'm calling the police," Rupert K. said.

"Are you mad?!" Rupert X. said. "The girls will get in here quicker than the police ever will. They'll see P. sat there, dead! They'll think we had something to do with it. You heard what Griffin said—he suspects foul play! What do you think he meant by that, by the way? Seriously."

"I don't know."

"No, wait. Griffin doesn't like me. Never has."

"What does any of this have to do with you?"

"Isn't it obvious?" Rupert X. said. "Griffin is going to accuse me of this." Clearly "this" meant Rupert P. Not a great nickname as far as nicknames went, but probably one of the nicest ones Rupert P. had ever had.

"What?" Rupert K. said.

"You know . . . because of the things I would say to P. sometimes."

"You mean constantly telling him you were going to kill him if he ever made eye contact with you?"

"Jokes! Those were hilarious jokes! See, that right there. Why does everyone always take me so seriously all the time?

Do you think P. ever told Griffin I said those things? Griffin would know that I was only joking, yeah? Griffin's not an idiot."

"Our friend is dead and this is all you care about? I'm calling the police. They'll get everything sorted."

"The police will investigate us!" Rupert X. said. "They'll read through my journal. Do you know how many pages I've filled detailing my absolute hatred for P.?! They'll think I had something to do with his death!"

"Well, maybe if you weren't such a homophobic twat . . ." Rupert K. said.

"I am not homophobic! I was always pleased anytime P. and Griffin were off doing their thing. It got him out of my hair."

"Right."

"See? If you—my bandmate—think I'm a homophobe, then I've no chance with the police. Fuckin' P.—even in death he's managed to ruin my day."

"You're such an arsehole," Rupert K. said. "Our friend is dead. He's *dead*."

"Maybe he's just sleeping," Rupert L. said.

"SHUT UP!" Rupert K. and Rupert X. said together.

"L., we need to get rid of him. Take him somewhere before any of the fans find their way in. Are we agreed?"

"Okay," Rupert L. said.

236

"You're mental!" Rupert K. said. "The both of you have gone mad. I'll have no part in this."

In all the insanity there were so many emotions running through me, but most of all was the feeling of pride. I was so proud of Rupert K. He was reacting in pretty much the same way I'd reacted with my own friends. Which told me, more than anything, that we were obviously compatible and possibly meant to be.

Once Rupert K. was out of the room the energy shifted. With Rupert P. dead and Rupert K. out, Rupert X. took control. You could see it in the way he stood, breathed, seethed. "Right," he said, turning to Rupert L. "Right. What time is it?"

"The time is 9:38!" It was the mechanical voice of Rupert L. And it came from two places: Rupert L.'s wristwatch, and Isabel's.

The four of us couldn't get any more frozen in that closet, but I swear we turned to stone. The boys turned to the closet and stared at the doors. It looked like they were staring right through them, at four fans trying not to piss themselves with fear. And here I was, holding a neon-orange suitcase, probably visible from space.

My heart sped up and beat so loud in my ears I thought for sure the boys could hear it, beckoning them to open the closet, just like Isabel's stupid watch had.

I mean, who even wears watches anymore?!

Could they see through the slats? Were our lives over as we knew them? We held our breaths. We held our breaths so long we were going to pass out, and soon Rupert P. wasn't going to be the only dead person in this room.

"How many of those stupid watches have you packed?" Rupert X. said.

"I didn't think I'd packed any . . ." Rupert L.'s eyes were squinty, his face screwed up. When Rupert L. was thinking hard you could see it. It was the phenomenon most commonly known as Rupert L. Constipation Face (RLCF). He came closer to the closet, slowly. And then he sniffed. "Did we pack the perfume too?"

We were all wearing The Ruperts' perfumes.

We were all fucked sideways.

"I don't know. Will you please just come here?"

But Rupert L. didn't turn back around. He kept coming closer. His hand was on the doorknob, ready to pull, when Rupert X. yelled, "Oi!"

Rupert L. turned.

"We need to focus. You've still got his Twitter passcode, yeah?"

Rupert L. nodded.

"Good. We'll need to post on his behalf. Let's go to the

bedrooms and gather as many sheets as we can. We need to wrap him."

"We do?" Rupert L. said.

"I don't know, but it sounds right. Now come help me!"

The boys disappeared down a hallway heading toward the bedrooms, and almost as soon as they did Erin pushed open the closet doors and we got the hell out of there.

19

When we got back to our hotel room everyone around me was breathing sighs of relief, but I felt different. I felt like I couldn't breathe at all.

I went straight for the bedroom and locked the door behind me, falling onto the bed that Isabel and Erin had already claimed for themselves. It got me thinking about strange bedfellows. Which made me laugh. Which in turn made me realize that I was maybe going crazy and/or having a weird kind of panic attack. My heart was racing. It was all I could hear as I stared up at the ceiling, hoping for answers there that would quell the questions running through my mind. And there were a lot of them. Here's an abridged list:

Had I really just pinned a dead body on The Ruperts, thus betraying the de facto loves of my life?

Was I going to hell?

How had I started this day having milk and toast and ended it by stuffing a body into a way-too-flashy suitcase?

Were my best friends actually my best friends? Was this what it meant to be part of a group of girlfriends? Kidnapping, murder, disposing of bodies all in a day's work? Did the fact that I was so reluctant to help make me a terrible friend?

Did I actually know my friends at all?

Did I know Erin?

And the most important question of all:

How did Rupert Pierpont die?

What Erin had said—or, more appropriately, what her dad the doctor had said—was worming its way through my gray matter until it was all I could think about.

A person couldn't strangle himself. Someone killed him.

Someone standing on the other side of that door.

I started to laugh again.

I don't know why, so don't judge me. It was just . . . My body felt weird. Shaky, fidgety, like I was lying on a trampoline while people all around me jumped.

People who looked an awful lot like my friends.

My teeth chattered and my cheeks tickled. I was having a full-on freak-out, so if you really think about it, laughing was the least offensive thing I could've been doing at that moment. The thing is, I recognized this feeling. I was on the brink of a breakdown.

I had one of these before, shortly after my dad died, when life felt impossibly heavy and my thoughts spiraled so far out of control that I was basically catatonic with fear. It was the kind of fear that pulled all the breath out of you with one continuing scream. The kind the made the walls move in, the kind that shut you up and shut the world out. The kind that sends you to therapy.

I had to pull myself together, rein in my reeling mind, before things got really bad.

I wanted to go home. When we'd all made the decision to come to the hotel I was secretly happy I'd get to skip Thanksgiving this year. I couldn't handle another Thanksgiving like the one I'd had last year. Just a few months after my father's death, me and my mom in our cramped apartment, eating silently under the fluorescent kitchen light. It was so pathetic and my mom and I knew it but pretended we didn't. Trying to make small talk over the cold gravy had given me anxiety.

But I would still choose a Thanksgiving like that one over the one I was currently experiencing.

I took out my phone and began typing a message.

Hi mom.

I held the phone in front of my face, waiting for her reply, turning the screen on again every time it dimmed to black.

Hi honey. Thanks for checking in. Busy over here. So glad you're having fun.

But I wasn't having fun. I wanted to tell her that, but my finger only hovered over the screen. Finally, I texted back.

Yeah. Lots of pillow fights.

I kept turning the screen back on, but after a while I realized she wasn't going to be texting back. Probably had to deal with a patient who had a wishbone stuck in his throat or something.

It was becoming increasingly clear to me that one of my best friends had murdered our least favorite member of our most favorite boy band, and any way you spin that it's simply unforgivable. Maybe I chickened out when we should've called the police, but I wasn't just going to barricade myself in this hotel room with a murderer.

So I made up my mind. This time I was going to stick to my guns.

I was going to get the fuck out of Dodge.

Damnit, I was starting to sound like Annie Oakley.

I opened the door, walked right through it, and didn't stop until I was facing my friends/a possible murderer.

"I am so done," I said.

"Oh, an encore performance," Isabel said. "Good. I had so much fun at the matinee."

"Eat a dick, Isabel!" I pointed my finger at her. Actually, it was more like my entire arm. It stretched out before me like a plank, the point of my index finger stopping just inches from Isabel's face. "I can't stand this anymore. Am I the only sane person here? Because none of you seem to understand what we just did. We moved a dead body! We could still very well go to jail if all this goes sideways! We *incriminated* our favorite people in the whole world. They're going to get into a lot of trouble! They're ruined. They're over! Rupert Kirke didn't deserve that. He didn't do anything wrong!"

"They're all the same," Erin said.

"You eat a dick too, Erin!" I yelled. "I am so done. I cannot. I have lost the ability to can. I am consciously fucking uncoupling myself from this situation. You guys want to wreak havoc on our world as we know it? Fine! Count me out! I'm not going to hang around with one of you—one of you who likely murdered Rupert P. Yes, he was a ginger and he was a flop but he didn't deserve to die!"

"She's right," Apple said. "I do kind of feel bad over what we just did to the boys. Maybe we should send them an Edible Arrangement?"

"Ugh!" My face was damp. I didn't know if it was sweat or snot or tears, but I didn't care. I wiped my face and pushed my hair back. I know I looked crazy, with half my bangs probably sticking up, my cola-stained sweater, my tear-streaked face. I didn't need a mirror—their expressions were enough to let me know that my freak-out was concerning them. Good.

244

"This is crazy," I said. "You're all crazy." I kept pointing. Pointing seemed like a very good idea at the time. "You're crazy! And you're crazy! And you're crazy!" In my mind I heard Oprah's voice. *You get a car! And you get a car!* My mom watched that episode on repeat so many times, weirdly happy and envious. It wasn't healthy.

Shit, what the hell was I even talking about?

"I'm leaving this hotel room and I am not stopping until I find a police officer, and then I'm telling them everything," I said. "So long. Farewell. Auf Wieder*fucking*sehen good night."

I turned around, swung open the door, and found Michelle Hornsbury standing on the other side of it.

"Hello," she said.

20

Michelle Hornsbury walked past me into the room and I was powerless to stop her. It was the shock more than anything that paralyzed me, and I saw that it paralyzed everyone else too.

"Michelle, hi," Erin said.

"Ethel, hello."

"Erin," Erin said.

"Erin, yes, of course, forgive me, I'm afraid I'm not in the right headspace at the moment, as you might say. It's been a troubling couple of hours on my end. Rupert quitting the band and all."

She hadn't stopped moving since she came in. She opened some doors, bent down to look under the desk, rounded the couch. She didn't miss a corner. I thought it was because she wanted to check that the room met her standards. I know better now.

"You know, you never actually gave me your room number when you left me out with the vultures in front of the hotel."

"Oops," Erin said, shooting me a furtive glance. "Guess I forgot."

"No worries. Lovely boy at the concierge desk was a very chatty fellow. He gave it to me."

"Look, I don't mean to be rude or anything, but what the fuckall are you doing in our room?" Isabel said.

Michelle Hornsbury sat on the couch and flashed Isabel a smile. "Why, Erin invited me to stay the night."

"Would you excuse us for a minute?" I said. I opened the door to the bathroom and Apple, Isabel, and Erin followed me in.

"Is Michelle Hornsbury really staying with us?" I said.

"Hashtag-NOPE," Apple said. "Hashtag-whodoesthat bitchthinksheis. Hashtag-thestarfuckinggolddiggingsuccubus trampgoes."

"Crisis, stop with the hashtags," Erin hissed. "This isn't my grandmother's Twitter."

If I could've added my own hashtag right then, it would've been hashtag-mess. Getting rid of Michelle Hornsbury was just another thing on the list of clusterfucks we were dealing with today, seeing as how she'd entered our hotel room and parked herself on our couch without any of us actually inviting her in.

"Wait, let's talk this out," Isabel said. "Think of all the shit Michelle Hornsbury could dish. I could fill my site for days."

"No," Erin, Apple, and I said simultaneously.

"She can't stay," Apple said.

"So we're agreed," I said. "Michelle Hornsbury goes."

Erin and Apple nodded. A moment later, Isabel gave in and nodded too.

"Great. Let's kick her out."

Michelle Hornsbury stayed. I have no good excuse for why Michelle Hornsbury stayed, except to say that somehow, in the time we had decided to kick her out, she'd put on silk pj's, curled up on the couch, and had a Kindle in one hand and a mug of tea that had mysteriously materialized in the other. After that none of us had the heart to kick her out. She was a sad, beautiful statue.

Also, she was Michelle Hornsbury. Even though she had no discernible talents, she was still famous, and that made her intimidating. The only one of us who probably could've stood up to her was Isabel, but she was also the only one of us who wanted her to stay.

And maybe Isabel had a point. Maybe sitting through Michelle Hornsbury's stories about the boys would be kind of cool.

*　　*　　*

"Terribly small, I'm afraid," Michelle Hornsbury said, snickering devilishly while the rest of us stared at her in awe, and at least one of us tried desperately not to believe her.

Michelle Hornsbury took a deep breath and let her laughter subside. "I'm sure you all want to talk about Griffin's video. I'm just not sure I can bring myself to do it."

Griffin's video! I'd forgotten about it in all the madness. And by the way the rest of the girls perked up, it seemed they'd forgotten about it too. Isabel whipped out her phone and found it on YouTube immediately. We all crowded around her to get a better view.

"Sorry," I said to Michelle Hornsbury. "We haven't seen it yet." Technically true.

Isabel clicked PLAY, and we finally had the video and audio together. Griffin sat in front of a white wall, all earnest and emotional. When he showed the video on his phone it was just the one I'd suspected—the same one that'd we'd all seen on Rupert P.'s phone. Michelle Hornsbury started to cry again.

"Alright, I'll talk about it!" she said. "That weasel Griffin Holmes has always had a crush on my Rupie. It's been clear from the start. But I'm certain he did some fancy CGI on that video or something. You girls don't actually believe Rupert would go behind my back?"

"No."

"Course not."

"Never."

"Rupie was not gay. He loved me. We loved each other."

She looked so convinced of her own words that I realized that she believed them. Was Michelle Hornsbury a professional beard who didn't realize she was a beard? This whole time I thought that she and Rupert P. had an understanding of what their relationship actually was: a front meant to convince the world that he was straight, a great ticket to fame for her. A win-win for both of them. But now I thought she may have been one of the few people in the world who wasn't aware of her own role in the relationship. And as I looked at Michelle Hornsbury, beautiful and poised and so elegantly English, I suddenly felt really bad for her.

I felt bad for her and Rupert K.

I wondered where he was, what he was doing. Did he call the police like he said he would? Like I said I wanted to. We'd both wanted to do the right thing, but if his story ended up anything like mine, he hadn't done the right thing either.

I took my phone out and checked his Twitter to see if he'd posted anything. It was a long shot in the middle of this shitstorm, but he was the most prolific tweeter in the Ruperts.

And then I saw it. He'd tweeted something twenty-two seconds ago.

Bright Lights, Big City.

I read it again and then a dozen more times. It was what we'd talked about on the roof. Was this a message for me? Did he want me to meet him on the roof?

I stood quickly.

"Where are you going?" Erin said.

"I need to be somewhere."

"Let her go," Isabel said. "I want to see if she'll actually make it out the door this time."

I did make it out the door, Isabel, thankyouverymuch. I headed for the roof.

21

Rupert K. was sitting against a low wall, his head in his hands.

I stood before him, over him, and didn't say anything. I only watched as he sat, crumpled against the wall, knees bent up to meet his face, shoulders heaving. He had his inhaler clutched in his hands, though if he'd just used it or was about to, I couldn't tell.

Finally he looked up at me, and despite the circumstances and the way he looked, it delighted me that he wasn't surprised to see me there.

"You read my tweet."

I nodded. It *had* been for me. I knew it. "Are you okay?"

"Yes," he said, and then immediately amended, "No."

I sat beside him, folding my feet underneath me to stave off some of the cold from the concrete. I wanted to ask him if he was upset because of Rupert P., but it felt wrong asking him a question I already knew the answer to. Deceptive, somehow. So instead I asked, "Do you want to talk about it?"

He searched for his words, unsure of what to say but determined to say something. He wrote that tweet for a reason after all. He wanted me here. He *needed* me here. "Ever since the band, things have been a little crazy in my life," he began. "I mean, one day you're in India, helping build a school for poor children, and then the very next day you'll be at the Teen Choice Awards, accepting the award for best smile. It's great, but it's also really screwed up, and somehow I've got used to it. The surreal has morphed into my reality when I wasn't looking, and now this is my life. But tonight . . . I don't think I can handle my reality anymore."

I said I wouldn't ask him this, but screw it, I asked it anyway. "Is this about Rupert P.?" He looked me in the eye so fiercely I didn't have time to be scared, because I knew that I'd scared him first. "I saw Griffin's video," I added quickly. I had to make sure I cleared up the fact that I was asking about Rupert P., the closeted boy bander who'd just quit, and not Rupert P., the closeted boy bander who'd just croaked. "Did you know the two of them were together?"

"Yeah, I knew. Rupert would never admit it, but I was his best friend. I think I was his only friend. I told him to let Michelle go, that it wasn't fair to her. And that our fans would understand if he wanted to come out. I supported him one hundred percent, whatever he wanted to do." He buried his face in his hands again. "I told him he could always come to me if he wanted to. I don't know why he didn't, and now . . ."

"And now what?"

"And now it's too late."

"Why?" I wanted him to say it. I wanted him to say it so badly so that it would be out in the open, a secret that was spilled instead of one that we both held, and both continued to keep. He looked at me, his green eyes glassy. He was going to tell me Rupert P. was dead. He was going to let me in. Maybe we could figure out what to do together.

But a noise tripped us out of the moment.

"What was that?" Rupert K. said.

We heard it again, a sound coming from one of the doors. Voices. Scraping. Thudding.

"I can't be here," Rupert K. said, standing and overly paranoid. "I don't want anyone to . . ." He stuck out his hand. "Come with me."

Rupert K. wanted to be alone, but he still wanted to be with me.

He wanted to take me somewhere.

He wanted to take my hand.

I let the moment linger, let my field of vision fill with the image of him standing above me, looming large and reaching out to me. And then I gave him my hand, obvs.

There were three doors we could see, and we ran to the

one farthest from the one where the noise was coming from. We slammed through the door and ran down the stairs, not knowing where they led but taking them like there was a fire behind us that we had to outrun. I was flying high/down floors, and all I knew in that moment was the feel of Rupert K.'s hand in mine. I know there was a lot going on; there was a giant dead redheaded elephant in the room to think about, but shit—I had given Rupert Pierpont enough thought for today. And to be honest, it was more thought than he even deserved. Mayherestinpeace.

The real newsworthy thing here was the fact that I was holding Rupert K.'s hand and we were alone together, practically having an adventure.

We must've taken the service route, because we kept passing equipment in the hallways—giant spools of cable, mopping apparatuses, large rolling bins. We were in the bowels of the hotel, the dark corners not meant to be seen by any of the guests, let alone one of the biggest stars in the universe. We checked every door we found, but they were all locked, so we kept going until we found one that wasn't. And when we did, we went through it.

The indoor pool.

Totally empty but still lit, water shimmering, a million diamonds. It slowed us to a halt. It quieted our breathing. And for the moment, at least, I think it eased both of our minds.

We looked at each other, me and Rupert K., and for the first time since finding Rupert P. in his room there was the shadow of a smile on his face.

"The purpose of the whole thing is to defeat the evil goblin— he's this huge giant who rules the kingdom and has a million minions. So in every level you have to defeat some of his minions, and they come in all forms—sometimes they're warlocks, sometimes they're beautiful sirens. The siren levels are brilliant. There's something about beautiful girls being totally evil that I really dig for some reason."

"Strong female characters?" I said.

"Exactly. I care very much about the feminist cause. I consider myself a feminist, actually."

"I think that's amazing."

Rupert K. and I sat by the edge of the pool on chaise lounges, and he was telling me about his favorite thing in the world—*Goblin Gerald's Kingdom*, a computer game. Of course, I already knew this was his favorite thing in the world, and I'd even tried to play the game myself a couple of times before giving up completely after I realized I really did not care about dragons and swords and witches. But I let him keep talking about it because the important thing you have to realize here is that he was sharing something with me. He was sharing his *favorite* thing. If you switched a few things up and squinted a little, this could even look like a date. And also, how cute was he, talking about what a feminist he was?

I hoped he couldn't tell that I was totally swooning. Was it a visible thing when girls swooned? Did we suddenly look faint? Were we all red and puffy-faced, our eyelids aflutter? All I know is if it was possible to look swoony, I did.

"By the way, are you aware that your shirt has a huge stain on it?"

I looked down at my white sweater, marred with a full bib of Coke. I was completely mortified. "Crisis," I said under my breath. "This is embarrassing."

"It's no biggie."

Rupert K. stood to walk up to the edge of the pool, and in the meantime I wondered if it would be too forward of me to take off my sweater right in front of him. I concluded that it would be.

I took off my sweater.

It was only when I looked down at my tank top that I remembered I was wearing my special Rupert K. shirt. His stenciled and faded face was smiling back at me, and I scrambled to put my sweater back on before the actual, three-dimensional Rupert K. turned around.

"You alright?" Rupert K. said.

I popped my head through the neck hole. "I'm great!"

"So now you know what I like to do when I have a moment to myself," he said. "What about you?"

"Me?" *I go to school, I come home, I check Twitter and Tumblr and Isabel's site for updates on your every move, I write fanfic about you that you'd consider very embarrassing. Who am I kidding—that* anybody *would consider embarrassing. I watch hours of YouTube videos of you. I make gifs of you goofing around and smiling. I eat dinner. Repeat steps three to five and then I sleep. I wake up and the cycle begins again.* "I don't have too many hobbies."

"Come on, there must be something Sloane Peterson enjoys."

Well, in the movie Sloane Peterson liked . . . "Fast red cars. Ditching class. Museums. Nice restaurants. Random dance parties in the middle of heavily populated city squares."

Rupert K.'s eyebrows dipped, his eyes narrowed. "Well, that's rather specific."

And then I decided to tell him something real about me. The real me. "I also like to write."

"Really? That's amazing. What do you write?"

"Fiction." Fanfiction was still fiction.

"Wow. I couldn't write a word, not even with a gun to my head."

"It's not that hard."

"Don't sell yourself short. You think up whole characters . . . whole worlds."

"I tell lies."

His lips twitched into a smirk, and I commenced with the swooning. "That's a funny way to think of it."

I gave in. If he wasn't selling me short, then neither should I. "Okay, yeah, I like to write. I like stories. I'm good at telling them."

"That's the attitude. I'd love to read one of your stories one day."

This was the part of the conversation where I totally LMAO in my head because Rupert K.? Reading one of my fics about him?

HAHAHAHAHAHA no.

But it got me to thinking about my most popular fic—the one about the "I do" tattoo on his forearm. The only tattoo he had. My entire fic was an imagining of what that tattoo meant to him—what those words meant to him. "I do" meant he was a take-action sort of guy. It meant he was a romantic, maybe. It meant he was waiting for the day when he could say those words to the love of his life and he etched them onto his skin so that he'd be reminded every day that every action he took was in preparation for meeting that special someone.

"Can I ask you something?" I said. "What does your tattoo mean?"

He scrunched his eyebrows, and I mentally kicked myself for being so random. I was so obviously bad at talking to boys.

And I was so obviously weirding him out. I was about to take back my question when he rolled up his sleeve.

"This?" Rupert K. said. "This was supposed to say Idobabli."

"What?"

"Idobabli. It's the name of the hero in *Goblin Gerald's Kingdom*? I wanted to immortalize him on my arm, but that needle is really quite more painful than they let on. I had to stop the tattoo artist almost as soon he began."

"Oh."

That was . . . I don't want to say stupid. I would never say anything that Rupert K. did was ever stupid. So I'll just go with quirky. It was adorably quirky.

"I think it's really great that you write," he said. "I think creativity is the most important trait a person can have. I probably sound like a snob, since I say that as someone who makes a living off of his creativity."

"No, not at all, you don't sound like a snob at all."

"That's not entirely true anyway. I wish I were more creative than I am. It's not like we get to write our own songs. And I never played my guitar on the album. They hired professional guitarists for that."

"But you get to play it when you tour."

Rupert K. shrugged and shook his head. "Not really. My guitar's not plugged into anything when we're onstage. Can't really run around and entertain the crowd when you've got wires and cables tripping you."

"But you sing," I said. "You've got the best voice in the group."

"Thank you," he said. "Yes, I sing. At least there's that. But like I said, we don't write our own songs, so I'm not singing the music I'd like to."

"You don't like the music you sing?"

He leaned forward. "Can I tell you a secret?"

I leaned forward too. "Sure."

"I hate it," Rupert K. said.

A punch in the face. Those hurt the most when you don't even see the blow coming. "What?"

"It's not about the music anyway. It's about the screaming girls."

"What do you mean?"

"The girls who come to watch us sing aren't doing so because they like our music. They just want to be part of the moment. A moment that's much larger than them, and even larger than us. Every girl goes through a phase like that. It's never about the music."

What Rupert K. was basically saying was that the reason I was in love with him was because I was just going through a phase. It was one thing when Civil War Bartender said it, and another when Erin said it, but to have the actual object of my affection spell it out for me was something else altogether.

It was bullshit.

"The music of The Ruperts isn't exactly going to be known long after we're gone, is it?" Rupert K. went on. "No, what I want to play is music that matters. Folk dubstep—that's where my heart lies."

"Folk dubstep sounds . . ." Not stupid. Again, nothing Rupert K. said or did was stupid, but I honestly couldn't think of another word just at that moment. Maybe it was me. Maybe I just didn't understand the concept of folk dubstep. It was probably me. "Interesting."

"I think you're amazing."

I sat back again. I'd never loved his non sequiturs so much. I'd been shocked by a lot tonight, but this shocked me more than anything. "You do?"

He nodded and scooted even closer to me so that our knees were touching. I didn't know if it was the contact, but I suddenly felt warmer. "In my line of work you meet a lot of girls and you don't meet a lot of girls. That probably doesn't make any sense."

"No, I get it. You guys have millions of fans, but . . ."

"None that are as amazing as you." I watched as he put his hand on my knee. I watched it like I was outside of my body, looking down at a scene that I was only imagining, a scene that couldn't be real. "You're smart, you're artistic, and you're beautiful. You're everything I'd want in a girlfriend."

He was so close that I had a perfect view of the California-shaped birthmark on his neck, the subtly different shades of brown. I'd never loved California so much. I was enthralled by everything about him. He reached out and put his palm on the side of my face, his thumb caressing my skin slightly. He could feel how hot my cheek was. His own cheeks were red too. Redder than usual, I mean. He leaned in slowly.

Rupert K. was going to kiss me.

He was fishing for the kiss.

And then he caught it. His lips were on mine, soft and pillowy with just the right amount of pressure. The perfect kiss.

My feelings could best be described by Track 9 from The Ruperts' album: "WHOA WHOA WHOA."

But the whole time he was kissing me I kept picturing Rupert P.'s dead face. Damn Rupert P., ruining *everything*. Even in death.

I pulled back. It may have been the hardest thing I'd ever had to do. But I couldn't go on kissing Rupert K. knowing I was keeping this huge secret from him. He needed to know my role in Rupert P.'s death. I needed to tell him.

And I would, just as soon I finished kissing him again.

This time I was the one who leaned toward him, but before I could get to him our phones started to go off, both at the same moment. We both took out our phones, checking our new texts. And I knew by the look on his face that we'd both just read a variation of the same headline.

THE RUPERTS SINGER RUPERT PIERPONT PLUMMETS 16 STORIES FROM HOTEL ROOF TO HIS DEATH.

22

What had the boys done?

That was all I could think. I know that we kidnapped Rupert P.——I know that he died in our room——but this was next-level crazy. Us fangirls——we were allowed to have the crazy. We had a monopoly on it. But when the boys acted crazy, that shifted the balance of things completely. The record that I'd been playing forever suddenly scratched, and I was left to wonder if I could ever play it again.

I had just been on the roof.

Was that noise Rupert K. and I heard . . . Was that Rupert L. and Rupert X. hauling up Rupert P.'s body? Did they throw their bandmate off the roof of a hotel to try and make it look like a suicide? Had I really spent the last two years of my life worshiping the dumbest boys alive?

Yes, I think I had.

Rupert K.'s face was stuck, unflinching, his eyes glued to his phone screen.

"Rupert, I'm sorry." Forget what Erin said about girls apologizing too much. This time was different. I meant it and I needed to say it. "I'm so sorry."

I really was. You have to believe me. Looking at his face right then made my stomach twist. I decided to tell him everything.

"Rupert, there's something—"

He stood too quickly, cutting off my words. "I have to go."

"Where are you going? We can talk about it."

"I have to go," he said again. And then he was gone, slamming through the pool doors and out of my life again.

After a time I made my own way to the door, down the dimly lit corridors. The closer I got to a door labeled LOBBY the louder the sound was. I recognized the noise right away: feet hitting the floor and taking off, running in every direction; orders being yelled, juxtaposed with steadier voices trying to keep the calm; and of course, there was the screaming, the constant ringing. It was the first stirrings of pandemonium.

The actual pandemonium greeted me once I opened the door. The sounds were nothing more than a buzzing dissonance in my ears, as distinct as the noise glass makes when it shatters. People whizzed past me in every direction. On the other side of the glass doors the entrance to The Rondack was madness. Bodies frantic and flashing lights and lots more police than there had been earlier. I was drawn to it, the cacophony, like any other person pulled into becoming a voyeur by chaos. But I had to stop just short of the doors when a cop stepped in front of me.

"How did you get in here?" he said. His hand was already on my shoulder, gently pushing me toward an exit.

"I have a room here."

"Sure you do. You can't be in here."

I dug into my jeans pocket, thankful that I had one of the room keys on me. I showed it to the cop, who looked kind of disappointed to see that I wasn't lying. "Go back to your room and await further instruction from the hotel staff."

"Wha—"

"You can't leave right now, miss." Something over my shoulder caught his eye, something much more important than a wayward teen girl. He got out of my way.

I had to go back to the girls.

Even before I walked through the door I could hear the crying. I didn't know who it belonged to, but I guessed it was Michelle Hornsbury. Maybe her crying sounded British (can crying sound British?), or maybe it was the fact that none of my friends would be crying over the current circumstances. When I walked inside, Michelle Hornsbury was sitting in the middle of the couch bawling, and Erin, Isabel, and Apple surrounded her, lending clearly apathetic shoulders to cry on and tapping her back with unsure hands. I guess they'd long given up the charade about caring for Rupert P., even for Michelle Hornsbury's sake.

"I guess you guys heard what happened." It was a dumb thing to say, I'm fully aware, but it was all I could come up with.

A new wave of sobs spilled out of Michelle Hornsbury.

"We didn't just hear about it," Isabel said. "We saw it."

"What?"

"Check the window."

I had forgotten our room faced the front of the building. I went straight to the window and looked down. The street was congested with people and police cars and ambulances, and I couldn't even see the pavement anymore. Every inch was covered, even with people who clearly weren't Strepurs (men, oldies, sane people), all of them clambering close with outstretched cell phones. The scaffolding was folded over like used tinfoil, all bent metal and splintered wood. And in the center of it—limbs bent in every unnatural position imaginable—was the body of Rupert P.

My hand flew to my mouth.

"I think I'm going to be sick," Michelle Hornsbury said, leaping up to go to the bathroom. Once she was out of sight Erin stood up and looked at me. "Where the hell have you been?"

"Just . . . around."

"The most important thing ever happens and she's just *around*," Isabel said. "Did you see what *Rupert P.* supposedly posted on Twitter a few minutes ago?"

Apple shoved her phone in my face. On the screen was Rupert P.'s apparently final tweet.

> Goodbuy cruul world . . . (Going 2 off meself now.) . . . Buy 4evr.

"Who wrote this?"

"Rupert L. and Rupert X. were talking about Rupert P.'s Twitter password," Erin said. "It was obviously their idea. And judging by the glaring typos it was Rupert L. who wrote it."

"You retweeted a suicide note?"

Apple snatched the phone out of my hand. "All the cool kids are doing it."

She was right. The tweet had only been posted ten minutes ago, but it had already been retweeted over 160,000 times, with even more favorites.

"I don't want to be here anymore, guys," Apple said. "This isn't fun."

"This stopped being fun hours ago," Erin said.

"We can't go," I said. "The police are downstairs. They said they're not letting anyone in or out."

"They won't even notice us, we can slip right past them," Erin said. "But what are we going to do about Michelle Hornsbury?"

Right. Michelle Hornsbury. Our loose end. I hadn't heard her crying in a while. "Why isn't she crying anymore?"

The four of us looked at one another. Normally not being able to hear Michelle Hornsbury's oddly British crying would be a kind of blessing, but given the circumstances, it was more suspicious than anything. We all went toward the bathroom without having to consult one another. Erin knocked on the door.

"Michelle? Everything okay in there?"

Nothing for a minute. And then the door opened. Michelle Hornsbury walked out with something orange pinched in her fingers. Tighty-whities, well, tighty-oranges, as it were. The name "Rupert Pierpont" stitched across the back.

"What the bloody hell is this?" Michelle Hornsbury said.

23

I was going to kill Apple.

Poor choice of words, all things considered, but really, we were *all* going to kill Apple. If only she didn't have to collect Rupert P.'s nastiest shit for her shrine, we wouldn't be in this hashtag-mess. Michelle Hornsbury held up Rupert P.'s underpants for further inspection. It was probably the closest she'd ever gotten to them.

"That's nothing!" Erin said. She was the quickest of all of us and snatched the thing out of Michelle's hands.

"Are those pants?"

"Pants?" Isabel said. "Have you seen pants before, or . . . ?"

"Pants!" Michelle Hornsbury said. "What you Yanks call underwear."

"Definitely not underwear," I said.

"They're Rupert's," Michelle Hornsbury said.

"Definitely not Rupert's," Erin said.

"They have his name stitched into them!"

Shit shit shit. Quick. Somebody had to think quick.

We stared blankly.

"All Rupert P. fangirls have underwear like that, right, Apple?" I thought it was a good way to go, but as I said it I realized I shouldn't have brought Apple into this. If this situation taught me anything, it was that Apple could not be trusted to make sane decisions when it came to Rupert P., dead or not. If I had only glanced in her direction before I said her name, I would've seen that she was hovering behind Michelle Hornsbury with an end-table lamp clutched over her head, ready to strike.

At her house in Connecticut, Apple had added a punching bag to her gym and named it Michelle Hornsbury. I should've known this was going to happen.

Erin and Isabel seemed to see it just as I did. We tried to motion to her. Isabel shook her head from side to side slowly. Erin mouthed the word "no" and I tried to discreetly make a "put down the blunt object" motion with my hand.

Of course, Michelle Hornsbury saw all of this. She looked up. "What the hell are you doing?!" She stood and ran to the corner of the room, hiding behind Rupert P.'s death chair, ironically enough.

Apple put the lamp down and walked over to Michelle Hornsbury. Well, I shouldn't say "walked," exactly. She stalked.

"So you found your dead fake boyfriend's underwear in our room. You want a prize or something?"

"I'm not sure I like your tone," Michelle Hornsbury said.

"You don't like my *tone*? Well, I don't like that you're practically accusing us of murder."

"Uh, Apple," I said. "She really didn't say that. Like, at all."

"Didn't she?!"

"Apple, honey, maybe you should stop talking," Erin said.

"No, she needs to hear this."

"Girl is gone with the wind," Isabel muttered. She folded her arms in front of her chest and rested her weight on one leg. "I am so here for this."

"You!" Apple continued, walking closer to Michelle Hornsbury. "You think you know everything now, don't you? You think finding Rupert P.'s underwear in our room is evidence that we did something wrong?"

"Well, I wouldn't call it *not* evidence," Michelle Hornsbury said.

"You think something's up?" Apple moved even closer to her, close enough to make Michelle Hornsbury inch away slowly. "You think something's fishy. Well, guess what, Michelle Hornsbury: It's our word against yours, you dig? If you even think of going to the police, the four of us will say that we were together the whole time, braiding our hair or some shit, and that just leaves you out to dry, doesn't it?

Because maybe we could've been your alibi, but we're done playing nice! You know, I never liked you from the start, right after Rupert P. picked you up from whatever street corner you were standing on and helped you wash the dried splooge out of your hair like the sweet angel that he was, and now I know why! It's because you're a bitch. A sussy bearding basic discount-bin bitch!"

This whole time Apple had been inching Michelle Hornsbury across the room and we'd all followed along with her, careful, apprehensive. Apple swung open the door. "So you can take your dead fake boyfriend's *pants* and kindly *get the fuck out of our room*." With that she took the underwear out of Erin's hand and threw it out the door for Michelle Hornsbury to fetch.

"You're mad!" Michelle Hornsbury said.

"Quite frankly." Apple let go of the knob, and the door swung shut in Michelle Hornsbury's face.

24

Wow.

I didn't know about anybody else, but I was taken aback. Even Isabel looked shocked, her mouth hanging open in proud awe. "Well gag me with a blueberry-flavored prophylactic," she said. "What did I just witness?"

"Apple went *in*," I said.

"Slay a bit!" Isabel said.

"Can everyone hold up with the boss bitch accolades?" Erin said. "What the hell was that with the lamp? Don't tell me you were trying to kill her."

"Another dead body is just a drop in the bucket at this point," Apple said.

Well, that put another mark in my Apple-did-it column.

"Great going," Erin said. "Did you get your rocks off, Apple? Because thanks to that little display, Michelle Hornsbury is going to go directly to the police with Rupert P.'s underwear in hand—evidence that you *handed* to her, I might add—and make us official persons of interest."

Apple only shrugged. "I didn't *hand* it to her. I threw it in her general direction. I did what needed to be done."

"We need to leave," Erin said. "This isn't cute anymore."

"But all the fun's about to start," Isabel said.

"What are you talking about?" Erin said.

"One of The Ruperts supposedly flung himself off a building, and we all know it was the other boys who actually did it. This is the biggest news story of the century, and I have a front-row seat to all of it. I need to update my website."

"You're vile," I said. It just came out. I didn't mean to start a fight with Isabel. Mainly because she scared me. But I had to say it. What we were doing was wrong. Even if we hadn't killed Rupert P. Even if his death really was an accident. "Us staying quiet about all this is wrong."

"I can't with this broken record," Isabel said. *"We got away with it."*

"The other boys are going to go down for it."

"Well, they were stupid enough to throw Rupert P. off a building!"

"Are you even a fan of theirs, or is every bad thing that happens to them just more fodder for your website?"

"We *all* went to their room to dump Rupert P.'s body," Isabel said. "So check yourself before you start asking who's a fan."

She was right. But the night wasn't over yet. Isabel's heart may have been nothing more than a frostbitten tumor between her lungs, but mine still worked. I still had my morals. I was still a fan. I could still do something to change the outcome.

"I'm going to confess. To everything."

Erin stepped in front of me before I could reach the door. "Think about what you're doing," she said. "Isabel and Apple and I are all sticking together on our story."

"Really? So if I confess, it's still your word against mine?"

Erin didn't say anything to that, and I think, despite everything that had happened, that shocked me the most. "You're my best friend."

Isabel let out a snarl of a laugh.

"What's so funny?" I said. I was tired of being afraid of Isabel. "You know, I could just go to the police and tell them you did it. I'll just tell them you wanted to destroy the boy band for hits and retweets."

"You'd lie like that?"

"Who said it's a lie?" I said. She smiled and I hated it. "He didn't die accidentally, Isabel."

"She's right," Erin said. "It would've been impossible for Rupert P. to use the tights to kill himself. Someone killed him."

"Oh, and now *you* think it was me too?" Isabel said. She turned to me. "Now I get it. Why you're so eager to point fingers. It was you, wasn't it?"

"What?"

"It all makes sense now."

"You're crazy," I said.

"Am I? We have no idea where you were when Rupert P. died."

"I told you, I was in the bar."

"That's not what Erin says."

I turned to Erin, not even a little bit surprised that she'd talk to Isabel about me behind my back.

"You weren't at the bar," Erin said. Her voice slow and steady. Deliberate. "I know you weren't at the bar because I was."

The thing about lying is you can be really good at it and still get caught.

This just happened to be the worst possible lie to get caught in. Isabel was enjoying it. She was the bull, suddenly awake and pawing the ground. It was up to me to stand my ground or run with my tail between my legs.

"Okay, I wasn't at the bar," I said. "I was with Rupert K."

Quiet. And not even like an awed quiet, more like an I-love-the-way-you-lie kind of quiet.

"What?" Erin said.

"I went up to the roof and he was there. We talked. When I came back down I found you all in the hallway, and that's when we all walked into the room and found Rupert P. dead."

"And let me guess," Isabel said, "you were with him when Rupert P. quote-unquote jumped off the roof too."

"Actually, yeah, I was."

"You expect us to believe that?"

"This is exactly why I didn't tell you in the first place. I know it sounds crazy, but it happened. He tweeted 'Bright Lights, Big City'—it was something we'd talked about earlier, so I knew where to find him."

Erin had her phone out instantly. "He didn't tweet that," she said.

"Yes, he did."

"Erin's right," Apple said. "There's no tweet like that on his feed."

"Then he must have deleted it."

"We all would've seen it, though," Erin said.

"No, you guys were too busy listening to Michelle Hornsbury's stories. I saw the tweet as soon it went out. He probably just deleted it like two seconds later."

"You imagined it."

Isabel. On her hind legs now and smiling. Her smile this time wasn't one of a beast about to pounce, but of one who'd already devoured her prey, satisfied. All I was to her was something stuck between her teeth. "You imagined the tweet. Just like you imagined meeting Rupert K. You're literally crazy."

"No, I'm not."

"Erin told me about the time you spent in that psych ward freshman year."

I stared at Erin. A dagger through the heart, twisting.

"It wasn't a psych ward," I said in a low voice. It was after my breakdown, my moment of paralyzing fear after my dad's death. My mom took me to her hospital, but I wasn't even admitted. "It wasn't a psych ward," I said again. Erin was the only one I told. Everyone else just thought I'd been out sick for a couple of days. How could she tell Isabel? "You know nothing about that."

"You know what else Erin told me? That you like to fantasize about Rupert K. You imagine he's with you all the livelong day. Face it—all of your lies have facilitated your slow spiral into insanity."

I was too embarrassed to be fully angry. "I'm *not* crazy."

"Sure," Isabel said. "And you also didn't kill Rupert P."

"I did meet Rupert K. He told me about his hobbies, he told me what direction he wants his music to go in . . ."

"Let me guess, video games and folk?" Isabel said. "It's in all of his interviews."

"Folk dubstep."

"Doesn't that sound made-up to you?"

My heart sped up, my breath trying to catch up.

Isabel was wrong.

Just because she spoke with authority didn't make anything she said true. She didn't know anything. "I did not kill Rupert P."

"Girl, you're being real messy right now. You're consumed by your obsession," Isabel said. "The rest of us—we know how to handle it, but you? You go insane."

"I don't—"

"You hallucinate."

"Stop it."

"And now it's escalated to murder."

"No!"

"I feel bad for you." She walked up to me. "You're full-stop psycho and you don't even know it."

My eyes found Erin's, always finding her, but only for a second. She looked down. Even Apple was looking at me funny. I knew it wasn't good when Apple of all people thought I was crazy. "Apple, Isabel's just talking shit."

Apple's eyebrows knit together. "Okay," she said. What she didn't say was, *I believe you.* What she meant was, *I'm afraid of you.* "We're all a little crazy right now," she said, the most unconvincing giggle in the world pinned on the end of it. "I'm going to get my things."

I turned to Erin, but she still wouldn't look at me.

This wasn't happening.

I did not imagine meeting Rupert K. on the roof both times.

I did not imagine us going down to the hotel pool.

I did not imagine the biggest superstar on the planet kissing me.

I brought my fingers to my lips, trying to feel something there, even though memories—real or false—were intangible. It was the perfect kiss, just like I'd always dreamed it would be . . . I know how that sounds. That it was too perfect, that it was the kiss I dreamed of because I literally dreamed it up. I didn't.

I *didn't*.

I looked down at myself, at my clothes, at my hair. I looked crazy. I kept telling myself I wasn't crazy, but what Isabel said was gnawing at me. Maybe she was right. Maybe I'd told one too many lies. I'd always made up stories. Had the lines just blurred between the real ones and the fake ones?

Maybe I was a little crazy. I could admit that—we all were—but was I crazy enough to kill?

I pictured Rupert P., the veins straining in his neck. I heard his breath cut out, the strangled noise it made, I saw his amber eyes go wider than they'd ever gone before and then stay unblinking forever, and I saw myself pulling the tights.

"We should get out of here," Erin said, breaking through my thoughts. I brushed past her, my former best friend, and grabbed my bag. Everyone else did too. None of them said anything to me as we all left the room. None of them said anything as we waited in front of the elevator doors.

And none of us spoke when the doors opened and The Ruperts stood on the other side of them, handcuffed, accompanied by a pair of cops.

25

An officer spoke first. "Take the next one."

We all roundly ignored him. Of course, Isabel was the first one to move forward. She crossed the threshold between us, the lesser people, and walked right into the elevator, the realm of the boys, rendering the cop's efforts to continuously hit the DOOR CLOSE button totally futile. She may have been the first one in, but don't kid yourself—we all would've done the exact same thing. It felt like we'd seen the boys all throughout the day, in different incarnations, but this time it'd be for real, enclosed in a small space, no place to hide. No cops were going to get in the way of that.

The doors closed behind us.

"Bloody fans," Rupert X. muttered under his breath.

"Don't say another word, Rupert," Rupert K. said. It didn't surprise me that he'd be the only one to take his Miranda rights seriously.

There was just enough room for us girls to stand facing the boys, about a foot between us. That feeling in the pit of my stomach of suspended gravity—of my stomach climbing up to my throat—wasn't just the elevator descending. Standing in front of The Ruperts, I knew the four of us girls were more or less thinking the same thing.

Was this all there was?

They were just boys. Take away the band, the lights, the fame, and the screaming girls, and they were just boys, chosen for us to obsess over. When they chuckled we made gifs, and when they hugged each other we wrote overblown analyses. But they were just boys who we'd looked at through a prism.

I knew I wasn't the only one who felt this way about the boys now, who felt like our perception of them had totally changed. Apple's favorite was gone, and they were the ones to throw him off a roof, so this couldn't have been that exciting for her. My theory that Isabel stopped liking them a long time ago and now only followed their every move for her website still held strong. Maybe she still had a thing for Rupert L.— aesthetically he wasn't unappealing—but he was a mouth breather of the highest order. (We already knew this, but in person, in an otherwise silent, enclosed space, it was impossible to ignore and increasingly irritating.) How could Isabel stand him?

Up close, Rupert X. was pale. Too skinny. Very possibly addicted to an illicit substance. Erin looked at him with such hatred in her eyes. She wasn't even trying to hide it.

"You look quite familiar," he said to her.

"Fuck you," Erin replied.

In the hard golden light of the elevator I saw the different shades of Rupert K.'s forehead, a bumpy terrain dusted in makeup. I hadn't noticed it the other two times I'd met him that day.

A scary thought, considering Isabel's hypothesis that I'd imagined it all.

Had I really hallucinated the whole thing?

He didn't say anything to me, but he stared at me. His eyes were locked on mine.

Once upon a time I would've loved this moment. I would've fantasized about looking into Rupert K.'s eyes and he looking back into mine.

Now I wasn't so sure.

These were boys who made us do bad things.

Made us turn on one another.

Made us stupid with delight, and then just stupid.

Isabel took out her phone and pointed the camera right at them.

"Oi, what are you doing?" Rupert L. said. "Aren't you girls fans?"

"We're your *biggest* fans," Isabel said.

The doors opened at the lobby, and the temporary quiet, where the only sound was that of Rupert L.'s breathing, was replaced by the continued noises of the pandemonium I'd heard the last time I was there. It hadn't subsided at all. In fact, it was louder now. The madness just outside the glass doors had seeped its way inside, and there was no way to avoid it.

We all stepped out of the elevator, and us girls stood back as the cops led the boys away. They bowed their heads, looking down to avoid the flashing camera lights. The glass doors opened and everyone was screaming, despair that their favorite boys were being taken away or happiness that they were finally getting to see them. It was impossible to tell the difference.

Rupert K. turned back around. He was being dragged forward, but he turned his head to see me. The expression on his face was inscrutable. Did he recognize me? Was Isabel just playing mind games with me? Was I playing mind games with myself?

We watched as the cops ushered them to the back of a police car, glowing with all the flashing lights that were bouncing off of it.

None of this was right.

I had to help him.

26

"I have to help him."

"Keep saying it," Isabel said. "Maybe you'll start to believe it."

For once I ignored her. I marched through the doors. It had started to rain, which made all the lights—cameras, the blue and red flashes from the cop cars, the beams from the helicopters—reflect off every surface, totally blinding. It took my eyes a moment to adjust. All there was were the flashing lights and thousands of drenched, crying girls. For a moment I wondered if it actually was raining at all, or if it wasn't just the collective tears of every Strepur in New York.

I spotted the girl from earlier in the day when we were making our way to the front of the hotel, the one who'd said it wasn't fair that we'd gotten a room. She was hugging one of her friends, and she was crying too, but when she saw me she stopped. Her eyes connected with mine and I could swear she hated me. Her eyebrows settled low, her lips formed a tight line, just shy of a pout. As if somehow she knew exactly what my part was in all of this.

"I didn't mean to."

I don't know if she heard me. Probably not. It was practically Armageddon outside after all. But either way, she only spurred me on further.

It took me a moment to find a police officer. Finally, I spotted one being engulfed in a sticky blob of blubbering girls. Every time he pushed his palm out to keep the girls from coming any closer it got swallowed up, lost for a scary moment before he was able to retrieve it again.

"Excuse me," I said to the cop. He didn't hear or he was too busy, so I had to say it again, louder this time. "Excuse me!" It felt like my voice was louder than it had ever been before. "I'd like to confess something."

"What's that?" the cop said.

Yeah, what's that? What was I going to confess? That me and my friends had kidnapped Rupert P. earlier? Despite everything, I still didn't want to rat them out. But I could still help Rupert K. while minimizing the damage.

"I was with Rupert Kirke."

"Who?"

"Rupert Kirke? He's one of The Ruperts? I was with him when Rupert P. . . . . jumped. I'm his alibi."

The cop rolled his eyes. Couldn't say I didn't expect that. "Get in line, miss. Every girl here is Rupert's alibi."

I looked around, and it was only then that I really stopped to listen to what the girls around me were screaming. It wasn't some unintelligible noise of collective anguish. They were saying something. I could pick words and sentences from the air.

"I saw him! He didn't do anything wrong!"

"I was with Rupert the whole time!"

"I was with Rupert!"

"I was with Rupert!"

"I was with Rupert!"

"Ignore her, she's simple," Erin said, suddenly next to me, smiling up at the cop and pulling on my elbow. "She's just sad, like the rest of us."

She steered me away. "What the hell do you think you're doing?"

"You know it isn't right." We were crossing the street to meet Apple and Isabel, and it almost felt like that time we'd waded through the crowd at the *Today* show to get to Apple's tent. It seemed like so long ago. "The boys are going to go down for this and they didn't do anything wrong."

"They threw a body off a roof," Erin said. We were on the other street now, back with Isabel and Apple. "I know he weighed one hundred and five pounds soaking wet, but from that height that scaffolding still felt the fall."

"According to Twitter, twelve girls were injured," Apple said. "One girl lost her ability to clap."

"Which is to say nothing of the hundreds of girls pledging to kill themselves if the cops don't let The Ruperts go. Fuck, sometimes even I'm embarrassed to be in this fandom," Isabel said.

"I can't live with myself knowing Rupert K. is going to go down for something that I was a part of! He needs to know the truth. *Someone* needs to know the truth," I said.

"The truth stays with us," Isabel said.

"Isabel's right," Erin said. "We can't tell anyone anything. Promise."

I took her hand and led her away from the other two girls. Before I promised anything I needed to know something.

"Do you believe I did it?"

My sanity was riding on her answer. Literally. She still knew me best. Despite her secrets, and her betrayal. Despite her allegiance to Isabel and her warped ideas about boy bands and teen girls. Erin may have stopped being my best friend, but I couldn't ignore the fact that she'd still held the title not one hour ago. "Just tell me," I said. "I need to know what you think."

"Any of us could've done it," she said. "We all had motive. I even told you I wanted to 'kill the boy band,' which in retrospect was a really poor choice of words."

"Yeah, but the difference is, I don't actually believe that you killed Rupert P." I never really suspected Erin. Maybe I let my imagination wander a few times, but despite everything, everything she'd done and all the new things I'd learned about her, I knew Erin wasn't capable of murder. "Do you believe that *I* did?"

The rain was turning her light hair dark, and she kept blinking through it. She sighed and bit her lip, the red of it faded by now. She seemed to think of that just as I did because she dug a lip gloss out of her pocket. Michelle Hornsbury's Pink Lemonade lip gloss.

"You know what?" I said. "Don't answer that. You were wrong about so much today already."

"Look—"

"No, you listen to me now." It was so easy to say that, and I suddenly wondered why I'd never said it to her before. "Maybe obsessing over a boy band is stupid. But so what? You say that us fans are the worst thing that's happened to society. But all we're doing is loving cute boys. Is that really so bad?"

"Fans have turned love into something medieval."

"But that's love. It's crazy and great. Being interested in cute boys is what we're supposed to be doing at this age. You know what we're not supposed to be doing? Kidnapping people. Murdering them. Inciting riots outside of hotels that are direct results of the bad choices we've made. You say our stanning has gone too far, but you're the one who took things too far, Erin. You ruined people's lives . . . You're a life ruiner."

The wailing sirens, the girls; I still couldn't wrap my mind around the destruction we'd caused. So much had changed since the afternoon. Including our friendship. "You told Isabel that I hallucinate that Rupert K. is with me sometimes."

"I fucked up." She looked like she meant it, sad enough to cry, and then actually crying. Or maybe that was just the rain, an illusion of false tears on her face. The rain couldn't make her less beautiful, though. I hated that even then I was thinking that. "I'm sorry, okay?" Erin said. "I'm sorry. I'm sorry. I'm so sorry."

Erin was saying sorry. What a time to be alive indeed. Strangely, it didn't make me feel any better. Maybe Erin was right. Maybe girls apologized too much.

"Say something," she said. "Forgive me."

I wouldn't give that to her. I wasn't ready to.

"Please," Erin said. "I know you. You're too nice not to accept my apology."

"Fuck nice," I said.

I turned and started to walk away.

"Where are you going?" Erin said, calling after me. But I did not turn around. I went back to The Rondack.

27

I didn't know what I was doing, going back to the scene of the crime. I guess I needed time to myself, to reflect on what I'd possibly done. I didn't really believe I'd killed Rupert P., but visualizing my friends murdering him actually made me believe that maybe I was capable of it too. And Isabel and Erin were a convincing pair; if they thought I'd gone crazy, then maybe I had. I mean, how do you know you're really crazy unless someone tells you that you are? I *did* dream of seeing Rupert K. all the time.

Maybe I *had* hallucinated seeing him tonight.

It didn't help my sanity any that when I opened the door to our hotel room Michelle Hornsbury was there.

She was just standing there, staring at the chair. The one that Rupert P. had once sat on. And she was weeping. Seeing her like that freaked me out. It felt like something out of a horror movie, like seeing a little girl with pigtails in a hallway: You didn't realize just how creepy something like that could

294

be until suddenly it was. I jumped, and Michelle Hornsbury did too when she heard me.

"Michelle," I said, breathless. "What are you doing here?"

She looked scared to see me too for a second and wiped her eyes quickly, but then she squinted, her brows knitting together. "I thought you girls had left," she said in a tear-clogged voice. "Are you going to stay the night? I know this was originally your room, but you left and, well, you know what they say—finders keepers and all that. I'm afraid I've already claimed the bed, you'll have to take the couch."

Relegated to the couch. Again. I shook my head, trying to get back to the matter at hand. "Wait, *what?*"

Michelle Hornsbury shrugged. "I was *invited* to stay in this room," she explained slowly. "I wasn't just going to leave because Orange unceremoniously kicked me out."

"Apple."

"No, thank you, I'm not hungry."

Could this night honestly get any more bizarre? It was never going to end. So long as I was in this hotel it seemed I was destined to spend my days in some weird *Twilight Zone* dimension where friends turned against you, boy bands were dumb, and beards came alive. Total mindfuck. And I obviously didn't do well with mindfucks. I didn't even know why I'd come back. To see the room one last time? To punish myself? All I really wanted to do was go home and forget about all of this. But seeing Michelle Hornsbury, I knew why I couldn't leave. All the times I'd said I'd go to the police, and even the one time I actually did, nothing changed. I was still responsible for what happened to Rupert P. Whether I only helped to kidnap him, or whether I actually did black out, go stark raving mad, and kill him. The more time that passed with that hypothesis in my mind, the more I believed it.

And nothing would change—everything would continue to not change—until I actually did something to change it.

I had to tell someone what I'd done. Even if no one would believe me.

I cleared my throat. I didn't normally clear my throat before confessions, but people on TV did and the moment seemed to call for it. "Michelle," I said. "I think I killed Rupert P."

She turned to me, her face screwed up in cloudy confusion. "What?"

"I think I might be going crazy." I just let it all out at that point. No holds barred. Confession was a go. "Last year I got really depressed—my mom calls it my 'bad way.' My dad died and after that I kind of had a breakdown. But what if it really was more serious than that? I mean, I've always imagined Rupert K. as if he was standing right next to me, but I always thought that was just because I have a really good imagination— I write a lot, it's my thing—and don't most Rupert K. fans fantasize about him sometimes? But then when Isabel told me he never tweeted that 'Bright Lights' thing I really got to thinking. He could've just deleted it before any of the girls saw it, but what if he didn't, you know? What if I imagined I was with him when really I was here, in this room, strangling Rupert P.? He was a douchefuck—mayherestinpeace—but he didn't deserve to die. I went from a crazy fangirl to literally a crazy fangirl, I think." I took a breath. I needed one. "And if it wasn't me then it was definitely Isabel, who I think may actually be bloodthirsty. I wouldn't put it past her."

"Oh, you poor thing," Michelle said.

That was not the reaction I had been expecting from the fake girlfriend of the dead boy bander. I expected backing away slowly and threats to call the police. Maybe even screams. Maybe even Michelle Hornsbury beating me up. But not this.

"You didn't kill Rupert P.," she said. "I did."

I swear this was what she said. Honestly, I'm not trying to place the blame on someone else. By now I hope you've seen how much I was willing to sacrifice by telling her all this— just to make it right.

"What?"

"Whew, you don't know how good it feels to get that off my chest," she said, heaving a big breath. "Thank you."

297

"What do you mean you killed Rupert P.? How? You couldn't have."

"Rupie and I had a complicated relationship."

The mother of all understatements.

"It's true, what Griffin Holmes said on that video. Rupie was gay. I knew it all along. But I didn't care. Rupie needed a girlfriend, and I got to do a lot of things from my place on his arm.

"We went everywhere together whenever he toured, and usually he'd always get a room just for us. Well, at least just for me, while he was out doing . . . whatever. But recently he'd been distant. He still wanted me to come on tour with him, but only in theory. In practice he didn't want me there at all. He wanted me around but he didn't want me around. Do you have any idea how frustrating that was? To be there but to also not be there? I should've just ended it, I know that now, but I was used to this life. I got to go all over the world—I wasn't just about to stop."

As she spoke, Michelle Hornsbury swept her hand over the edges of the big chair in the room. Rupert P.'s death chair. Now she sat down in it, which added an extra layer of queasiness to everything she was saying.

"So recently Rupie had been booking a room for me for a night. We'd walk into the hotel together a couple of times to be seen together, and then my trip would be cut shorter than the boys'. But this time he didn't book me a room. I confronted him about it. I said I needed someplace to stay while I was here, and he said that I could just roam around the hotel. That it would just be for a night. That this place had 'great amenities.' As if that was supposed to make up for the fact that I didn't have a bed to sleep in. Now tell me that's not a horrible way to treat your fake girlfriend."

"Fairly horrible," I said, though all I could think about was how screwed up the world of boy banders and beards was.

"He said that the hotel had been all booked up. That he'd really tried to get me a room but couldn't. But he had a room with the rest of the boys. And he had a room with Griffin.

"Two rooms!" Michelle Hornsbury went on. "It made me crazy! And then when I found him in a new room full of girls, well, I guess that was the final straw."

"How'd you know he was even here?"

"I heard you and Erin talking about it at the bar, the first time we met. After I left my purse at the table I went back for it, and you girls were bragging about having Rupert in your room."

"We weren't bragging."

"Whatever it was, I couldn't believe it. It was the third room he had access to in this bloody hotel. Which was three more rooms than I had access to!"

"How did you even get in here?"

"I went to the front desk and said I was one of the girls in your room and that I'd lost my key. The boy at the front really was easy to persuade. He gave me a new key, no problem. I've actually had a key to your room since then. I had to confront Rupie. He wasn't taking any of my calls, and now he was hiding out with other girls. I waited in the stairwell on this floor for all of you to leave, and then I went in the room. You can imagine how shocked I was to see Rupert all tied up."

"Yeah——"

"I wasn't shocked in the slightest! Rupie had always been a crazy bondage freak. In my mind, not only was he constantly off having crazy bondage fun with Griffin, now he was off having bondage fun with a room full of girls when he could've just been having it with me, had he asked! I suppose I just suddenly snapped. I completely lost my head. I choked him with the tights that had gagged his mouth."

Well, shit.

"But if you killed him, why did you stick around? Why didn't you just leave?"

"I knew word would get out soon enough and that if I ran it would look suspicious. I was actually hoping to have you girls caught. You'd already kidnapped him; the police would assume that you had killed him too. You were a troupe of raving mad fanatics after all. I figured if I caught you here with him that was my best chance to get away with it and place the blame on someone else. That's why I wanted to get you to let me into your room so badly. Sorry about that, by the way."

"Uh . . ."

"And then when I came here and he was gone I was shocked. Impressed. But shocked. You girls were pure evil dumping his body in the boys' room."

So it hadn't been me. It had been Michelle Hornsbury: part-time model, professional beard, murderer.

And I was alone in a room with her.

Maybe I was going to hell today after all. Literally—at the hands of Michelle Hornsbury. I glanced toward the door, but there was no way I could get anywhere near it without Michelle noticing. Her eyes bore into me like a cop's flashlight in my face, my heart speeding up. "Are you going to kill me?"

"What?"

I tried to keep my voice steady, but there was no hiding the fear in it. "Now that I know your secret, what's to stop you from killing me?"

"Well, gosh, I'm not a psychopath! Killing Rupert was an act of passion!" Michelle Hornsbury cried. "A mistake, really. I don't just go around killing people!"

"So why did you tell me?"

"For the same reason you tried confessing to me, I guess. Guilt isn't good for my complexion."

"Do you feel less guilty now?"

"A little . . . Maybe . . . Not really." She sighed, seeming tired. "All I wanted was a room," she said. "You have to believe me. All I wanted was one measly room."

Beautiful, posh Michelle Hornsbury. I'd never seen anyone so sad and pathetic. I'd also never been this close to a murderer. I needed to get the hell out of there.

"Can I ask you something?" Michelle Hornsbury said.

"Okay."

"Why did you kidnap him?"

At the end of the day there still wasn't a logical answer to that question. But I guess that was fitting, in a way. There was so little logic to fandom. At the end, the only thing left was passion. Madness. Maybe those two things weren't so different.

I shrugged. "He was a Rupert."

She dwelled on this for a minute. Her eyebrows rose and then fell just as quickly. She'd come to be satisfied by this answer, even though I couldn't possibly understand how she could be.

"Are you going to tell on me?" Michelle Hornsbury asked. "Because I should probably take this time to remind you that I know about the kidnapping, and then the disposal of the body in the boys' room. The punishment would still be awfully severe for you."

Always nice getting threatened at the end of the night. "No. I won't tell on you." I didn't know if that was true yet, but

I wanted to get out of there alive. Also, somehow, impossibly, I felt sorry for her. I knew she was a psycho, so there was still fear there, but now it was mingled with pity.

"So do you mind if I stay here tonight, then?"

"Go nuts," I told her.

She shot me a look and I winced, realizing what I'd just said. "I didn't mean it like that."

Michelle Hornsbury watched me carefully for another minute and then just up and walked into the bedroom, closing the door behind her and leaving me like I was another fan she couldn't deal with. At least she didn't kill me.

I counted my blessings and got the hell out of there. Outside the room, in the hallway, I dug into my pocket and found my white bead bracelet. A lot of crazy shit had happened since Rupert P. had broken it, but I'd gotten through the night without having to smack it against my skin to feel the sting. I'd have to find another way to commemorate my dad, and that was okay.

I left The Rondack and never looked back.

28

"That's quite a story," the officer said.

I nodded. "Thank you." And then as soon as I said it I realized I must've sounded like an idiot. He hadn't been complimenting my storytelling abilities.

"Probably didn't have to be so long, though," he said, "did it?"

"What?" This was not the reaction I was expecting. I was sitting on the chair beside his desk at the precinct, people bustling about all around us. It had taken a week since everything went down at The Rondack for me to muster up the courage to come down here and make this confession. Not to sound like a snob or anything, but honestly, I thought there'd be a bit more fanfare.

"Your story," the officer said. He looked at his watch, brought it right to his face, squinted, and then pulled it back farther, opening his eyes wider. "It took hours to tell."

"I thought it would be important not to spare any details."

"Yeah, but we're talking about hours here. Four hours of my life."

"I'm sorry?"

"An abridged version woulda done the job."

I was about to say something but then thought better of it. He really did seem kind of annoyed that my story had been so long, and I didn't want to annoy him any more than I clearly already had. I stuck my hands out toward him, palms up, wrists together. "Are you going to arrest me now?"

"Arrest you?"

"I just confessed to kidnapping and framing somebody for murder. And I just told you who actually did kill Rupert Pierpont."

"The girl who was in here before you did the same thing," the cop said.

My hands fell to my lap. "Excuse me?"

"Her story had her seducing all the Ruperts and then smothering Rupert Pierpont with a pillow in a sacrificial ritual. And it only took her ten minutes to tell it. *Ten minutes.*"

"Look, I'm sorry that my story was so long, but——"

"Your friends, this Erin and Apple and Isabel——they'll corroborate all this?"

"No, but——"

The cop closed a file on his desk and sat up a little, stretching out his right leg. "Few days ago we got a girl in here that actually planted her own evidence in the hotel to make it look like she had something to do with the murder. Another girl confessed to killing Rupert Pierpont in music video fashion on YouTube. Do you really think you're the only one trying to get The Ruperts off?"

"I didn't know——"

"There's hundreds of you girls," the cop said. "Making a mockery of the NYPD. But I'm forced to listen to all of you until we officially close this case. I honestly don't know if you girls just want attention or if you really do love those boys too much. But I'll tell you one thing: It scares me."

I watched him shake his head from side to side, a silent whistle escaping his lips. In that headshake I could see exactly what he was thinking about. He was wondering what happened to the good old days. He was wondering when girls got so gosh darn complicated. He didn't have a clue.

"Fans," he sighed. A bad word when he said it.

"Fans," I repeated, serious.

"You girls . . ."

Are never taken seriously.

". . . should find a nice hobby."

But we should be taken seriously. We can be amazing. And dangerous.

The cop was no longer paying attention to me, but that was okay, since I was no longer paying attention to him. "So you don't believe what I just told you."

"Four *hours*," the cop said, getting up, shaking his head.

He left. I found my own way out.

29

So the cops didn't believe me. Maybe I should've seen that coming. Or maybe not. Out loud, the story really did seem totally outrageous. But it still needs to be known, and that's why I'm posting it here. I guess you can consider all of this one long-ass PostSecret. So now it's out in the open, whether anyone chooses to believe it or not.

A short while after I left the hotel it was completely taken over by Strepurs. They infiltrated, just as Rupert L. feared they would. Running amok, with the police hopeless to catch all of them, Strepurs ransacked every floor of the place. No one is really sure what their mission was, but I think being packed so tightly together outside of the hotel, plus the trauma of a Rupert dying and the rest of the members being carted off to jail, set something off in those Strepurs. There was never any rhyme or reason to the things they did in their day-to-day fan lives; imagine how much less there was on the other side of a collective psychotic break. They managed to get into our room somehow and destroyed everything that may have once made it a crime scene. Michelle Hornsbury was swallowed up by Strepurs for the second time that day.

Things cooled down after that night.

Last I heard, Michelle Hornsbury was in Dubai and in a new relationship. John Mayer.

Rupert Xavier and Rupert Lemon were arrested and sentenced to twenty-five years in a maximum security prison for throwing a body off a roof and endangering the public, but with any luck they'll be out in twenty for good behavior.

Rupert Kirke's case was a little different. He'd told the prosecutor and the media that he'd been with a girl the whole time. A girl whose name he did not remember. For a while, the media had a field day basically calling him a skank for being with a girl and not even knowing her name.

Rupert K.'s team of lawyers interviewed a lot of the girls who had come forward to say they were the ones who had been with him when Rupert P. died and had been thrown off the roof. The press called it a modern-day Cinderella story. Thousands of girls came forward, from all over the world, hoping that crystal slipper fit on their foot. But Rupert K.'s lawyers couldn't go through all the girls. It wasn't feasible, they said. And then, miraculously, Rupert K. did remember her name. He said he'd been with a girl named Sloane Peterson. He said she liked red cars, museums, dance parties in town squares, and writing.

The media had a second field day, and every blog, newspaper, and entertainment news show made fun of him for spending that night with the female lead in *Ferris Bueller's Day Off.*

His case looked pretty bleak for a while there. But a maintenance man at the hotel came forward and corroborated Rupert K.'s story, saying that he'd seen Rupert K. and a young woman running through the halls near the hotel's indoor pool. Rupert X. and Rupert L. eventually admitted that Rupert K. wasn't with them on the roof.

Rupert K. wasn't charged with a crime. He's currently working on a solo album. Folk dubstep. He posted a SoundCloud of his first single on Twitter. It's called "Are You the Girl?" I can't bring myself to listen to it yet.

As for what happened to us four girls, it's a lot less interesting.

As you may have guessed, none of my friends came forward with any information about what happened that night at The Rondack. Once they left the hotel, they never looked back.

Apple took down all her Rupert P. posters and found a new band to obsess over. Six Stages of Grief was an American boy band trying to bring back the whole emo/pop/punk scene. They weren't very big yet but they had a small following of devoted fans, Apple among them. She washed the auburn out of her hair, going back to her natural black. Her favorite member of 6SoG was Dashiell Bancroft. He was five feet one, showing a major case of premature male-pattern baldness, and had a chin that receded into his jaw.

Now that the members of The Ruperts were dead/behind bars/a solo artist, Isabel couldn't exactly continue to run her Ruperts update site. But with all the traffic she'd garnered from her night at The Rondack she had a strong enough following to launch a full-blown celeb gossip site big enough to rival the major outlets. I wonder if she'll link to this story.

I still see Erin at school, and we still talk, but it isn't how it used to be. I don't think it ever will be again. I never told her what happened when I went back to our hotel room and found Michelle Hornsbury there. She'd already made her conclusions about me, and I don't even know if she'd trust that what I'm telling you right now is the truth.

But that's just it, isn't it?

I could be making all this up. I could have spun this whole story so that it worked out in my favor. I could've assigned random roles and made Erin the Mastermind, Isabel the Enforcer, and Apple the Simple One just so that I could be the Innocent One. I know that if Erin, Apple, and Isabel were telling it, they'd probably (definitely) make me out to be the Crazy One. But if I were making all of this up, I would probably just make Isabel out to be the murderer or something, don't you think?

I've told you about everyone else, and if you've read this far I'm assuming you're interested to know about what happened with me. As per usual, my life isn't terribly exciting at the moment. I haven't written fanfiction since everything that happened with The Ruperts. Maybe one day I'll find some other fandom that'll inspire me to write about it, but until then I think I'll try my hand at real fiction. If that's the only thing that came out of writing this whole story down, then that's good enough.

But I've been thinking a lot about the future too. And if I'm being honest, I've been thinking about what Civil War Bartender said. I imagine myself going to my first college party. I imagine talking to a group of hip, counterculture coeds and the topic of The Ruperts getting brought up. Somebody'll say, "Hey, you guys remember The Ruperts? How lame were they?"

I imagine what I'll say.

I wonder if I'll lie.

ACKNOWLEDGMENTS

Thank you:

To Jenny Bent, my rock star agent, who does so much more than I thought an agent could do. You are so, so good and I am truly lucky and amazed to have you in my corner. To Gemma Cooper, who got this book straightaway and made things go smoothly over the pond. Eskimo! And to Victoria Lowes for putting up with all my emails. ☺

To my editor, Matt Ringler, who may be the coolest person I know and not only because he is king of the raccoons. Thank you for making everything about this experience *so* choice. #blessed #squad. I also have to thank Aimee Friedman and David Levithan, who, along with Matt, not only rallied behind this book but turned their lives into what I imagine to be a particularly zany episode of *Three's Company* in order to acquire it. I am forever grateful.

And thank you to all the amazing people I've met at Scholastic, which I can confirm is a magical wonderland of a place: Yaffa Jaskoll, Alexis Lunsford, Alexis Lassiter, Jacquelyn Rubin, Jody Stigliano, Tracy van Straaten, Caitlin Friedman, Rachel Feld, Bess Braswell, Lauren Festa, Lisa Quach, Vaishali Nayak, Emily Heddleson, Antonio Gonzalez, Lizette Serrano, Emily Rader, Alan Smagler, Lori Benton, and Ellie Berger. And to Jennifer Abbots, a most perfect human being.

To my awesome UK editor, Rachel Petty, and everyone at Macmillan UK for their support.

To those who read early drafts and chapters: Esther Silberstein, Diana Gallagher, Richard Ho. Heroes, all of you. And to Chaya

Levinsohn, my first reader, always. I remember the exact moment we were walking through a bookstore and I asked you if you thought I'd ever have a book in there and you said, with so much conviction, yes. That was when I knew I could do it. Thank you.

To those who provided some excellent jokes: Steve Bluth and Jo Schwarcz. To Lawrence Lee of the Canadian Lees. My first partner in parody crime. (:-*) To Ruthie, Shira, and Sarah (you're welcome!).

To Akiva Moldavsky Z"L and Sonia Moldavsky. Mom, you gave me everything and now everything I have is for you. I love you. To Ari, Maayan, Tily, and to Yasmin Freedman, the original stan. Your fangirling ways are the stuff of legend, and way better than any fiction I could come up with. This book was an attempt to capture everything I loved growing up. And everything I loved growing up is inextricably entwined with you. I hope we never stop talking in movie quotes and singing our favorite telenovela theme songs.

To Berko Schnaiderman Z"L and Blanca Schnaiderman. To Felix ánd Valer. Tios Samuel Z"L and Vladimir. Tias Bella Z"L, Estella Z"L, Malka, Lidia. And to Raquel Fodor and Rebeca Schnaiderman, *con todo mi cariño.*

To Silvia, David, Rodrigo, Jordana, Kevin, and Berko.

And to Alex, who was very literally by my side throughout the making of this book. At the Tea Lounge when I wrote the very first line, in Herald Square when we figured out what the start looked like, on the road back from CT trying to pin down who Erin was, at Chagall's when we had the very important plot breakthrough, at Basil when we finally knew whodunit, and flying over the Pacific, doing the very last revisions. Thank you for being there. (And for telling me that I am an amazing story.)